STARSTRUCK

S. E. ANDERSON

BOLIDE
PUBLISHING LIMITED

STARSTRUCK

© S. E. Anderson 2017
Cover Art by S.E. Anderson
Edited by Michelle Dunbar, Cayleigh Stickler and Anna Johnstone.

This is a work of fiction. Names, characters, businesses, places, events, and incidents are either the products of the author's imagination, or used in a fictitious manner. Any resemblance to persons, living or dead, or actual events is entirely coincidental.

First published in 2017 by Bolide Publishing Limited

http://bolidepublishing.com

ISBN 978-0-9957789-1-7

For Joanna,
I cannot thank you enough

CONTENTS

PROLOGUE
IT ALL BEGINS WITH A LOT OF SAND   1
CHAPTER ONE
HOT-AIR BALLOONS RUIN EVERYTHING   8
CHAPTER TWO
A LITTLE PARTY NEVER KILLED NOBODY,
BUT THAT'S A DOUBLE NEGATIVE   22
CHAPTER THREE
IMAGINE RUNNING OVER A DUDE WITH YOUR CAR   36
CHAPTER FOUR
IN WHICH I GAIN A HEALTHY DISTRUST OF PARKS   47
CHAPTER FIVE
ALL OF THE ABDUCTION, NONE OF THE PROBING   58
CHAPTER SIX
DON'T EVER TRY THIS AT HOME   72
CHAPTER SEVEN
I FINALLY GET SOME ANSWERS AROUND HERE   83
CHAPTER EIGHT
MESSY THINGS YOU CAN'T CLEAN WITH A SPONGE   98
CHAPTER NINE
LIFE GIVES ME LEMONS   111
CHAPTER TEN
DANG ALIENS, ALWAYS GETTING THEMSELVES
ARRESTED   125
CHAPTER ELEVEN
CLOSE ENCOUNTERS OF THE COFFEE KIND   136
CHAPTER TWELVE
SOMEONE CRASHES MY DATE AND THE GLASS
CEILING ALL AT ONCE   151
CHAPTER THIRTEEN
I GET BEAMED UP TO THE MOTHER SHIP   165

CHAPTER FOURTEEN
IT'S A LONG WAY DOWN FROM OUTER SPACE,
BUT WE'RE ONLY AT LOWER EARTH ORBIT   180

CHAPTER FIFTEEN
ZANDER SEEMS TO WORK HERE, NOW   197

CHAPTER SIXTEEN
A TOAST TO MAKING AN ACTUAL EFFORT   211

CHAPTER SEVENTEEN
IT'S NOT A DRINKING PROBLEM IF ALIENS ARE
INVOLVED   225

CHAPTER EIGHTEEN
SHAKING IT OFF MIGHT NOT BE SO EASY   241

CHAPTER NINETEEN
THE SISTER I NEVER HAD NOR WANTED   254

CHAPTER TWENTY
WHEN BLAYDE CAME TO STAY   267

CHAPTER TWENTY-ONE
HOW NOT TO BEHAVE IN THE WORKPLACE   282

CHAPTER TWENTY-TWO
I ACTUALLY CAN'T HANDLE THE TRUTH   294

CHAPTER TWENTY-THREE
THE WORLD IS AWFUL AND EVERYTHING SUCKS   304

CHAPTER TWENTY-FOUR
WE FINISH THIS THING ONCE AND FOR ALL   314

CHAPTER TWENTY-FIVE
I GET MY FINAL BOSS FIGHT   326

EPILOGUE
WHERE SOME THINGS FINALLY GO RIGHT   337

STARSTRUCK

BOOK 1 OF THE STARSTRUCK SAGA

PROLOGUE
IT ALL BEGINS WITH A LOT OF SAND

The commander raised his binoculars and surveyed the desert. The bleak landscape spread out for an eternity before him, flat as far as he could see, broken only by the crumbling buildings of the city. "Where are you?"

"Um, sir. W-what are your orders?"

The commander drew in a sharp breath. His second might only be a kid—on his first posting, no less—and maybe he hadn't seen the kind of action that kept the commander awake at night, but he had to keep his face straight. If he thought that skirmish with the fugitives was an actual attack, he was kidding himself. Besides, the men counted on them for strength and guidance, not fear and weakness.

His team waited in silence on the roof beside him. Most were looking anywhere but at the commander, avoiding eye, or any other kind, of contact. He did not blame them.

"I want you to find those fugitives." The commander's order flew off his tongue like sparks from a fire. "They must be within the city limits or someone would have spotted them."

"But, sir, we searched the burg, and there was no sign of them."

"Then look harder," the commander hissed, raising the binoculars again. He scowled at the empty wasteland. It was the same as always, as it had been for months ... well, until today.

"Maybe they've, um, braved the desert?"

The commander resisted the temptation to slap him. How his superiors thought the boy ready for the post was beyond him. Maybe it was meant as a slight, giving him children to command, like he was a babysitter rather than a decorated war hero. "Can you see them out there?"

His number two swallowed. "Um, no, sir."

"Then they're not there, are they?" The commander shifted his gaze back to the horizon, daring the universe to put the fugitives in his field of vision. "They're in the town. They can't be anywhere else, which makes me wonder what you are still doing here." He turned and glared at his number two. "Find them."

"Sir!"

A call from the street below made him lower his binoculars. He marched to the edge of the roof and looked down at the cracked pavement, ignoring his second-in-command as the boy scampered off to follow his orders. A soldier looked up at him, clutching a rifle against his chest like a shield.

"What?"

2

"They've been sighted, sir." His voice cracked. "They're making a run for it on foot, but they're not moving very fast. They've taken to the desert, by the east bridge."

The commander spun on his heels, turning from his perch to make his way to the staircase. He gave a curt nod to each of the men standing by, gesturing for them to follow. He would need every soldier assigned to this middle-of-nowhere dump he had been defending for half a century. The atmosphere had been quite cheerful until today, the day when everyone under his command learned what it meant to be tested.

But they'd been seen, finally, and he could take as long as he wanted to get to the East End. The desert was eternal, without shelter or cover until one reached the mountains, and that took at least three days by 'craft. If they were on foot, all his men needed to do was to keep them in sight, and he would have them.

He ran through the list of rewards he would receive for capturing the elusive pair. Money? Land? A promotion would be in order; he deserved that much, at least. Somewhere nice, somewhere where the sun shone, instead of burning like fire on his constantly covered-up skin. There was a little place he liked not too far away, with sandy beaches and a deep ocean, a post that required plainclothes rather than camouflage.

He marched through the ghost town, realizing how high the sand had risen since his first day all those years ago. It had been a vibrant place back then, with a market on this very street and flags flying from the windows. Now, all that remained were crumbling memories; the rising sands were devouring what lingered. Soon, all they would leave would be a gigantic dune—the only dune for thousands of miles.

"You have them?" he asked as he reached the squadron at the east bridge. The soldiers huddled in a mass, each trying to mask their fear. The broken bridge had all but crumbled away, leaving a cement perch over an ocean of sand, a perfect vantage point from which to see ... well, more sand. Only today, just for a change, there was something else out there.

Each of his soldiers bore a mark from the so-called attack: a red-raw neck; a lump or two growing on their head; a small mark in the shape of a cigarette burn, accompanied by the scent of scorched clothing and skin. Their wounds were minor, however, which meant he would capture the two most wanted criminals in the universe without losing a single man. He did wonder how they had managed to get through the fight with such light injuries, though. According to legend, the fugitives could kill hundreds in a single minute—some even said the blink of an eye—though he was sure the stories were exaggerated.

The felons dashed across the arid desert. They wore desert clothes, loose layers of cotton wrapped around their bodies to help them blend in with the sand. The man's turban was coming undone, fluttering in the wind he created by his sheer speed. The woman danced lightly across the sand beside him; unhindered by the wrap, she was so graceful, she almost floated in the air. It was enough to make the commander freeze as he watched her shrinking from view.

"I have them in my sights, sir," the sniper announced. His finger hovered above the trigger. The commander found himself staring at it, that lonely digit, reveling in how something so simple could bring such vile things to an end. The rest of his companions stood further back, eyes wide with terror, faces contorted with fear, and legs paralyzed by both. This man had no welts on his arms, no marks or bruising on his neck. No wonder he could still think clearly. The commander ran a hand over the burn on his right wrist, sliding his sleeve to cover it.

"I see them." He grinned at the sniper, his binoculars trained on the two figures. "Shoot to incapacitate. Then have a retrieval squad pick them up."

The sniper fired a single shot. A loud, piercing sound broke the silence. Almost instantly, the man fell to the ground, a red spot spreading from the middle of his back, soaking through his cotton garb. The commander sneered. Just minutes away from glory.

His sneer faded when the man stood up; he didn't seem to notice the bullet, even though the splotch of blood spread. The man fled across the desert unhindered by the wound, his feet pounding rhythmically. "Shoot him again," the commander ordered, mortified. He clutched his burn as if he could reflect the pain back tenfold upon those who bestowed it.

The shot rang out, seemingly louder this time, but the man kept running, despite fresh blood saturating his shirt. "Again." Finally, losing his temper he commanded, "Kill him!"

This time, the bullet hit the small of the man's back, but he didn't fall. Instead, his hand reached across his back, as if to swat a fly, smearing the blood without slowing his stride.

"This is clearly the wrong approach," the commander said, forcing himself to keep his composure, though fury flooded his words. "Arms at the ready."

"What, all of us?" a soldier asked.

"Yes, all of you," he snapped, raising a hand in the air. "Ready ... aim ..."

The soldiers had barely raised their guns when the targets just ... disappeared. They had not fallen, nor had they escaped upward. The commander scrutinized the landscape, but there was no trace of them; in their place, an unfurled turban floated to the ground in the breeze.

The commander's fury burst the dam of self-control, and he howled. He ripped off his helmet and slammed it on the ground. It hit the pavement and rebounded, ramming into his shin. He felt none of it; his anger eclipsed his pain, the fury burning through his veins like acid, stronger and hotter than he had ever felt before.

Everything he had heard about them, everything he wished he hadn't known but had learned to fear about them ... it was all true, and there was no better truth than the one he had seen with his own eyes. One second they were there, just out of reach, the next, gone. Just ... gone. Bullets didn't even slow them down. No wonder they had a knack for evading the law.

No wonder they needed to be taken down.

For the first time in his life, the commander dropped his head into his hands, a sob ringing across the empty wasteland, heard only by the cowards behind him. He picked up his helmet, and, seeing the burn marks upon it, shouted words into the desert that his men could not understand. Then, without thought, he tossed it into the desert, watching the dented metal tumble in the air, before falling into the sand and lodging itself there to be covered up by time. With that, the commander fell to his knees, rubbing his webbed fingers over his irritated, sunburned scalp.

They had escaped once again. And with them, his dreams.

Goodbye, money.

Goodbye, land.

Goodbye, promotion and plainclothes.

And he had so wanted that quiet posting on Earth.

CHAPTER ONE

HOT-AIR BALLOONS RUIN EVERYTHING

Before there was the universe, before the endless cities, the ships, or the Dread, before the Alliances and higher dimensional parties, there was only sleep.

I was pretty happy just sleeping.

Sometimes, I wonder what would have happened if I had taken the day off and just slept. If I had called in sick to work, sick to the party, and had never left the apartment at all.

I think about that a lot.

I awoke to the sound of a jackhammer. It broke

through the morning gloom, tearing me painfully from sleep. The noise made my entire nightstand shake and with it, my mattress and pillow. It jolted me awake quite violently; I should have known then what sort of day I would have.

I wasn't fully aware yet, my brain was still waking up, but I knew enough to throw out my hand and try to stop the dreadful noise. Ugh. My other hand clutched the sheets, begging the universe for just one more minute of warm, comfortable sleep.

The universe denied my request.

I finally found the alarm clock and slapped it as hard as I could. No such luck; the music kept playing. So I did the only thing that seemed logical—I hit it again.

And again.

By that point, my hand stung, and I concluded it wasn't the alarm clock making the ruckus. My phone vibrated all over the place. I fumbled for it, missing it completely. Finally, my fingers found its cold surface, and I dragged it under the covers. I accepted the call and held the tiny speaker to my ear.

"'Lo?" I grunted, expecting a full word to come out.

"Sally?" came the anxious voice on the other end.

This early in the morning, I had no idea whose voice this was. It could have been Sir Patrick Stewart or God himself trying to wake me. Whoever it was—I was mad at them.

"Who is this?" I mumbled.

"Marcy," the voice replied, worried as ever—or could it have been cheerful? People who could be cheerful at this ungodly hour were not to be trusted. "I wanted to know if you had a grill?"

"Hold on, what?" I sat up way too fast. The blood rushing from my head gave me the worst morning headache in human history. And the cold—the cold! I shivered as my skin made contact with air. "You want a grill? What on earth for?"

"For tonight. Jenn's is busted."

"Tonight?"

There was a painful silence on the other end of the line. I used the pause to my advantage, pulling the sheets over my cold, exposed shoulders. Finally, Marcy spoke again, slowly this time, the worry all the way back in her voice. "It's my birthday," she said, but then her cheery self returned, "Birth-day par-tay. My birthday party. Tell me if any of this rings a bell? Like, if there's something you'd like to say to me?"

"Marce, I would absolutely love to jump into a rendition of the birthday song, but not this early in the morning."

"Well, sorry," Marcy replied, mock-hurt, "I assumed you'd be at work."

"At four in the morning?" I grabbed the alarm clock and looked at its glowing blue hands. Definitely on the wrong side of the quadrant. "I can't remember my own birthday at this hour."

"Um, Sally, you'd better check your clock."

"I'm looking right at it," I gave the thing a shake, nothing compared to the pounding it had received five minutes earlier. "It's 4:03 am, and it's still pitch-black."

I turned my head to look at my window—my dark window—and saw a strange sliver of light in the darkness of the universe.

Or maybe it wasn't the universe. Maybe it was the

tarp draped over the window.

"It's 9:30!" Marcy screamed. "Sally, get up now!"

I swore as I flew to my feet, words so harsh that I could hear Marcy shudder over the phone. Then she was the one screaming, yelling at me to hang up and get dressed. Advice I could not process with my head reeling in shock.

Late, so late. I staggered as I tried to throw on my pants, but as most people who have tried getting dressed in a hurry know, trying to put on pants faster takes longer: The pants paradox. I practically fell over trying to get the legs all the way up. I realized then I hadn't turned the light on, so I threw out an arm to hit the switch.

Soft yellow light illuminated my small bedroom. The place was the cheapest I could afford, but it was comfortable, with enough space for a bed and closet. The floor was a mix of clothing I hadn't washed and clean clothes that hadn't made it as far as the shelves.

The first shirt I tried had a stain down the front, which I didn't remember getting, but I had no time to think about that now. No time for a sniff test. Off went the stained shirt, and on went a passable-for-clean one.

I rushed into the living room, hoping there was some food I could grab, but it seemed my roomie, Rosemary, had eaten the apples that were usually in the bowl on the counter.

"Oh, Sally, do you have a minute?"

Speak of the devil. Rose poked her head out of the bathroom, her hair wrapped in a tight, white towel turban. Her nose was red and puffy, and she wiped it repeatedly with a too-small piece of toilet paper, which only seemed to make it worse.

"Allergies?" I asked. "Wait, no, I don't have time. We'll talk later."

The irrational part of me—which was quite loud when I was in a whirlwind of panic—was mad she wasn't in the same rush I was, and the fact she was trying to delay me rubbed me the wrong way. I glared at her, shooting imaginary daggers her way, trying to get her to back off so I could dash out.

"It's super important. I need your advice, it's—"

"Look, Rose, not to be rude, but I'm about to lose my job," I said, already halfway out the door. "Tell you what, if I'm fired, I'll be back in an hour. We can talk then. It's that or this evening. Or you can text?"

I didn't wait for an answer. My stomach growled as I ran down the stairs, wishing I'd had time to eat something, anything. By the time I'd reached the street outside, I was fully awake and completely ravenous.

It was then I saw the tarp. Only it wasn't a tarp but a deflated red-and-yellow hot-air balloon draped across the roof, hanging over my window, and my window alone.

What. The. Heck.

"Is that yours?" asked a voice next to me. I turned to see Jules, my next-door neighbor, standing next to his car.

Jules was an overall stand-up guy. He never bothered me, and I never bothered him; he kept my mail for me when I went to visit family, and I fed his fish when he went on vacation. He kept his parties at reasonable sound levels, and I never complained about how late they ended. It was a good situation.

"The balloon?" I scoffed. "Yeah right. That thing might have just cost me my job."

"Oh, crap. Good luck with that."

I didn't have the time to ponder further. I jumped behind the wheel of my car and sped to my demise. I probably ran a few lights, but I impressed even myself at the full one-eighty I pulled to get the last spot in the service parking lot at the mall.

In that minute, nothing mattered more than getting to work on time. I had only one chance at this. I could be late so long as I showed up before Valerie Price did. And, if Ms. Price was already here, then beating my co-worker, Justine, to the store was just as good.

I caught my reflection in the rearview mirror. My hair was a wreck. I rummaged through the layers on the passenger seat, found an elastic between two Subway napkins, and threw everything into a messy bun. It looked pretty good, honestly.

If I called in sick, would I be in the clear? Maybe, but I was here now.

Of course, I know now that wasn't the best decision. The best decision would have been to stay at home and figure out why a hot-air balloon was draped over the effing building. But, you know, hindsight is always 20/20.

Breathe in, breathe out; you can't walk in there looking like you got chased by a bear. After all signs of outward panic were gone, I slipped out of the car, straightened my blouse, and marched into Price's Boutique.

I scanned the shop floor, trying to assess how deep in shit I was. The store was empty—thank your highest entity for that—of customers, at least. The imposing silhouette of my boss grew from behind the register, and I rushed to relieve her of my job. "I am so sorry I'm late, Mrs. Price."

The look she gave me told me my apology had fallen on deaf ears. Perched behind the desk like some kind of overstuffed hawk, she glared at me with those beady eyes of hers. I felt as if I was going to be sent to the principal's office or something.

This was not the first time I had gotten such a look from her, either. She had made me feel uncomfortable since day one. The way she scrutinized my every single movement, or the passive aggressive notes she left for me to find. I always felt as if, at any minute, she would swoop and pluck me up in her blue-varnished talons and drop me into a nest thousands of miles away where no one would ever find me.

"Ah, Ms. Webber, how kind of you to grace us with your presence." A smile stretched across her face. Oddly enough, this reminded me of the Grinch, right before his heart grew two sizes larger.

But alas—this wasn't a Christmas miracle. It wasn't anywhere near Christmas, and nothing miraculous ever happened to me.

"I really am sorry," I repeated, getting to work on sorting out the poorly-folded shirts on the display closest to me. "My alarm clock died. I can assure you this won't happen again."

There was a snort from the back of the room, and there she was—a tall girl of seventeen, her hair pulled back in pigtails because she knew it increased her sales. They swung like pendulums as she moved the broom back and forth across the floor using short, jerky motions.

I could almost feel my hair fluttering in an imaginary wind and my eyes filling with fiery rage as I glared at the girl.

"Justine," I mumbled.

It was petty, really. We were close in age but lived very different lives. Part of me sort of resented the fact that she didn't have to work for a living. Though we didn't talk much, I knew she came from wealth. Her mom wanted her to work to understand the plight of the working class.

Justine said that a lot. Mostly when she was on the phone with friends lucky enough not to have moms who made them work—her words, not mine.

So, you can understand my—albeit petty—feud with Justine. Right?

Not that any of it mattered because that was the last day I ever saw her.

"Justine has been here since eight," Mrs. Price said, lifting a battered Cosmo and pretending to pay no attention to me, or, at least, not wanting to seem like she cared. Which she didn't, so it wasn't a hard act to pull.

"I'll buy some batteries for my alarm clock as soon as my shift ends."

"No need," she said. "Go and buy them now. And don't bother coming back."

I guess it didn't come as much of a surprise, but it still hurt. A lot more than I expected, actually. Bile rose in the back of my throat as I built up to say something, anything, that would sway my now-former boss. I wanted to scream and shout and throw a tantrum.

But I was so tired.

My stomach twisted in knots. All I wanted was get out, far away. Get in my car and drive until I reached the edge of the horizon.

I couldn't think of anything to say so I just stood there, frozen, mouth agape, my mind racing through every possibility. What was there to say? No, please? There was no hope there. You'll regret this? Too theatrical. It would come back to bite me.

"Um, okay, thank you."

Are you kidding me, Sally?

Talk about a weak exit. With a sudden burst of dramatic flair, I ripped my nametag from my chest, slamming it on the desk. A little too dramatic, but it was too late now to search for a middle ground. I left the store in a huff, only just realizing I had destroyed my blouse. And now, I couldn't feel my arms or legs.

Once I was out of the mall, I dropped my pace from a 'dramatic storming out' to a 'shuffle of shame.' It felt like I was walking through thick gel; everything was heavy and dark around the edges. When I finally got back in the car, I just sat there, staring forward, brain numb.

I made eye contact with my reflection and froze as a sense of dread washed over me. Dang, she looked worried. And tired. Her sand-colored hair was stacked in a weird knot on the top of her head, dry tendrils floating down to frame her somewhat gaunt face. Her lips looked as if the blood hadn't reached them in a few days. The only sign of life was the brown eyes, which met mine and held my gaze, begging me not to let go.

It was like looking at a stranger.

I didn't know when I got back on the road. Everything was running on automatic, like I wasn't really in my body anymore. I gripped the wheel tight enough to turn my knuckles white and my fingertips red, forcing myself to follow the way back home.

I had been gone not even an hour, but the hot-air balloon was already gone. A mystery I would probably never find the answer to. Maybe Rosemary would know something about it.

Except she had gone too; her room was completely cleared out. As a matter of fact, half the furniture was missing from the apartment—the rug under the coffee table, the cat statue that sat by the door; all the little tidbits we had accumulated over the years were just … gone.

Holy shit. Had I been robbed, on top of everything else? A quick check showed my things were here; my laptop was still on the edge of my nightstand, and the old TV still comfortably in its place in the living room. Only Rosemary's things were gone.

That's when I saw the note, a napkin placed strategically on the kitchen counter, black scribbles in a fast cursive announcing, "we're eloping."

Luckily, there was more, a note in the trash on a page ripped from a yellow legal pad. Some words were scratched out. The writer had obviously stopped and started a few times, scribbling over the failed beginnings before tossing it out entirely. But there was some sense to it.

Sorry, Sally, I couldn't risk you spilling the beans to my mom. Sally, I wanted to say something this morning, but you were in such a rush. Ben and I are going to Vegas, and we're not coming back. I've taken my stuff and left this month's rent on the bed. Wish us luck! — Rosie

That's when I burst.

Call it a nervous breakdown. An anxiety attack. Panic attack. Or all the above. My mind shifted from clear thought to murky territory, running the events of the morning through my head over and over, a highlight reel of personal failure. Suddenly, I couldn't breathe anymore; my lungs refusing to do their work. I hiccupped as my eyes filled with tears. It was illogical, all of it, but even so, I couldn't stop. The energy welled up inside me and spilled out in such an ugly way, the terror shaking me back and forth and making it impossible for me to think straight.

I sank to the floor and let it spill. Everything hurt.

What was I supposed to do now? A college dropout with no prospects and only a few dollars to my name. I had nothing going for me, no ambition, no dreams, no passion. There was no direction whatsoever for me to go in.

Loser. Loser. Loser.

The rational part of my brain shut down, leaving me with anger and tears—tears that burned and drained me. And in the back, dark thoughts I couldn't find words for.

The weight on my chest pressed down on me, choking out my air. I couldn't breathe. I couldn't do anything but weep and try to keep myself together.

I didn't know how long the attack lasted, but slowly, it began to let up. The tightness in my lungs eased, and

I breathed deeply again. My eyes stung like they had been doused in salt, even on the backside of the eyeballs.

What was I going to do?

I needed a job, fast. I needed to get out of retail, focus on a career, but there wasn't much available for a girl without a degree. Maybe I could apply for a job at the new power plant that was opening outside of town? Nah, they needed someone with experience— and probably some kind of university diploma. So, retail work it is, I guess.

I shuffled to the couch and saw Rosemary had taken half the cushions. Great. I guess they were hers in the first place, but I still wished they were here. I wished she were here, too. We weren't the best of friends, but we enjoyed each other's company. And right now, I didn't want to be alone.

I pulled off my shoes and discovered my socks were two completely different colors. I shrugged it off. I'd had those kinds of days before, though never to this extent. With my feet now freed, I stretched on the couch and tried to ease my aching body.

I needed another roommate. I couldn't afford this place on my own, and that was when I had a job. I needed someone to split the rent, or I was going to be out on the street in less than a month.

The best thing to do would be to call Marcy. She'd know what to say; she always did. And I really, really needed to hear her voice.

She picked up after not even a whole ring. "Sally? What happened?"

"What makes you think something happened?"

"Come on."

"Fired," I replied, my false confidence making it sound like pride. I reached into the candy bowl on the table and popped a peppermint in my mouth. At least Rose had the decency to leave those.

"Oh. I'm sorry."

"'S'okay."

"No, it isn't."

"I'm telling you, it's okay," I said, sucking on the candy for a minute, feeling the cool taste of mint across my tongue. I probably should have started with one of those; it was already starting to soothe me. "I was going to leave eventually, anyway. Price had it in for me."

"Is that a peppermint in your mouth?" When I didn't answer immediately, Marcy kept going. "Yup, thought so. You only eat candy when you're worked up. So, what can I do?"

"Find me a new roommate?"

"What happened to Rosie?"

"Vegas."

"With Ben?"

"Who else?"

"So, they finally eloped?"

"You knew?"

"I read into the situation," she replied casually, but there was a definite hint of pity in her voice. "Anything I can do?"

"I guess your party will cheer me up. What time is it again?"

"Starts at seven. And we'll be at Jenn's."

"I'll be there. But why were you asking me about a grill? You know what I own better than I do. Did Jenn's break or something?"

"Nah," she scoffed. I expected her to go on, but she offered no answer. Instead, there was an awkward pause. "So, no grill?"

"You know I don't have one."

"Drat." She sighed heavily, the sound saturating the microphone for a split second. "Well, Mike says he has a friend that could bring one if we ask nicely."

"Do you even know how to grill?"

"I will soon. I'll be on WikiHow for the rest of the day. What are you going to do 'till party time?"

"I'll figure something out. See you then," I said, hanging up quickly.

If I had stayed on any longer, Marcy would have coerced me into coming over or convinced me she needed to come to mine. And I didn't want that for her, not on her birthday. She had been planning this party for months; it's not every day you turn nineteen.

I felt guilty about the abrupt responses, but I hoped Marcy would forgive me. Right now, my body felt limp and useless, my mind slow and numb. Not that I was all that surprised. I was used to the letdown the universe dragged me through. I'm not the kind of person to blame it on divinity, chaos, or destiny. I guess I didn't blame it on anything. I had long since accepted my lack of luck as being my lot in life, though I wanted something or someone to blame it on right now.

Curse you, universe! I shook my fist in the air, falling back into the cushion-less couch and right back into sleep.

Anyways. This is getting pretty dark. Let's skip forward to the party. That's where things get really interesting.

CHAPTER TWO
A LITTLE PARTY NEVER KILLED NOBODY, BUT THAT'S A DOUBLE NEGATIVE

I like parties when they're small get-togethers, but Marcy's idea of a party is a little bigger than mine. By the time I had gotten to Jenn's, the house was already bursting with people. I pushed my way inside, searching through the throng of party guests for my friend.

"Hey, have you seen Marcy?" I asked the first person I made eye contact with.

"What?" he shouted, leaning closer. The music was loud enough to raise the dead.

"Marcy?"

"Who?" He shrugged and went back to his conversation.

I gave up on searching the house and slipped out the rear door. The overflow of the party was in the garden, which was where I finally found her, hanging out by the tables. She was mingling around a cheering mass, enjoying the company of friends and meeting strangers—friends of friends of friends with access to Facebook and Twitter and the like.

Marcy exuded radiance. She glowed with every step she took, excited at the commotion and energized by the crowd. Above all, she looked happy.

She was one of those people who stepped into a room and immediately made you gravitate toward her. She was probably one of the shortest people I knew (which isn't saying much, since I don't know that many people), only about five feet tall, but she stood out no matter what. Her shoulder-length, straight black hair had been featured in a shampoo commercial once, and she jokingly told people she was a hair model from then on.

I'd believe her.

Marcy grew up with an overflow of love, and it's still spilling out of her. She glowed with it. Anyone coming to the party tonight not knowing her would leave with her name forever engraved in their memory.

"Sally!" Marcy gushed, rushing over to give me a huge squeeze.

"Happy birthday, Marce!" I hugged her tight enough to break a rib.

"You have got to taste my burgers," Marcy said, handing me a plate with a blue bun on it. "I spent the afternoon baking."

"Blue burgers?"

"I'm a sucker for alliteration," she snickered. "Oh, Sal, this is the Mike I've been talking about. Mike, Sally. Sally's from Bridgeton, like me."

"Pleasure," I said, shaking his hand. Mike nodded, repeating the sentiment. He was a tall, thin man with a smile wider than the width of his shoulders.

"Mike brought the grill. He works at Starbucks down on sixth."

"Nice to meet you," he said, not letting go of my hand. I pulled away. My palm was clammy now. Gross.

"You should talk to Jenn about her grill, though," Marcy said. "Turns out she had a dream before it went missing. Something about you needing it to fly away in a hot-air balloon. It's pretty trippy."

"A balloon?" I stammered, the coincidence too striking to not bring it up. "You know, just this morning I—"

There was a noise behind me, a scrambling of feet as flocks of people stepped aside to let someone through. I turned and practically jumped out of my skin.

"Who is the host of this event?" The woman's deep voice rose above the crowd. People parted awkwardly before returning to their own things. "It is essential that I know. It is of the utmost importance." She looked around at our shocked faces. "Well? Speak up. Is Harris here?"

"I'm the host," Marcy said, scanning the woman from head to toe and returning a dazzling smile. "But I don't know any Harris. We can spread the word, though. Are ... are you all right?"

The stranger leaned forward, trying to hide the fact that she was out of breath. Marcy threw out a hand to support her, and the woman smiled, clutching her chest as she slowly regained control.

She was tall, and I mean incredibly tall. For a second, I thought she might have been an Amazon warrior. She would fit right in with them; her muscular figure showed through her soft silk blouse and tight black pants. Her hair was long and dusty blonde, pulled back into a tight ponytail to reveal ears with at least five piercings. Each. Golden coins and geometric shapes jingled whenever she turned her head, making me think of a pirate queen. She scanned each of us with her piercing gray eyes, casually raising a hand to pluck a leaf from behind one of her gilded ears.

"Any of you know who I am?" she growled, showing her teeth. Marcy stood her ground, glancing at Mike and then at the stranger, worry lining her face before she hid it behind a smile.

"Never saw you before, mate," Mike said sternly. "Who the heck are you?"

"Sorry, sorry." The stranger's snarl melted into a grin. It was like a light bulb going off in her head, and she relaxed enough to let her shoulders slump. "I'm trying to lay low, if you know what I mean."

"Boyfriend?" Mike urged.

"Nope."

"Girlfriend?" Marcy interjected.

The stranger shook her head.

"Cops?"

"I hope not." She laughed heartily. "Nothing like that. Bodyguards, you know?"

"Um, no." Marcy lifted an eyebrow. "Bodyguards?"

"No bodyguards?"

"Um, no?"

"Cool, cool." She nodded slowly, wrapping her mouth around the vernacular as if trying to force an American accent. The switch in tone was both sudden and unsettling. "Okay, so, like, my father's rich, ya know? He's got me tailed everywhere, like, to make sure I don't get into what he supposes is trouble. I've got to make sure the coast is clear, like, before I can even begin to think about enjoying myself. So, um, where am I exactly?"

"Marcy's birthday party," Marcy said, extending a hand. "And I'm Marcy."

"Danir—Dany," Her grin widened. "Sorry to, ahem, crash the party. Harris brought me along, but knowing my dad, like, he could have been bribed to report my every move. Doesn't look like he has, though."

"You could always hang out around the grill," Marcy offered. "No trouble to get into over here. Unless trouble is what you want."

The entire situation was incredibly weird. I had a feeling there was more going on than Dany was saying, but that was probably just me being paranoid, per usual, when people started hanging around Marcy. I'm a little protective of my girl.

Dany removed more leaves from her shirt and hair. She looked as if she had run through a forest to get here. One thing was obvious, though: she had certainly been captivated by Marcy's glow.

The woman laughed again, and all I could think about was how much she looked like she should be out on the high seas, but with Wonder Woman by her side. I dropped my gaze to my plate, trying not to stare. Not that I would have said anything, but the burger was charred black; no amount of blue bun could hide that.

"Well, happy birthday, Marcy," Dany said. "Sorry, I don't have a gift on me. Harris was really vague about what was actually happening tonight."

"Saving the food will be gift enough," she said, gesturing to the grill. "Show me how you do this ..."

"Me?" The woman laughed again, "I've never seen this contraption before in my life."

"What, a grill?"

I watched the two of them slip into each other's orbit, realizing quite suddenly that I didn't know anyone else, except maybe Jenn and Mike, the former being somewhere in the hubbub and the latter disappearing into the house.

I grabbed a beer from the ice bucket and scanned the crowd, clutching the bottle to my chest. At what point had I lost track of Marcy's other friends? Close as we were, I always felt awkward at Marcy's parties, knowing fewer people every time. Maybe it was enough to have shown my face—binging science fiction on Netflix under a heap of blankets awaited me back home.

Watching a good sci-fi filled me with an odd sense of astrolust. I loved it, but when the show was exceptionally good, it left me feeling empty inside, like there was a little hole that needed to be filled with adventure, spaceships, exploration, and the unknown. But I wasn't very good at science, never kept up in math, and although I loved school, I was awful at it. Sadly, I was born too early for space travel to be an everyday thing. Thankfully, Netflix existed to fill all the gaps.

I wanted to go home and fill my head with images of an invented universe. But no—no—I was here for Marcy. So long as she wanted me here, I'd stay.

Jenn emerged from the house, shouting something about having some music. She placed tall, expensive speakers out on the porch, hooked up her iPod, and blasted some Lady Gaga. Just like that, people started dancing, somehow balancing blue burgers and dance moves.

I stood by myself, swaying from side to side, trying to eat my burger so Marcy wouldn't feel bad. She lounged by the grill with a large spatula in her hand, laughing, as Dany stood frozen, staring wide-eyed at the speakers by the door. There was something off about that woman. Not a dangerous off, but something definitely strange.

"If I had a nickel for every time I saw a girl as beautiful as you, I'd have exactly five cents," someone said, moving into my field of vision. He looked as awkward as I felt. His cheeks were red and his smile feeble.

Holy crap—it was Matt.

I had first met him in a creative writing course in college, one of those electives I didn't think I'd enjoy. The course had been great and the company even more so. Embarrassingly enough, I had developed a small crush on the guy who always took the front row and who was always excited to share his progress. How he was at Marcy's party, I did not know, but this wasn't a dream; it was real.

Ok, Sally, keep your cool. He approached you, not the other way around. Just say something good.

"Sorry," I replied sheepishly, waving my blue burger in the air. "That was cute, but I'm not interested."

Crap, no! Don't say that! You like this guy!

But, then again… he did use a pickup line. And not a very good one, either.

"Ugh." Matt sighed, and glared at Mike who stood

28

a short distance away, proudly holding up two thumbs. "I'm sorry. I was told it was a good conversation starter—looks like I was sorely misinformed!"

He shouted the last part in Mike's direction, though he was nowhere to be found. Matt looked at me again, smiling as much as he could. It was probably too much. "It sounded cool when Mike said it." He shook his head. "Look, can we try again? Forget I said that last bit?"

"Sure."

Matt walked away, and, for a minute, I thought he wasn't coming back. I groaned internally. I really sucked at this.

"What about this weather we're having?" he said, striding casually back to my side, as if he hadn't been standing there.

"You want to talk about the weather?" I scoffed, feeling my eyebrows drift up my face. "Come on, you can think of something more interesting than that."

"Do you believe in life after death?"

"Religion?"

"I still have trouble believing it's been over ten years since Firefly's been off the air."

"And science fiction." I grinned. "All fantastic topics of discussion."

"Matthew Daniels," he said, extending his hand, "but most people call me Matt."

I held back the urge to tell him I knew who he was, and shook his hand as if it was my first time meeting him. Which, I guess, it was. We never actually spoke during the course.

Yeah, crushes are weird. Right?

"Sally Webber, pleasure," I replied.

He was a bold-looking man, his dark brown hair shaggy around his temples, framing a soft baby face and the most piercing blue eyes I had ever seen. He was dressed in comfortable jeans and a t-shirt that looked like it had been worn since the birth of time. The image on the front was of a white triangle with a circled X, an old math joke that never really got old, even if the picture had faded with time.

"I'm not sure if you remember," he said, "but we had a class together. Creative writing, I think?"

Holy shit. Was I blushing? I hoped not.

"Oh, yeah," I said, all casual-like. "You wrote that sci-fi piece about the white hole."

"I can't believe you remember that. So?"

"So, what?"

"Well, I recall asking you a few questions."

"The weather is fabulous for this time of year; yes; and no, definitely not. Why are you opening that old wound again?"

At that moment, the lights dimmed and the music faded. Jenn brought out the cake, her voice carrying over the crowd, hushing us all before we realized we were supposed to join in. She carried it to the grill as people flocked around her, singing Happy Birthday at the top of their voices, painfully out of tune. The sparklers cut a sharp contrast to the darkness, jumping into the air and shining on Marcy's beaming face. The world cheered as she blew out the candles.

Someone brought plates over, and Jenn placed the cake on a nearby table so she could cut it. I stuffed the rest of the burger in my mouth just before the cake reached me.

"So how do you know Marcy?" Matt asked, using his plastic fork to slice off a bite of dessert.

"We grew up together," I explained, adoring the taste of chocolate sponge on my tongue. It had always been my favorite. "We're from Bridgeton, Virginia."

"Oh, cool," Matt said. "Both of you go to U-Frank?"

"Yeah."

"What's your major?"

"Undeclared," I said, lowering my voice, "but I dropped out."

"What? Why?"

I shrugged. "It wasn't for me. I was going through a lot, and it wasn't where I wanted to be. And why am I even telling you this?"

Why was I telling him? I didn't tell strangers anything, and here I was babbling away. He didn't seem to mind, though. I guess I liked that, and it explained why I couldn't really stop.

"Maybe it's my irresistible charm?" He grinned, completely awkward, and for some reason it made me laugh. I blamed that on the beer.

"Yeah, maybe, and you?"

"Communications major. Currently interning at Grisham Corp."

"The new power plant?"

"One of the fortunate few." He laughed. "I'm going to need all the help I can get to pay off those darn student loans."

We took a break from the conversation to scarf down more cake. The chocolate was perfect, fluffy, and moist; the icing sweet but not too sugary; and I found myself wondering if I could take some home. It was amazing, the perfect cake, and certainly my favorite—

And then it hit me.

I sputtered, tossing my fork like it was a poisonous viper, and glanced around. The music. The blue burgers. The cake.

Shit, shit, shit.

A look of worry crossed Matt's face. "Is something wrong?"

"I have something I need to do." I spun on my heels and marched to Jenn, who was cutting and handing out slices from a second cake, pressed my knuckles on the table, and leaned forward. "Why chocolate?"

Jenn shrugged. "Last minute change. Marcy said she wanted it that way."

"But Marcy's favorite is Angel food," I pointed out, my voice going high-pitched.

"Guess she changed her mind?"

"Chocolate is my favorite."

"Oh," Jenn said, as though she could not care any less.

I, however, was freaking out.

"Marce," I snapped, storming toward the grill. My friend was sitting on an empty table with Dany at her side. They were laughing, cake untouched, barely able to hold their paper plates straight.

"Marcy!"

"Heya, Sal." Marcy smiled. "Have you met Dany?"

"Yes," I said, my voice icier than I would have liked. "I have."

"Is everything all right?" Her smile faded into worry, and she slid off the table, putting her hand on my shoulder. Dany looked in the opposite direction, holding the spatula up to her face as if to examine it.

"No, not really. You do realize this is your birthday party, right?"

"Um, yeah?"

"So, why are you pandering to me?" My heart raced. I felt mad, a blob of lava boiling in my gut. "No, don't give me those eyes. Coloring the food? Chocolate cake? Since when have you liked chocolate cake?"

"Who doesn't?" Marcy nudged Dany. "Chocolate cake?"

"A rare delicacy," Dany said quietly.

"But over angel food?" I urged. Marcy's gaze fell, and I knew I was right: Marcy was a poor liar. "I don't need a pity party."

"It's not a pity party—"

"So why does your music mix sound like you stole my iPod?"

"You have good taste."

"You hate pop," I snapped. "Marce, don't worry about me, seriously. I got fired, that's all. I'll be okay."

Marcy glared at me. She put her hands on her hips and dared me with her eyes. I couldn't help it—I laughed—and so did she.

"You're right," I said. "It sucks."

"This really isn't about you getting fired." Marcy smiled, but it was cold and fading fast. "I ... I'm worried about you, Sal."

"About what?"

"About you." She clasped my shoulders. "You're wavering. Flickering out. I've been watching for a long time, Sally, and since John—"

"Don't you dare bring him up!"

"Since John, you've been falling apart. First, you stopped eating, but I guess that was a normal reaction. Then the dropout, followed by job after dead-end job. It's been years now, Sally—two freaking years! When's the last time you saw your therapist?"

I ripped my arms from hers and backed away. "I … I have to go."

"Sally, please." Marcy grabbed my arm. "I wasn't saying that to make you angry, I just … I want you to know—"

"What?"

Marcy let out a heavy sigh. "Look around you, Sally. How many people do you know here? Have you made any friends? Anyone at all since we moved here?"

"Arthur."

"He's your mailman. He doesn't count."

I couldn't look at her anymore. I jerked my arm free and stormed away, doing a much better job of it than I had at work that morning. Marcy and Dany followed me, though why Dany thought she had anything to do with this, I didn't know.

I made a beeline toward the exit, only to have another obstacle thrown in my way. An annoyingly handsome one.

Matt sprung up, interposing himself between the doorway and me. "Hey, Sally, are you okay?"

I tried to smile, but it never reached my eyes. "You're my friend, right, Matt?"

"Um … yeah?" He looked frightened.

I snatched the phone from his hands, added myself as a contact. I turned the phone around and held it out to take a selfie. I held up the phone, showing Marcy before handing it back to Matt. "Now we're friends. Feel free to call or text or do whatever it is friends do." I spun around. "See, Marcy? I can make friends."

"Sally, I ..."

I still could not believe she would turn her own party into an intervention for me. It was a low blow. An awful tool to play, made worse by her trying to drag John into it.

My face was hot and sweating like I was running a fever. My skin prickled, the hair standing at attention all the way up my neck and down my arms. I would not have been surprised to see steam spouting from my ears: I needed to get out of here—fast.

"Yo, you good?" someone asked, sticking their head out of the kitchen at the sound of the slamming door.

"Just smashing," I replied.

I shoved through the revelers in the hallway, slammed the front door behind me, and climbed in my car. Soon, I was speeding down the roads leading to home, trying to put as much distance as I could between me and that dreadful party. I was still fuming from the bitter memory of Marcy when I rammed a man with my car.

CHAPTER THREE
IMAGINE RUNNING OVER A DUDE WITH YOUR CAR

I don't think I will ever forget the sound my car made. That awful crunching noise. First, the initial impact with the body, then the windshield shattering, followed by the dull thud as he hit the ground behind me.

I had just run someone over.

All the way over.

I slammed on the brakes. The car screeched, and I lurched forward, my momentum halted by the seatbelt. My hands shook as I gripped the wheel, my heart pounding from shock. I trembled in the seat, staring into the rearview mirror, begging... pleading for whatever I had hit to get up and wander off.

But nothing moved.

I forced myself out of the car, flinging the door open and tumbling into the road. I had never seen so much blood before. The street glistened with it, and I refused to believe a human could have spilled so much. I must have hit a bear. I must have hit—

But it wasn't a bear. It looked like a mass of bed sheets someone had used to clean up after a murder—with the body still inside—wrapped like a mummy, face down on the street.

I sighed in relief. Obviously, someone had left the body there to get run over, destroy the evidence, and—wait—no. Why was I relieved? Someone had been murdered, and I was being framed. How had I missed it lying in the road like that anyway? I was sure the street had been empty.

I needed to call 9-1-1.

And then the body did something I had not expected—it moved.

A hand extracted itself from the mess, slapped the ground, and used it to push up the rest of its body. The man underneath it let out a low groan. It was small and muffled and surprisingly calm. I heard the rasp of his breath, like fingers running down a washboard. I could have screamed right there, but no sound came out. It was as if someone had stuck their hand into my back and wrapped a fist around my spine.

Sometimes, Don't Panic does not apply.

Slowly, he turned his face in my direction: his nose was crooked and probably broken, stones had been pushed into his skin deeper than should have been possible. I saw the bewilderment as his eyes met mine. I took a step back, an involuntary move on my part, but he did not break eye contact. Instead, he stretched out another arm, bracing himself, but could not support himself and fell back with a grunt.

This time, my reflexes kicked in, and I ran to him and kneeled at his side. I didn't want to move, or even touch him. At least, not until I knew the extent of his injuries. I reached for my hip, struggling to pull out my phone from my tiny half-pocket.

"I'm here, I'm here, it's okay," I tried to say in a soothing voice, but it wasn't convincing. Actually, it failed to sound anything but completely terrified. "Can you hear me? Can you say something—anything?"

With his face still on the concrete, voice muffled, he let out a string of gibberish in a language I didn't recognize, and then punctuated it with a laugh.

Of course, none of this made sense.

"What on earth?" I muttered, which somehow piqued his curiosity.

"Oh … Earth!"

The stranger rolled onto his back, sprawling on the street like it was his bed. He looked up with a broad smile that lit the night.

I guess I had been wrong: He wasn't as injured as I first thought. Maybe it had been the harsh light from the streetlamp making his nose look broken. With a brush of his hand, most of the stones and blood fell away, revealing a pristine face, no cuts or bruises to speak of.

"I've been here before," he said, letting out a long breath of relief, as if I hadn't just run him over. Had I? I was starting to doubt my recollection of the events. Though the blood around us told another story.

His voice was accent-less: I couldn't pinpoint where he was from. He pronounced words as if he were reading them from a dictionary. He breathed deeply, staring at the stars. Vibrant, silvery-green eyes reflected the sky above him. His smile became a thin line.

"Dude, are you okay?" I asked, reaching a hand out and then snatching it back as I realized what I was doing. He said nothing.

I finally wrangled my phone out of my pocket to call emergency services. Before I could hit the call button, his hand shot out and grabbed my wrist.

"Blade," he hissed, his eyes wide in terror. "I need blade."

The word came out of his mouth like a hymn, or a parched man begging for water. I ripped my arm from his grasp.

"You're fine; it's okay," I said, quite possibly a lie.

"Never been without blade," he choked out. A thin line of blood trickled from his mouth. I wondered if a rib had punctured his lung or his stomach, knowledge that came from too many years of watching hospital shows. How much time did he have left? He laughed gently, and blood oozed out of his mouth, trickling down his chin, staining the street with yet another red puddle. None of this seemed to bother him, though. Instead, his eyes swept back to me, wide and determined.

"Stay with me," I said. "I'm going to get you some help."

"Don't ... don't call anyone." His voice was raspy, but he was definitely pleading. "They can't help."

"Of course they can. Don't give up now."

"I'm fine, really." As if to prove it, he pushed himself up, groggily, and turned his head one way then the next, making his neck bones crack. He looked like a man getting up in the morning, stretching his muscles, a peaceful look on his face. And he wasn't wearing a sheet, but a toga thingy, a wrap of some kind, like you might see in the desert. The cotton sheet shifted, exposing a bit of skin here and there. I couldn't see any cuts.

"Have you seen Blayde?"

"Um, no," I said, scanning the ground. "You sure it's not around here?"

I sure hoped not but, for now, I'd play into his delusion; stay on his good side just in case he was a psychopath with a new way of abducting people. While logic told me that something was off, my gut was sure there was nothing to worry about. I stood, extending a hand to help him up. He took it, his legs cracking like his neck when he put his weight on them.

Finally on his feet, he brushed himself down. The bloody wrap stuck to him pretty much everywhere, and the sand clinging to the patches of blood wasn't coming off either. He lifted a hand coated with sticky, bloody sand and grimaced before wiping it on his wrap.

"She wouldn't be on the ground," he explained quickly. "She's about yay tall"—he held his hand to about my eye level—"and tends to get a little intense when she doesn't know where I am. Then again, I never lost her before …"

"This is your blade we're talking about?"

"My Blayde, yes."

"I haven't seen one around here."

"Her. Blayde is a her."

"Your knife's a woman?"

"Oh, no." He laughed, pointing at me. Had I done something funny? Maybe the look of realization spreading on my face was something different for him. "It's Blayde. With a 'y' sound. B-l-a-y-d-e. She's my little sister. She's not here?"

"Oh, Blayde." I laughed, though in my back of my mind I was still debating whether the man was psychotic. I felt a little relief in the fact that he wasn't a knife-wielding maniac. "I've never heard that name before. What ethnicity is it?"

He ignored me, going to the edge of the road and shouting into the park. "Blayde! Blayde!" He shouted at the sky, the trees, and at anything that would listen, but he must have realized it wasn't getting him anywhere because he stopped.

"You could try calling her," I suggested.

"That's what I am doing!"

"With a phone, I mean."

"Blayde has our phone." He glared at me. "Wait a minute, do you have something to do with this?"

There was a sudden fire behind his eyes that wasn't there before, making me take a step away, shivering. He looked absolutely terrifying in that desert garb. At least, I guessed that's what it was, based on my experience with movies and such. It was soaked with blood, and his face was covered with sweat and twisted with fear.

Holy shit, he was scary.

"No," I said, stepping away from him. He looked taller now. While he wasn't a giant, he still towered over me like a mountain.

"What have you done with Blayde? Did you run over her too?" the stranger growled, pretty much saying the worst thing he could have said.

"No!" I sputtered, "No, no, no ... Oh shit. I hit

41

you with my car. No, I ran you over. I felt it. Heard it. I … but you weren't there, and then … where did you come from?"

"You'll get answers when I get answers," he snarled, a threat hanging on his lips, "Now, tell me, and tell me quickly. Where. Is. Blayde?"

And that's when it hit me, all at once. The thing I refused to believe, what his jovial smile and quick recovery had pushed to the back of my mind.

I had hit him with my car.

I lost control of my breathing as the truth hit me. The morning's panic came back but stronger, a panic attack of the likes I hadn't felt in years. Everything was so clear now—the body crunching against the impact of my car, the blood in the street. I fell to my knees, clutching my chest and willing myself to calm down, but it was too much to process.

"Oh … no, hey," he said, his voice soft and reassuring, going from terrifying giant to sweet teddy in five seconds flat. He crouched beside me, putting a warm hand on my shoulder. "It's okay. I'm okay. See? You didn't hurt me. I'm all right. And you're all right. You're going to be fine."

And the attack slowly began to subside.

He waited until I had calmed before removing his hand. The stranger sat beside me in the middle of that empty road, staring up at the sky as I composed myself.

Why was this happening to me?

And why on earth was it happening to me?

"Do you know what it's like to be alone?" he whispered. His voice was so low it felt like it was woven from the frozen air. "With only one person in the entire

42

universe you can count on? Just one?"

I didn't answer, but the truth was, I did. Marcy had been right, even if I couldn't admit it. But I had a feeling his question ran a little deeper than that.

"Do you have any idea what it's like to lose them?"

It didn't sound like this Blayde person had walked off like I had or taken off somewhere distant. It sounded like she was dead.

"I've had my losses," I said, unsure if his questions were rhetorical, if he really wanted an answer or just wanted to talk to a wall. "I've felt like I've lost my world before. My universe. But I didn't, not really."

"Now, I know what that feels like, too."

And so, we sat and stared at the stars for a little while longer, neither of us knowing what to say. I wanted to take him to a hospital, make sure he was all right, but he had made it seem like that would be the death of him.

"I'm Sally," I said, finally breaking the silence. "Sally Webber. I don't know who you are or if you believe me, but I am truly sorry. Really, I am. And not just about hitting you with the car."

"I'm Zander," he said, his eyes still riveted on the sky.

Did he see something up there? What was he even looking for?

"Zander who?"

"Just Zander."

A gust of wind blew down the street, chilling my skin. Zander ignored it. He ignored a lot of things, actually. He was an odd sight, for sure. His clothes had an otherworldly feel to them. His tunic slipped over his head then wrapped around his waist; his loose-fitting pants were stuffed into worn leather boots, old and cracked in places, with long strips of cotton wrapping up his calves to keep him from tripping over his clothes.

His face didn't seem to fit his choice of clothes, however. While the wrap was light, his face seemed chiseled and hard, like that of a Greek statue. Blemish-free and a gentle brown that could have been a dark tan, his skin had sand stuck to it in places, and gravel in others. He scratched the stubble near his ear, dislodging small particles of sand and revealing dirty fingernails. His eyes reflected the stars as he stared up. He ran a hand through his hair, which billowed from the top of his head, defying gravity. And although his arms were bloodied, there were no cuts. No marks. Not even scars.

"I'm glad you're not hurt, Zander, whoever you are," I said, teeth chattering. "I could never have lived with myself if I had ..."

"You don't even know me."

"Yeah, but still, I'm in shock, right? Actually running someone over ..." I shuddered. "It's the sort of thing that'll haunt your nightmares forever."

"Not the worst thing to haunt your nightmares, but I see your point." The edges of his smile were taut, and the expression didn't reach his eyes. It was an expression I knew well.

"So, um, how come you're not hurt? If you don't mind me asking? I mean, the blood ..."

"Oh, this?" He chuckled. "Costume."

"But, the street."

"Costume," he insisted, brows furrowing. "Nothing

happened."

"Right," I agreed, knowing he wouldn't let me push it any further while fully aware it was a lie. "So, um, you want to call Blayde?"

"Oh, that would be great. Thanks," he said, taking the phone I held toward him. "If I can remember her number, of course."

"Ha, gotta love smartphones," I joked. "I only know my house number from when I was a kid. I'd be a mess if I were ever stranded."

"Oh, ha, true," he agreed, smiling politely, as if he had no idea what I was talking about.

"Blayde, hey, it's me," he said, after a whole minute of fumbling around. Judging by the response time, he had managed to reach an answering machine. "Jump got interrupted. Not my fault and not yours either, but we'll talk about that later. I'm in—hey," he shouted to me. "Where are we?"

"Franklin."

"No." He shook his head. "What country?"

"Country? Um, the US."

"Yeah," he said, returning to the call. "The US, on Earth. Franklin. There're lots of trees. I'll be waiting. And Blayde? Be safe, okay?"

Zander hung up the phone, handing it back with a tip of his head.

"Is there anything else I can do for you?" I asked, still shaken. "Anything you need? Can I offer you a ride somewhere?"

He laughed. "That's kind, but no thanks. I'm fine, really. I'll be on my way."

"Are you sure?"

"Yup." Zander nodded. "But, hey, thanks. Here."

He reached into his pocket, pulling out a handful of coins in different shapes and sizes. Some were hexagonal—I couldn't think of any countries that had hexagonal coins—while some looked more like poker chips, only smaller. Finally, he selected six small coins that I didn't recognize. They looked like something out of an old movie, old fashioned but in perfect condition, as if they minted only yesterday.

"For all the trouble I've caused," he explained. "Thanks again!"

With that, he tore off into the park, disappearing between the trees before I could call him back, leaving nothing but bloody sand in his wake.

I stared at the coins in my hand. What on earth had just happened?

And where had all that sand come from?

CHAPTER FOUR

IN WHICH I GAIN A HEALTHY DISTRUST OF PARKS

You know that moment you wake up and everything is good with the world? When you snuggle in the sheets and think that life might just be perfect? And then wonder why you need to get up, and if you could stay like this forever, or if anybody would even notice if you were gone?

I guess I didn't deserve that kind of comfort. When my eyes flew open the next morning, I felt the weight of everything on my chest. I had lost my job. I had gotten into a fight with Marcy. And, to top it off, I had run a man over with my car—or something. That part wasn't so clear.

Luckily, one of those problems could be rectified right now. I fought against the bright light from the sun as I struggled to find my phone, which wasn't on my nightstand where I usually left it. Nothing was where I usually left it. I was still entirely dressed, well, except for my shoes, which were nowhere to be found.

I guess yesterday was pretty rough.

I got up, shuffling out of my room, trying to find my purse through the blur of morning vision. I found it in the sink. One of my shoes was balanced on the drying rack beside it; the other one was unaccounted for. Luckily, the water hadn't touched my purse, so my phone was safe.

Everything on the phone's screen punched my anxiety button. For starters, the clock announced it was already 11:30 A.M. On top of that, there were dozens of missed calls, all from the same number. Marcy, of course. She was probably peeved I hadn't called her back, and the guilt for how I had acted last night hit me again tenfold.

My stomach knotted itself at the memory of the things I had said, or wanted to say. I had been stupid and rude, to the only person who was even trying to help. There would be a lot of apologizing to do, even if I did feel slightly offended at how easily Marcy thought she could change me. I didn't need any pity from her or anyone. But I loved her, and I couldn't believe I had stormed off like that.

I pressed the call button and hopped on the sofa, sinking into the softness of the seat. I needed to buy new cushions, I remembered. Rosemary's absence lingered in the air, weighing me down.

"... Out of your mind?" Marcy squawked. "Because I've been out of mine. I've been trying to call you all morning. How are you feeling, by the way? Any better? I'm sorry about last night. I thought I was helping, but, my gosh, Sally, I've been worried sick. I wanted to ...

I tried to …"

I couldn't help but laugh. "Relax, Marcy. I overslept."

"Overslept?" Marcy sputtered. "It's almost noon. Are you okay?"

"A little stressed," I replied, which was true, but it wasn't the whole story. I would tell her about that Zander guy when we met in person; it wasn't telephone talk. "I needed to sleep it off. It just took a little longer than I expected."

"Obviously."

Silence followed, during which we both waited for the other to speak until it became so unbearable that we both blurted out the words we were dying to say.

"I'm sorry!" They came out almost simultaneously, and we laughed at each other and ourselves.

"I shouldn't have blown up at you," I said. "I know you were looking out for me."

"Yeah, but I shouldn't have tried to intervene at my birthday party," said Marcy. "Look, Sally, I am sorry, okay? I was worried about you. You barely go out except to work or buy food. I just want you to be happy."

"I get it, Marce." I nodded, though I knew she wouldn't see it.

"Please tell me you didn't go clubbing afterward," she said, "I got so scared. I know what you're like when you're down, and I saw you with a beer, and I…"

"I don't do that anymore, Marce." I shuddered at the memory, "Let's not do this over the phone. You want some lunch? I did a poor job celebrating your birthday." I stood and stretched, feeling like I had just taken a hundred tons off my back.

"So did I," she pointed out.

"So … lunch?" I asked, hoping it would benefit both of us. I tiptoed to look out the high kitchen window. The day was beautiful, incredible sunny October weather. Except for the man on the bench reading a newspaper, the street was empty. It was a wonderful day for a picnic. "In an hour? I'll buy the cake."

"Sounds fab."

"The Jitterbug?"

"Nah, I'll make us sandwiches."

"That's perfect." I grinned. "Picnic, then? The usual place? I'll provide the rest."

"See you there!"

I hung up with a smile on my lips. Things were going to get better from here on out, I just knew it.

That was probably the moment I jinxed it.

Well, the conversation would be awkward. I wasn't the kind of person to take help unless I've asked for it. Marcy and I were going to have some hurdles to work through, but we've been the best friends for years and that wasn't going to end anytime soon, and certainly not over a small spat.

I got dressed in no particular rush. It felt nice to wear a clean shirt, and I wondered why I hadn't taken the time to do my laundry for the past few weeks. I piled everything in the hamper, impressed by how airy it made the room feel. Somehow, that made me feel better, too.

And so, I decided to clean.

It felt good, honestly. Cathartic. I took out the trash. I wiped down the kitchen and the bathroom. My mind wandered, and, for some reason, it kept going back to the man in the loosely-draped cotton robes saturated with blood and sand. Whenever it did, I had to clutch something to keep from falling over. There was something very wrong about that man.

I brought my mind back to cleaning and sorting. Finally, I assembled a bag consisting of a small bottle of champagne—Rosemary must have left it here—and Marcy's still-wrapped birthday present, which had never left my purse, along with paper plates, knives, and napkins. I even left the house on time.

First up—the bakery. Just across the park, it made the best cakes you could possibly imagine. Just perfect for Marcy. She would get the angel food cake she had sacrificed to cheer me up. I had even left with enough time to wait in line if it was busier than usual.

I couldn't help but relish the amazing weather. We'd had a sweltering summer, but now, the city was cooling off, making it comfortable and sunny with a slight breeze. It had, however, rained through the night, leaving puddles in my path. I wove around them, keeping my feet dry.

Had it washed away the blood on the street?

The tightness around my spine was back, forcing a shiver through my body. No matter how hard I tried to keep it out of my head, my mind wandered back to the events of last night, but I didn't want to see them again. I'd rather forget them entirely. With a deep breath, I reined in my thoughts and tried to ignore the images burned in the back of my mind.

I crossed the road, smiling politely at the man on the bench. He rolled his eyes and went back to his column. My path took me through the park which, to my surprise, was practically empty. The gravel path was mine this morning, the full heat of the sun blocked by the thick, shady trees. I reveled at the thought of sitting near the river, Marcy's famous homemade sandwich in hand, in weather better suited for May than October.

As I walked further into the depths of the foliage, where branches hung so low and were so close together that the sun barely reached the path below, I realized that I hadn't seen anyone else. Even the birds were quiet. Okay, so maybe they migrated a few months earlier than usual. The squirrels, normally so noisy with their skittering along the branches, were nowhere to be seen. I could hear nothing but the quiet crunch of gravel. That and the quickening of my heart.

And then, suddenly, people were there.

Where the park had been empty seconds before, three people now stood, right in the middle of the path ahead of me. They chatted amicably, as if they had been there all along.

Now I was seeing things. Somehow, they were just there, fully materialized out of nowhere, and all I could do was stand frozen, my jaw practically on the ground.

Oh, you have got to be kidding me.

Was I imagining it? Hallucinating? If I was, it was extremely convincing. They looked real, but they couldn't be. People don't just—

Two of the strangers were female, both with their backs to me, but I was close enough to make out every separate hair, every fiber of their clothing. It was more than my mind could have conjured on its own. The third fixed his eyes on me, his face too detailed to be a dream.

I knew who he was immediately. There was no way I couldn't. His face had been permanently engraved in my mind since the night before.

Zander. The man in the bloody rags.

The man I had hit with my car.

His hair was different; that was the first thing I noticed. He was better groomed, each dark chocolate strand shouting a personal "screw you!" to gravity, reaching for the skies in a gentle swoop. He was dressed in a dark, formal suit with a battered black leather jacket, yet somehow, it didn't seem to clash with his outfit. He had a strange half-smirk on his face, a mix of confusion and amusement.

What was he doing here? And, more importantly, where on earth had he come from?

He grinned. "Would you look at that." The women spun around at his words, both wore varying degrees of shock on their stern faces.

The taller of the two had hair as astonishing as the man's, a vibrant mix of reds, purples, and blues feathered over jet-black. She wore a leather jacket, too, but hers was brownish-red and in a much better shape, almost new. Her features were incredibly sharp, as if her sculptor had forgotten to smooth the edges of her face; she had a pointed nose, high cheekbones, and thin eyebrows, almost invisible. They contrasted with her wide lips. Something about her face made her ethnicity impossible to pinpoint, as if she were a mix of everything the planet had to offer.

The woman beside her turned slower than her friend, but I recognized her as quickly as I had recognized the man—she was me.

Another Sally—the same face, the same me. She was prettier, though, much prettier than I had ever been. All the pimples and scars were gone; even her fingers seemed longer and more elegant. She radiated confidence from every pore, her smile one of cheer and excitement. She scanned me with wide, surprised eyes, but her smile never wavered.

"I remember this," she said, turning back to Zander, who lifted an eyebrow. "But now? No, this isn't right. We should go."

"You sure?" he asked. "We're here, aren't we?"

"Not the right here," the other woman said. "We've overshot a little. Is this ...?"

"Before," the other Sally replied. "We'd better go before we mess anything up."

As suddenly as they'd arrived, they were gone.

Just like that.

Of course, like the dumbass I was, I just stood there. I couldn't move, and I wasn't sure I wanted to. My arms trembled, causing the plastic bag I still carried to rattle against the side of my leg.

I did the deep breathing techniques I had learned in therapy, but they weren't helping. Focus, focus, I tried to tell myself, but I couldn't ignore that I had seen another version of myself pop in and out of existence like a glitching hologram.

I didn't know how long I stood there. It could have been hours. I probably would have stood there forever if a voice hadn't interrupted the silence.

"Ms. Webber?"

It came to so suddenly that I lost my balance and

practically fell over if not for the stranger reaching out to steady me. Things just kept getting weirder. The man wore a trench coat and dark Fedora, the image of a noir movie cop. He stood in the middle of the gravel path, the shade obscuring his face. Even when I did catch his features, they looked like they were shifting around.

His arm was on mine for far longer than I was comfortable with. I pulled it back, wary of the stranger.

"Who's asking?" I said, relatively pleased that my voice wasn't shaking like my hands were.

"Detective Madison." He pulled a badge from his breast pocket and flashed it in front of my face too quickly for me to make anything out. "I wondered if you could answer a few questions?"

"What about?" I asked. I slipped my hand into my pocket, wrapping my hand around my house keys. Not very effective if anything came to that.

Maybe I was just paranoid, but there was definitely something wrong with his face. Very wrong. So wrong that I kept wanting to look away without knowing why.

"Have you seen this man?" He reached into his jacket and pulled out a large, glossy photograph. And there he was again, the man it seemed impossible to forget—Zander.

He glared at me from the printed spots of ink, from the mug shot he was posing for. A thick cut crossed his nose, red and purple and bulbous, but it was nothing compared to the state of his jaw, which, though cleaned, was mangled beyond recognition. Even through the sorry state of his face, he seemed to sneer at the camera.

"I haven't," I replied truthfully. While it looked like the man called Zander, it simply couldn't be him. Those cuts would have left scarring, but the man from last night had a perfect jawline.

"Are you sure?" the detective urged. "Look closer."

"Never seen him before."

"It would have been in the past few days."

"No, I'm sure," I said, forcing myself to keep cool. "I would remember someone who looked like that."

"It's a felony to withhold information from the law," The man was adamant now, his voice harsh and cruel. "If you're not telling me something—"

"It's a felony if you work for the police or the FBI," I snapped. "You never said what agency you were with. I'm pretty sure you're supposed to tell me that. I know my rights. Well, the gist of them, and I don't have to tell you anything."

The man scowled. "This is a matter of life and death, Sally Webber. If you don't tell me, hundreds, nay, thousands could be in grave danger."

I felt a jolt of terror roll through my body. "And how do you know my name?" I wanted to run, but my legs wouldn't let me. He didn't respond. "Who are you?"

"Don't say I never gave you a chance." He tsked under his breath, reaching into his jacket again. This time, he pulled out a gun.

Holy shit—a gun! An actual freaking gun!

"Now, hold on," I said, stumbling backward as he advanced, weapon drawn. I threw my hands up, even though I knew it wouldn't do anything. The trembling in my legs intensified.

"Why are you protecting him?" the man asked, waving the weapon in my face, close enough for me to smell the pungent odor of a recently fired gun. "You don't even know him. Who he is. What he's done!"

"Look, let's just talk this over with level heads, all right?" I said, my voice a high-pitched squeak. My panic level was out of control. "I don't know what you're talking about. I know that's not what you want to hear, but it's the truth. You have to believe me."

"Terrans are liars, and awful ones at that," he replied, sounding bored. "Tell me where Zander is, and I'll spare your life."

I didn't believe a word he said, but I wasn't about to tell him that. "He asked for directions," I lied, spurting out the first thing that came to mind. "He wanted to find his way to Chicago. Drove off in a red car, that's all I know. I swear."

And then he pulled the trigger.

CHAPTER FIVE

ALL OF THE ABDUCTION, NONE OF THE PROBING

I awoke for the second time that day. Only this time, there were no bed sheets and no comfy blankets. No, this time, I woke on a cold metal floor, and I was already out of breath.

It was like waking from one dream into another, though I knew this was far too real. I had been shot by an Inspector Gadget look-alike. I quickly checked my body with trembling hands: I wasn't injured, and I didn't feel drowsy, just angry. I opened and closed my mouth like a fish out of water, and the putrid taste of an ashtray coated my tongue. And yes, I do know what one tastes like, but that's another story.

Had he used a … a stun gun on me? Were those things even real? I guess they had to be, seeing as how I wasn't dead.

I was in a dark room, lit by weak light strips lining

the top of the walls. It wasn't very wide, about the size of my bedroom back home, but the walls were gross— metal, covered with condensation, scratched in places, and covered with what I really hoped was just rust.

And I wasn't alone.

In the chair nearest the door sat a woman who could have been a student at U-Frank, wearing brown Ugg boots and a comfy sweatshirt. On the single bunk, against the wall to my right sat an androgynous person with a pixie haircut wearing jeans and a long-sleeved t-shirt.

They looked fucking terrified.

I scrambled up and backed against the wall. Bad idea: the gross wall water of water pressed against my shirt, slowly seeping through. I didn't know these people. I didn't want to. Had they been the ones to take me?

That's when it dawned on me, a little late, you might say—I had been kidnapped.

Well, shit.

"Don't be cat," said the Ugg boots girl. "Everything will be lemonade, just stool calm."

"What?" I asked.

"Don't worry about her," the pixie person said. "Her translator's on the fritz. Some words get jumbled. I'm pretty sure she wants you to stay calm. We're not going to hurt you—we're in the same position you are."

Ugg boots girl nodded. As she did, she lifted a hand to push some of her silky blonde hair behind her ear, flashing fingers that looked closer to an iguana's than a human. It was as if her skin ended at her wrist: The rest of her hand was completely reptilian, a dark emerald-green tone. Her other hand and the rest of her body looked completely human.

Holy shit. A lizard hand? I was dumbstruck. The repitilians really are among us? How high up does this go? My jaw dropped open. I must have looked terrified—I was, after all—because pixie person gave me an apologetic look.

"What did they get you for?"

"For?" I stammered.

"I flew through the Ordran territory to get here, got a bounty on my head for that. And Miko," they said, indicating the Ugg boots girl, "she skipped bail. She's been hiding out here for years, though they wouldn't have caught her if her skin wrap hadn't gotten damaged and she ended up on Instagram. What about you?"

"Holy shit!" I said, sliding down the wall and falling on my ass. "You're aliens!"

Aliens. Real aliens. Okay, don't panic. That's the best place to start. But what else was I supposed to do when confronted with undeniable proof that aliens exist? My eyes were hooked on the lizard hand, if you could even call it that. It looked so ... wrong.

It looked alien.

And yet, the two of them looked at me, exchanging quick, scared glances.

"You're ... Terran?" Miko squawked. "Flowers. This spelunking!"

"You have got to be kidding me." The pixie ran their hands through their hair. "They can't take Terrans. They're breaking—I can't tell you how many laws—"

"Spigot?" Miko snorted. "You really think what they're doing to us is legal? We're free tiramisu. We should be able to do what we please."

"No, they want you for tax evasion. That makes good sense," pixie cut said, "but the Terran? They can't take Terrans. It's so many different shades of illegal."

"Excuse me?" I sputtered, trying to make sense of the situation. "But who are they?"

"Bounty Hunters," pixie cut explained, signaling for Miko to shush. "Or mercenaries. You know, the kind of people who don't care what side of the law they're on, so long as they get paid."

"I've been abducted?" I shuddered, the full realization dawning on me, "Oh shit. I've been abducted. I'm on a spaceship and I ... I ..."

I had been abducted. By fucking aliens.

Today was not my day.

Yesterday wasn't either; I really hoped the rest of the week wasn't going to be more of the same. Then again, the past two years had been disappointing. It was entirely possible this was just the next step in my rotten luck.

"Don't worry," Miko said softly. "They don't flan you."

"Who are we kidding?" said the pixie. "They don't care. They've taken her anyway. Though what the Alliance wants with her, I don't know."

"Maybe it was an accident?" Miko suggested.

"Maybe ..."

Pixie stared at me as if expecting me to do tricks or something. I wasn't going to give them the pleasure. I stood, propping a hand on the gross wall to steady myself.

"We're on a spaceship," I muttered, running my

hand over the LED strip like a moth attracted to a flame. We didn't have a window and it didn't feel like we were moving, but it was a spaceship—and I was on it.

Also, spaceships existed. Cool.

Too bad I only knew this because I had become the most recent in a line of alien abductees.

"Wait a second. You're both speaking English?" I spun around to face them. "Does everyone in the universe speak English? Is this like Star Trek?"

"By gremlins alone," Miko said. "Ugh. When they ...um ... grab me, my translate got ... jumbled? Taylor, help."

"Miko got zapped in the head; it fried her chip," the pixie, named Taylor, explained. "Some of the words come out backward."

"Chip?"

"Translator," Taylor said. "That little implant that does wonders for interstellar travel. If you can afford it, that is. I had to learn English the hard way."

"That had to be an interesting language class," I muttered. "You speak it really well."

"Thanks, I've had fifty years to work on it."

"Fifty years? But you look ..."

"Skin wrap," said Taylor. "I'm wearing a human suit so I can fit in? Wow, you really are Terran. This is tourism 101."

I shuddered. If I was so ... Terran ... then what did that make them? Their words were alien to me, even if they spoke English, and yet, they looked just like anyone else. Minus the lizard hands.

How many others were out there taking human

form and roaming the streets? And what did they want with our planet?

Though, selfishly, I had to focus on myself right now. I couldn't think about aliens roaming the streets. I needed to figure out why the hell aliens had decided I was worth abducting.

"So, what do they want with me?" I asked, facing my fellow captives.

Taylor shrugged. "What's your name? Maybe it's something to do with your—"

"Sally," I said. "Sally Webber."

"Never heard of you," Taylor said. "Have you encountered any weird artifacts lately? It's possible you were dealing with tech you're not supposed to have—"

"No weird artifacts," I said, shaking my head, "but the guy who shot me wanted to know about someone I ran into."

Miko leaned forward. "What kind of guy?"

"Um, it's a long story, I think," I replied. Taylor tapped a spot on the cot, and I sat next to them. I didn't think about how gross the cot was, or how the color was not the one it had been when it was made. I tried not to think about it as I put my rear on the formerly white fabric.

"So? Tell us," Taylor urged. "We have a whole lot of time on our hands."

"Well, um," I started, making eye contact with the alien beside me. Their eyes were gorgeous; deep silver I could see myself falling into …

No. Talk. Talk to keep the panic from settling in …

"So, last night I was driving home, and I hit this

guy," I said. "No idea where he came from. One second I was driving, and then boom, I ran him over!"

"Flowers!" Miko said, cursing under her breath while still concentrating on every word. "You might have killed someone important from the Alliance. That would explain why they flan you. The crown prince is spaghetti to be missing, last scarf here—did you run over the emperor's son?"

"Ha, no emperor, I'm pretty sure." My heart clenched. Was Zander a galactic royal? I hoped not. Running people over from a royal court was not a good idea. "No. He was fine. He got up and walked away. But then, this morning, the guy who got me was looking for him. He showed me a picture of the guy, and boy, did he look rough. Like there was no way the man I met—I mean, ran over—could be that person. There were chunks missing from his face."

"Did this guy have a name?" Taylor urged. "Miko might be right. He could be someone important. They might want to put you on trial."

"But he was fine!" I sputtered, trembling. What if these strangers were right? What if Zander was someone important?

But the man in the park—my abductor, I think I should be calling him—he said Zander was dangerous. Very dangerous. So maybe it was the other way around. Maybe they wanted me to help them find Zander. Which was ridiculous. I had no idea where on earth he could be.

If he even was on Earth. Thinking of him as an alien cast last night into an entirely new light.

"He said his name was Zander, but no last name,

and it could have been a fake ..."

The second the name came out of my mouth, both captives changed completely. Taylor stiffened, while Miko's face burst into a smile far too wide for her face.

"Do you know him?" I asked.

"Know him?" Miko said excitedly. "Him ... legend."

"A legendary dick," Taylor snapped, and Miko glared at them.

"I from ... outer planets," said Miko, very slowly, forcing her words to come out right. I waited. I wasn't in any rush. "Outer planets see him differently. Him hero. He not get harmed. He travels through space in... blinks. He and sister."

"Sister?"

"The stories say that millennia ago, there were two super heroic siblings who traveled the universe saving people, okay?" Taylor said rolling their eyes. "But they're folk tales. Stories you tell kids. These two have wreaked havoc for the Alliance. They're pretending to be the siblings, but they're criminals blowing things up and stealing shit. No one reads or tells those old stories anymore, anyway. Nobody cares."

"I care!" snapped Miko.

"So, wait, the guy I met is an intergalactic criminal?" I scratched my head. Zander had been nice; he didn't seem like a criminal. He didn't seem like a legend, either, though.

Then again, he didn't seem alien, and from what I could tell, the consensus said that he was.

"Interstellar, but I guess it's all the same to you." Taylor rolled their eyes, not trying to be as chummy as before. "Anyway, that's why they took you. They want

STARSTRUCK

information."

"Nuh-uh." Miko shook her head. "The Zander from the stories is a hero. If they took her, it's so he tries to save her."

"Wait, they want to trap him?"

"Probably," Taylor said. "Trap him, find him, whatever. You're here because of the mysterious Zander. Get used to it. At least you have someone to blame other than yourself."

I shuddered. I was doing that a lot lately.

"Couldn't it be some other Zander?"

"Nah," Taylor said. "No one gives children that name. It would be like a Terran naming their kid Adolph. Not gonna happen."

"So, wait," I said, addressing Miko, "what did you say this guy could do?"

"There's a poem about him in my language." She grinned. "It'll sound like nonsense in yours. Here ..."

She let out a shriek that could have torn apart my ears. Heck, I could feel my hair flying backward from the sheer force of it. She laughed, stopping quickly.

"What was that?" I asked, shocked.

"A little taste of the universe, Terran." Miko chuckled. "Right, let's see if I can gummy ... I mean, translate. Damn this chip. Okay. Here goes: There were once two heroes, valiant to behold. Brother, sister, never old. Ha, that rhymes in English too! Impressive."

"Yeah, impressive," I muttered.

"Right," she continued. "They appeared with no fanfare and left with no sound. They bled like mortals but never faltered. Where they stood, justice prevailed, and also they had a whole lot of faces."

66

"You're going great with this translation thing," I said, which made her smile. Now that my initial shock of her being not of this world had worn off, I began to see her as just another human. If we had met in college, we probably would have been friends.

"Thanks. It sounds better in my native tongue, though, a lot more sing-songy. It used to put me to sleep."

"I can imagine," I said politely.

"Right. I guess that last line would sound better with a poetic ring to it? Like, they bled like mortals, but always stood strong; under their changing faces, you could do no wrong. Something like that?"

"Classy." I grinned. I could see what she was doing. She was trying to distract me—us—from the fact we were being hauled to our deaths, probably.

"It ends by saying they would reward good children with presents and gifts," Miko explained.

"So basically, they're your Santa, right?" Taylor scoffed. "We were told a different story. You've got two criminals who can get into any place they want, travel from planet to planet unnoticed. Great at changing their appearances, huge tolerance for pain. But when they show up, people get hurt or worse—killed. The Alliance wanted them dead."

"Past tense?"

"Yeah, duh."

"All of this was over a hundred years ago in Standard Union Time. That's close to three or four centuries ago for Earth. Any truth about them would be kept by the Berbabsywell Monks, and we both know they're not talking to anyone anytime soon. If they ever did exist, they died a long time ago. As did the myths a few millennia before that."

"I don't believe that," Miko muttered.

"Well, keep believing in Santa then," Taylor spat.

"Santa's not real?" she asked, and Taylor sighed. "Shit. I thought he was a local deity. I've been leaving offerings of milk and cookies for nothing? No wrath is being appeased?"

"Seems that way."

"So who's been eating them?"

I sat on the cot, my mind reeling. Zander: criminal, hero, or just some dead guy? Had I met the legend or a man with the same name? I mean, Zander wasn't too rare of a name on Earth, but as for the rest of the galaxy...

A jingle blasted through the compartment.

Both captives turned to stare at me as I extracted my phone. Yes, my phone was ringing, in the heart of a spaceship flying us to our doom, and of all people who could have been calling, well, it was some unknown caller who decided this was the right moment.

"What are you keen vacant?" Miko urged. "Pineapple. Pineapple."

I picked up, cradling the phone close to my ear. My hand shook. "Hello?" I said, begging it not to be a spam call.

"Sally? Hey."

Oh, my God. Matt.

Sweet, beautiful, incredible Matt was calling me. I flew to my feet, taking myself and the phone to one of the free corners in our cell. I wasn't more than six feet away from anyone else, but it felt like privacy.

Oh, crap. Privacy. Did we have a bathroom in here?

Looking around, I saw there was no toilet or receptacle in this small room. Not to mention that I had Matt on the phone, and really didn't need to think about it.

"Hey, Matt, great to hear from you," I said. I mean, what was I supposed to tell him? Help, aliens kidnapped me because they think the man I ran over is an intergalactic—sorry, interstellar—super criminal?

"You feeling any better?" he asked, genuine concern in his voice. "Last night at the party, you looked—"

"Yeah, I was having a bad day. A hot-air balloon covered my window the day my alarm clock failed, so I was late and ... well, it's retail. I lost my job."

"A hot-air balloon did what?"

"In any case, I was suddenly unemployed, so it sucked pretty hard."

"Oh," he said, excitedly. "Wait, you need a job? What kind?"

"I've got retail experience, but that's about it. Why?"

"I might be able to fix you up with that." I could sense him smiling on the other end. "My boss, Mr. Grisham, has come to his senses and realized he's a bit overwhelmed, and needs a PA. Personal assistant? I mean, it's not very rewarding, but it pays great and Grisham is a fantastic boss. Heck, I think he's my mentor now. Want me to get you the info?"

"Oh, my gosh, really?" I replied, giddy, forgetting my situation and reveling in my luck. "Matt, you're the best."

"Aww," he said, "it's great that you say that, because, um, I didn't actually call to help you find a job.

I wanted to ask you on a date. Don't say yes just because I'm helping you, all right? I mean do say yes, but—"

"I would love to," I replied, forgetting I was in a spaceship, in a cell with two aliens. I was right down on Earth and happy.

"Perfect. When's best for you?"

"Um, not too sure ..." I said, looking back around the cell. Would I get out of here in time for a date? Would I get out of here at all?

"Friday?" he asked. "We can move it around if your schedule changes."

Like, if I don't come back from outer space?

"Friday sounds great!"

"Fantastic, I'll get us a reservation somewhere nice. Do you like Italian?"

"Multi Bene."

"Perfect. See you soon then, Sally."

"See you, Matt," I said, wishing the call would never end. "Oh, and Matt?"

"Yeah?"

Call the White House. Aliens are real and kidnapping US citizens, I wanted to say.

Find me.

Help me.

"I'm looking forward to it." I shuddered as he hung up the phone, propelled into my dismal reality as I remembered I was trapped.

"They let me keep my phone," I muttered.

"Pfft, Mercs don't know what that is," Taylor scoffed. "But I mean, no signal in space, so ..."

"But I have signal," I said, holding the phone up and turning around, finding five bars everywhere. It made no sense, there weren't any phone towers in space, unless …

"What if we never took off?"

The two captives looked at me with wide eyes.

"Where else would we be?" Miko intoned.

I tapped on the Google Maps app and grinned. "In Franklin—Echotree State Park."

"You're kidding me?" Taylor was by my side, staring down at my phone like it was a million-dollar bill.

"You know what this means, right?" I said, a smile creeping up my lips, "It means we're breaking out of this place."

CHAPTER SIX
DON'T EVER TRY THIS AT HOME

"There is no way out of here," Taylor scoffed. "We've tried."

"Yeah, well, you have a secret weapon now," I said, bursting with false confidence. Call it desperation, but there was a fire in my belly, and it was growing.

"What?" Taylor snorted. "A Terran?"

"Exactly," I replied, marching to the door. It was sturdy and probably reinforced. It looked like one of those doors on tugboats, all thick and metal and impenetrable. "Anyone have martial arts training?"

Nobody answered. A plan was forming in my head, growing from hours of TV marathons and action movies. I had no experience, but I couldn't just sit here. I felt like a caged animal, and it filled me with an insane amount of adrenaline and an urge to run, to get out, to free myself.

Heck, I really wanted to go on that date.

I indicated for Miko to stand up and hold her chair.

She gripped it tightly, giving me a quick nod of understanding. Good. I hoped she was up to the task.

"You can't be serious," scoffed Taylor, but I ignored them. When this goes pear-shaped, they would have every right to say, 'I told you so' but until then ...

"Help!" I shouted, adopting an awful falsetto impression, astonished at how terrible my voice sounded. "Oh gosh, is there somebody out there? I'm going to burst."

I screamed until my voice was hoarse and my throat dry and raspy, but I didn't give up. The words burned with every shout. Finally, I heard footsteps approaching. We all did, exchanging looks and nods. The sound echoed like gunshots on metal. Miko grasped the chair tighter.

"Oh, come on, shut uuuup. What is this about?" whined a gruff voice from the other side of the door. I clenched my legs together and hopped from foot to foot.

"I've got to pee," I insisted. It wasn't hard to fake—I really had to go. Call it a nervous bladder, then add it to the list of reasons I needed to get out of here. "Please, I need a toilet!"

"Well, hold it in?" It sounded uncertain. Perfect.

"I can't," I whined. "I'm going to wet myself, and you know how corrosive Terran pee is, right?"

No reply so I pushed the act a little further, hoping that, like with the phone, this guy knew hardly anything about my planet.

"Look, I'm really sorry, okay?" I said, still pushing the awful little girl voice. "I don't mean to cause any trouble. It's just the way I am. If I pee in here, it'll burn a hole through your ship."

"Don't let her do it, sir!" Taylor added in their most pleading voice. "I've lived with Terrans for half a century. I've seen what they're capable of. And their urine, it's—"

The latch clicked, and the door hissed as it opened. I took a step back, breathing deeply, knowing what was going to happen next and hoping, pleading, that this wasn't going to be the last thing I ever saw.

The second the door opened, before Miko even had a chance to strike, Taylor shoved their shirt over our captor's face, muffling his screams. It was then that Miko thwacked him with the chair. The echo reverberated through the cell, and he crumpled to the floor.

Okay, so that was easier than expected.

Taylor retrieved the shirt, putting it back on as Miko and I dragged the bounty hunter into the cell. Wow, the man was heavy. I was grateful for the help and impressed with Miko's strength. We flipped him onto his back. It was the man from the park—my abductor.

He looked different without the hat and trench coat. His ears pointed up and away from his face, like a bat, and I wondered how much of that face was his own. Did he have a skin wrap, like Miko? Just how alien was this guy?

I didn't care. I was mad that he had kidnapped me and gave him a swift kick in the gut. Go ahead, call me petty—you get abducted, see if you like it.

"What now?" Taylor hissed, glaring at the unconscious man.

"Now we get out of here," I said, surprised they were turning to me for leadership. Then again, I was the one who had gotten us this far. "We're in the forest, in Echotree, so we can run in a straight line until we reach the freeway and signal for help. But we can't let the others know we're out, so we must act fast. How many in the crew?"

"One other man that we know of," said Taylor. "There could be more."

Miko clung to her chair, holding two of the legs firmly. "I can scissor this."

"Thanks, Miko."

I wish I could tell you more about the ship. I mean, it's not every day you get to see an alien spacecraft. It's also not every day you get abducted and held in one. With getting out being priority numero uno, I didn't take the time to inspect my surroundings. All I saw were metal walls slick with condensation as we tiptoed through the hallways. Long wires and pipes followed the corridors. Every few feet, I saw patches of tape on the craft, really showing its age.

And it certainly wasn't a flying saucer.

We turned a corner, and suddenly there were voices. Lots of them. Angry voices. And horses? Why were there horses?

"Gruik, get back here," bellowed someone over the din. "The dragons are back. I'm not putting this on pause for you!"

I peeked into the room. It looked like a cargo bay, large and wide enough for lots of crates, but it fitted into a kitchen or dining room. There was what looked like a bar with a fridge on it and some dull-looking patio furniture. A lone man sat with his feet propped on a small, metal table, a desktop monitor in front of him.

It was hooked up to cable, and I saw our abductor was enjoying a recent episode of *Games of Thrones* while eating popcorn.

Miko didn't wait. With a murderous war cry that could have meant anything from "This is the end!" to "I will murder your family," she rushed into the room and slammed the chair into the man's head. Before he could turn around, he collapsed. She thwacked him again repeatedly until he stopped moving. The grimace etched on her face could mean only one thing—murder.

She turned and grinned at us, giving a thumbs-up with her lizard hand. Her long, blonde hair was still silky and straight, barely disheveled. There wasn't a splash of blood on her.

"Nice going," I said, trying not to act too freaked out, though my levels of panic skyrocketed when I saw the man on the floor. It was the man from the park bench, the guy casually reading his newspaper, or so I had thought when I had seen him this morning. I guess he was spying on me, too. Now that was just creepy. Who else was involved? Marcy? Matt? Dany?

Arthur?

"We need to get out of here," Taylor said, tugging my sleeve.

I didn't need to be told twice. I followed them to the door, a big metal thing large enough to dwarf a garage. My heart pounded at the thought of freedom.

It pounded even harder when I heard footsteps.

"Open the fucking door!" I screamed as the fake detective shuffled into the room, groggy but obviously furious. He held a hand to his head. His wig had been ripped, revealing parched, red skin underneath. "Do it now!"

Taylor slammed their hand against the red button, and the cargo door creeped open. The metal slab lowering into a ramp wasn't in the rush we were. Sunlight poured in, and I breathed a sigh of relief when I saw with absolute certainty we were still on Earth.

"Hurry it up!" I shouted.

"I'm doing what I can," Taylor snapped, banging the button even harder. It wasn't helping

"Pancakes," Miko snorted and slammed her chair on the button.

The door flew open with a defective clunk. Before I could thank her, the detective roared and rushed at us with a sudden burst of energy. I jumped out of the way and kept running.

The world outside, thankfully, was not the cold, uncaring void of space, but the warm woods of the local forest. Still, a shitty place to sprint through. But we ran anyway—we had to. Our abductor was right behind us. Right now, Miko and Taylor were not my friends—they were competition. All I had to do to be safe was outrun them.

The cold air burned my throat, making my breath shallow. My heart pounded so hard I could feel its beat in my fingertips. My feet slapped the ground as I ran; each stride was like stabbing myself with a knife.

Running absolutely sucked.

I didn't know how people did it in the movies. I had expected the adrenaline to help more. The only reason I kept running was because I knew that if I slowed down, it would mean getting abducted by aliens—again—and I wasn't going to let that happen. Even if it meant setting my lungs on fire and forcing my legs to move more than they had in the last three years combined. The only marathons I ran were on Netflix, and those were from the comfort of my couch.

I heard cars in the distance; a road, please, Lord, let it be a road. But as I ran, it sounded more like the road was coming toward me. The sound grew louder, rising until it was on top of me, and a car—my car—burst through the underbrush, flying over leaves and twigs. It let out a honk, and shock propelled me to the side.

It might have been old and battered with a huge dent in the fender from the incident the night before, but at this moment, it looked like a chariot made of gold. At its reins was Zander, complete with sandy robes and those big, red stains.

The car spun and skidded to a halt before me and the passenger side door flew open. I dove in, slamming it shut behind me, breathing heavily as I gripped my seat.

"Are you all right?" asked Zander, jamming his foot on the accelerator and throwing the car forward.

"I'm fine." I panted, trying to catch my breath as my head slammed against the headrest. "But we have to get the others."

"On it." Zander slammed his foot down on the accelerator, propelling us forward.

"This is my car."

"I needed a rescue vehicle. I didn't think you'd mind. Up ahead."

I leaned into the backseat and grabbed the handle to the back door when Taylor was upon us. The alien jumped in without hesitation.

"What's this crappy car?" Taylor asked, panting.

"It's my car," I replied. "Where's the guy?"

"After Miko," they said as they buckled their seat belt. "I think he had her. Who's that?"

"A friend. Which way?"

Zander didn't need me answering questions for him; he was already driving in the right direction, weaving through the trees like they weren't even there. I bit my lip, urging myself to calm down, feeling somewhat safe with Zander at the wheel and yet utterly terrified for Miko.

"Grab the wheel," Zander shouted, shattering my illusion of safety.

"What?"

"Grab it!"

I leaned over the stick shift and put both hands on the wheel. Zander, meanwhile, gazed out the window, searching for something. We saw it at the same time: Miko standing strong, feet planted like roots, swinging the chair like a fiery sword. The false detective dodged it easily, grinning like it was a grotesque game.

Without warning, the driver's seat was empty. My hands were the only ones at the wheel, and we were heading right for Miko. I swung the car around fast enough to miss careening into them but not fast enough to miss the scene that would change my life forever—the sight of Zander knocking out our captor cold.

But only after he appeared out of nowhere.

I hoisted myself into the driver's seat and slammed my foot on the brakes. Zander grabbed Miko and hauled her to the car, tossing her into the back just as Taylor opened the door, before climbing into the passenger seat beside me.

I guess it was my turn to drive.

"Petals to the medals!" Miko shouted.

"What?"

"Drive!"

"Yup." I floored it, and we took off into the forest, hopefully in the direction of my home.

Zander had made navigating around the trees seem easy. They tested my reflexes, forcing me to swerve at every turn. I didn't have any sense of direction; all I knew was that I had to drive and keep driving.

"Holy shit, you're him," Miko said with a fangirlish squeal.

"Who?" Zander asked.

"You're, like, him."

"What she means to say is that you're the guy everyone's after," Taylor supplied. "Thanks for the rescue, anyway."

"Can I get an eggplant?" she asked.

"I beg your pardon?" Zander stammered.

"Her translator's on the fritz," I relayed. "Makes her spout gibberish."

"Oh, I can fix that," he said. "Hand it over."

"It's in my pumpkin."

"Oh," he replied as if he understood.

"No offense," Taylor said, "but what the heck are you doing here? I thought you were some kind of—"

"I'm a lot of things." Zander glanced at her, and, though I couldn't see his expression, from what I could see of hers in the rearview mirror, he had given her a meaningful look. "I'm a lot of things, but I'm here to help. Speaking of which, you may want to cover your ears."

The draconic sound of a jet taking off above us shook the car and everyone inside. It hovered over the treetops, and it was coming for us.

I guess our abductors didn't care much for the 'alive' part of dead or alive because they started shooting at us.

Plasma beams. Actual plasma beams. Well, I think they were plasma beams, but I was too busy driving to check them out.

"Pickle," Miko shouted.

"We're all going to die," Taylor snarled, "in a car with the criminal that time forgot."

"Hey, come on," Zander said. I wasn't sure which part of the sentence offended him most. "Give me some credit. This has been just saved your life, and I'm not a criminal; I probably should have started with that. Oh, and no, you're not going to die. Well, you are going to die, one day, but—"

"Zander," I snapped. "What do we do?"

"You?" he said. "Keep driving. Don't look back."

"And where are you going?"

Before I could finish my sentence, he was gone, from the car at least, leaving the three of us to flee from the flying hell-beast of a ship as fast as we could.

"He's hot sauce." Miko chuckled from the backseat. She didn't seem all that scared anymore.

"Did you mean—"

"I know what I said."

The forest floor rumbled, and, just like that, the thunder was gone. Just ... gone. I breathed a sigh of relief.

"You think it's over?" Taylor asked.

"It's done." Once again, Zander had found a way to appear in my car without any kind of warning, making me jump a foot in the air. He didn't open the door. He didn't climb through the window. No sound to announce his approach; no flash of light. One minute he was there, when a second before he wasn't.

"Holy shit," Taylor said, snatching the words right out of my mouth.

"Don't you ever knock?" I asked.

He gave me a glowing smile. "When I'm not busy making sure everyone's in one piece and saving lives and all, yes, I do. You're welcome, by the way."

I grumbled my thanks, and his smile widened.

How was this man smiling? I was sure he had taken down an alien spaceship with his bare hands, wearing nothing more than a bloody toga. One that was still, somehow, dropping sand in my car—and now pine needles too.

"Is it over?" Taylor asked, pragmatic as always. Well, I say always, I hadn't known them for much more than an hour. But after an ordeal like that? It felt like the longest hour in my life, a real eternity.

"Yes," Zander said. "It's over."

I hoped he was telling the truth. In any case, I slowed the car. Just so there was no chance we'd ruin this victory by having me crash into a tree.

CHAPTER SEVEN
I FINALLY GET SOME ANSWERS AROUND HERE

"Will I ever see you again?"

Miko grasped Zander's forearms as she stood before him on the platform. Her hands were covered by pristine, white gloves now. Much better than having her lizard hand exposed for everyone to see.

"Probably not," he said curtly. He was still in the bloody, sandy robes. "I'm not staying on this planet long."

"Oh." Her face fell. "Well, thank you for saving us…"

I turned to Taylor, who rolled their eyes. The two of us sat on a bench, waiting for the train. Taylor was still on the run from—I never did get their names— more bounty hunters, but, for now, it was safe enough for them to recover their things and create a new identity elsewhere.

I was happy for them.

"Be careful around that man," Taylor said, jerking their chin toward Zander. "He might not be the criminal from years ago, but the bounty hunters want him for something. He's trouble, Sally."

"Miko seems to think he's the guy from her local legend."

"I was in a cell with her for three days." Taylor sighed, "Miko believes a lot of things. Believes in a lot of things."

Which was the moment Miko chose to grab Zander's face with both hands, bringing it down for a very large, very loud kiss. His eyes widened. For all we had just witnessed of him being an alien action hero, he was completely incapable of escaping her grasp.

"I'd love to trade numbers, you know." Taylor's cold exterior broke, and they put a hand on my shoulder. "I know I'm the first extraterrestrial you've met. Well, that you know of. I'd love to keep talking, but it's going to be tough with the new identity and all."

"I wouldn't even know where to start. With the questions, I mean, not with changing identities. I guess. I just ... where are you from? Which planet? What species? What brings you here? And ... I don't know. My mind's spinning."

"I've always known we weren't alone in the universe," Taylor replied, "so I can't imagine how hard it is for you to deal with the fact that, well, aliens exist. Though I guess we're not the only illegal aliens in this country, there'll be others." They paused. "My real name is Gorrin of the Second Setting House, the last offspring of Maveen. I was born on a small planet named Kel, in a binary system. My species? We call ourselves 'us' I guess. It's hard to translate concepts you don't have words for. If I weren't wearing my skin wrap, you'd probably pass out. My real body isn't exactly corporeal like yours. My life, my customs, the history of my planet could fill books on Earth, but, you know, it doesn't have a Starbucks. For me, Kel was kind of dull, which was why I left."

"Whoa."

I couldn't think of anything else to say. My head hurt from all this new information, and I felt exhausted. My hands trembled on my lap as I sat in silence. Miko returned, leaving Zander and his bashful-looking face to lean awkwardly against one of the trees lining the platform.

"That's us, Taylor." Miko indicated to the train approaching the station. My new friend nodded.

"I'd love to say we'll talk soon, but I think this is goodbye," Taylor said, getting up. I stood and wrapped my arms around them. I was hugging someone not born on my planet. It was pretty cool.

"You can track me down on Facebook once you're settled," I told them.

"I'm adding you the second I get home," announced Miko, next in line for a hug.

"I look forward to it." I grinned, squeezing her. Her grasp was tight and strong, and somewhere in the deep recesses of my mind, I knew that she could easily crush me if she wanted to.

I watched them climb aboard and waved as they rode away. Soon, their train was just a speck of dust on the horizon. They were gone, and I knew I would never see either again.

It was a weird feeling. We had been through something awful together, something no one else would ever know, something life changing. There was a new kind of confidence running through my veins that hadn't been there before, and the warmth was readily welcomed.

Plus, I had met aliens, which meant my personal world had gotten about a zillion times larger. It was kind of amazing. No, who am I kidding? It was incredibly amazing to know that we were not alone in the universe.

Or to know that some aliens had a thing for Starbucks, which I would never have expected. Maybe there's hope for Earth yet.

Zander was waiting for me by the tree line at the edge of the platform. I hadn't expected him to stick around. I honestly thought he would take off like he had last night, but I was glad he stayed. It was time for answers.

I walked to him, the thousands of things I wanted to say running through my mind. Why was he here? Who was he really? What was going on? Why was he able to do what he did? All questions I was desperate to ask. But when I reached him, I just stood there, mouth opening and closing like a fish. No words came out.

"Um," he started, the opposite of the self-assured man from the car. "Are you going to be all right?"

"Yeah, I think so. I just—I don't know where to start. I mean, you saved my life—why?"

"Oh, come on. He scratched the back of his head. "They only wanted you because of me. I couldn't let you suffer because of my mistake."

"You realize they were counting on that? It was a trap. If we hadn't gotten out, you might be ..."

"Not to sound boastful, but I did bring their ship down in four minutes and thirty-three seconds—by myself. Trust me, I would have gotten you out of there no matter what." He shrugged. "I guess they were counting on me having a conscience. I didn't realize I had gotten so ... predictable." He twisted his mouth around the word like it was rot on his tongue.

"Hey, would you like some coffee or something? Or dinner?" I offered, seeing the look on his face. "As a thank you for saving my life?"

"That's not necessary."

"I insist," I said. "Have you eaten since last night?"

"No."

"Then come on." I didn't know why but I had the urge to help him, maybe out of relief from being saved or maybe out of a need to have him around so I could fill my curiosity about the universe. I knew that if he walked away, it would leave me feeling guilty for the rest of my life.

Plus, I sure as heck needed answers.

"I don't want to impose ..."

"It's no bother. We'll see about getting you cleaned up, too. You can't walk around town like that."

"Oh?" He looked down at himself. "Is it the clothes? They don't seem to be the norm around here."

"Bloody rags haven't been the fashion for over a thousand years, and probably not on this continent. And why are you still wearing them?"

"I slept in them."

"I'll help you track down something to wear," I

assured him. "Come on, let's get you cleaned up. You've been walking around looking like an axe murderer for long enough."

I decided I would drive. I wasn't expecting him to get behind the wheel again, though it was obvious he knew where I lived seeing as he had taken my car from the street outside my apartment. I didn't want to think about how he knew these things. If he had been stalking me, it had helped to save my life.

I saw my canvas bag on the floor of the passenger side. He must have found it in the park and brought it along, which was very thoughtful for a rescue mission.

"Thanks," I said, pointing at the bag.

"Oh, you're welcome." Zander grinned. "Look, I'm sorry I wasn't around to stop that man. I … I … well…" He shrugged. "Actually, I don't have an excuse."

"You don't need one." I backed up the car, pulling us out of the parking lot. "You're not my keeper."

"Still, I knew there was a chance this could happen. The second they learned we had talked, I put you in danger. I waited in your park just in case."

"Just talking to you gets people abducted?"

"I have, well, I guess, um—" he stumbled over his words. "I have a few enemies. They don't like me."

"Why?"

"You know why."

"The mercenary dude said you were dangerous. He said if I didn't turn you in thousands would die."

"Sally, are you really going to believe the word of a man who tried to kill you over the one who stopped him from doing so?"

It was the first time he had said my name, and for

some reason, it struck me as odd. It was more than a name on his tongue. It was a spell, an incantation. Begging me, insisting that I believe him and trust him. It worked.

"Is it because you're some kind of historical criminal? Or a hero?"

"You've seen what I can do. The whole—"

"Teleporting thingy?"

"That thing, yeah." He smiled sheepishly. "Blayde calls it jumping. It fits better. Spontaneous atomic displacement sounded sad."

"So, they want you for that?" I shuddered. "Because you can teleport here and there?"

"I can go anywhere in the universe. Well, it's completely random, but hey, I won't bore you with the specifics. Some people are out to study me; some just don't want me out and about. But in a way, they're all asking the same questions. Who is Zander? Why does he heal so quickly? Why does he do those things the way he does? Why is it that every time he eats a pancake, half the universe suddenly thinks about whales?"

"Really?"

"It happened once, at least."

We turned the corner and arrived on my street. I pulled up onto the curb, and with a stutter, my poor car finally stopped. I didn't know if it would start back up again, but I patted the dashboard, thankful for it holding up this long.

"I do have a question for you, though," Zander said, fixing his gray-green eyes on mine. "What did I look like in the photograph he showed you?"

"You looked ... bashed up. Pretty badly bashed up

actually." Your nose was cut, and there were chunks missing out of your jaw, like, big gaping chunks. But that couldn't have been you, could it?"

"Was it a mug shot or a vacation shot? Hold on, was I holding a turtle?" I swear he said all of this with a straight face. "Or was I wearing … plaid?"

"Mug shot," I recalled, "and you were wearing a pink button-down shirt. With a … a palm tree on the pocket. Gold sunglasses hung from the front."

"Thank the Almighty." He sighed, a hand rising to support his head, fingers running through the greasy hair. He closed his eyes. "That's good."

"How is that good?" I tried not to be judgmental, but hey. "Why do you have a mug shot? Why was your face all—"

"They're not Alliance." He grinned. "The mercs were contractors. It means the bounty hunters are the only ones who know I'm here. No one's coming back for me. No one's going to bother you again—ever."

We exchanged smiles, and though I didn't get half of what he was saying, I understood enough to feel relieved. Hopefully, it meant no more alien abductions anytime soon.

"But what's the Alliance?" I asked, breaking our grinning match.

"Maybe we should get out of the car?" Zander suggested, unbuckling his seat belt. Why a man like him found the need for a seat belt, I'd never know. Maybe he assumed they were customary.

"Sure," I said and got out. Looking up at my apartment, I felt as if I had returned from a long, long trip. It was weird being home after everything that had just happened.

"So, the Alliance is, um"—Zander waved his hand in the air—"a group of planets. They're the closest union to you guys here on Earth, so they tend to think of Earth as being under their wing. You know, Earth might get tourists from time to time, but really everyone thinks this place is the boondocks. They've got rules against showing themselves to civilizations that aren't ready for contact yet, though I thought they had already. Wasn't there some kind of contact at Roswell? Fifty ... sixty years back?"

"The jury is still out on that," I answered. A smile crept on my face as I unlocked the front door to my building. "The government said it was a weather balloon."

"The weather balloon was a weather balloon." He rolled his eyes. "The ship, though. Typical. I've been to a few pre-contact civilizations, and it's always the same. If you find out too much and you're too primitive, the Alliance will talk to your leaders to keep it hushed up. Don't worry. As soon as you guys settle down, lose the wars and such, they'll come to you."

"There hasn't been any sign of intelligent life out there. Well, yet," I said as we climbed the stairs. "And you're telling me there are whole planetary alliance thingies?"

"Not always very good ones," he muttered. "But ... yes."

"So, the ship in the park?" I shuddered. "It's not going to make the news, is it?"

"Not if the agency has anything to do with it, no."

"The agency?"

"Travel agency," he said with a shrug. "Keeps the tourists coming, and keeps it safe for them to come back. Basically, it's the Alliance's branch out here."

"Right?" I unlocked the door to my apartment and was so, so glad I had cleaned up before leaving this morning. The place didn't look spotless, not by a long shot, but at least it didn't imply that I was a slob. No one needed to know that about me.

"Shower's through there," I said, pointing to the white door down the hallway. "And there are towels available, help yourself."

"Thank you," he replied. He smiled, and I realized I was smiling, too, despite my exhaustion.

I didn't even have anything that would fit him, clothing wise. I could tell that under his layers of wrap he was a large man, even my baggiest clothes wouldn't fit him. I had to do something I dreaded—I had to bring someone else into this mess.

I went to knock on Jules's door.

He had always been nice to me. He'd been helpful from the first day we met when he carried my table and sofa into the apartment and I could only pay him in pizza. And he wasn't the type to judge, which was a definite plus. Though I had never really understood how he could be constantly cheerful. He was the kind of neighbor everyone wanted. If anybody could help, he could—and better than that, he would.

So, I knocked on his door. He opened it with that winning grin he never seemed to lose.

"Sally!" He said it like I had made his day.

"Jules, it's good to see you," I replied, his cheerfulness rubbing off on me already.

"Hey, are you all right?" he asked, probably the state of my face. My hand reached up and felt the cuts. They only started to sting when I realized they were there.

"Yeah, it's fine, just a scrape. I'm sorry, Jules, I need your help. Do you have some clothes I could borrow?"

"Like ... your kind of clothes, or ..."

Of course, Zander decided to look out my apartment door. He was completely shirtless, probably only one step from shedding his bloody garments. My cheeks burned. He waved casually at Jules.

"Ah, yes. Well, I can help with that," Jules said. He grinned a sheepish smile and left for a second, coming back with a nice pair of jeans and a shirt, as well as socks and other helpful items. He even had a toothbrush on his pile of things.

"I hope these fit. What happened to um, the ...?"

Well, he had me there. I couldn't tell Jules that Zander's clothes, if you could even call them that, were covered in blood. At least with what Jules was imagining, there wouldn't be much of an inquiry, not that he'd believe me if I told him the truth.

Jules winked at me. I winked back, feeling slightly embarrassed.

"Thanks, bro," Zander said, a perfect imitation of the boys on campus.

Jules waved back. "Don't mention it, man."

I rushed back into the apartment, handing Zander the stack of clothes. He had peeled the wrap from his shoulders to reveal a heavily muscled chest, the likes you only saw in action films. It was more than just impressive. I could count every one of his abs—there was one too many, but I'll chock it up to him being alien—and his skin glistened with sweat. My stomach flipped.

"Um, towels," I said, walking to the bathroom and handing him the fluffiest one I could find.

"Thanks," he said, reaching to undo the rest of the wrap bunched around his waist. Sand fell on my bath mat; it'd probably never come out again. I spun around. While he didn't care too much for modesty, I sure did.

Come on, I'd had a weird day. I wasn't looking forward to adding alien genitalia to the list of things I'd seen.

"I'll get out of your hair," I muttered.

I sat on my couch in silence, listening to the shower run. The water washing sand off an alien, the man who had saved my life.

To think I had started this by running him over with my car. Now, he was getting cleaned in my shower, after doing who knows what to the aliens who had tried to abduct me.

Maybe he had killed them.

I realized I didn't care.

"Right," I said, pulling myself up. "This is obviously a crazy dream brought on by the shock of being fired from work. A panic attack on steroids. So, this? All this? It's imagined. My subconscious is trying to tell me something."

"I can assure you, it's real," Zander said, stepping out of the bathroom, drying his hair with the fluffy towel. He was dressed, thank goodness, and he cleaned up well. "But don't ask me to prove that."

"A dream would say that."

"And what kind of dream would invent a person

like me? Have you ever seen anyone who looks like me? Who dresses like me? Who can drive like me? Who can appear ... hold on, I may fail to sound convincing."

"So, what happens next?"

"I'm sticking around on this planet until my sister gets back," he said, plopping down on the couch. "As I was saying, jumping long distances is difficult and pretty random. It isn't an exact science. There's no system of guidance. Space is so big, you know? There's a lot of empty between the places with solid ground. When I jump, it takes all my willpower to find a spot that's safe to land. I never know where that is. Last night, we were in a bit of trouble, and I had to get off a planet in a hurry. Earth was in the right place at the right time, but I jumped before she did. I think the thwack with your vehicle made it impossible for her to lock on my arrival point. She has no idea where I am."

"But you left a message on her phone. She can track you down, right?"

"Sure, once she jumps to Earth, which is one chance in ... about one hundred and fifty-eight million. She has to get here first, right here, in whatever this town is. Consider space-time, and she might just make it in time to see your great-granddaughter buying her first house."

"Wait, what?" I asked. "Why that long?"

"Ever hear about the theory of relativity? Time dilation?"

"Vaguely."

"It'll take too long to explain, but basically, when you travel at the speed of light—"

"You can't travel at the speed of light."

Zander rolled his eyes "—or nearly at the speed of light, you age slower than those around you. We can go from one place to another in what feels like an instant, but sometimes years can pass between each pit stop. Like, I've been on Earth before, but ages might have passed for your people."

"So what will you do now? Are you going to jump to someplace else, find your sister?"

"No, I need to stay put. If I leave this spot—and by this spot, I mean this city, not your armchair—I could lose her forever. She needs to find me, not the other way around. She's better at jumping. She can't decide what planet to land on either, but if we get separated, she always tracks me down eventually. We usually jump simultaneously, so we don't end up in completely different galaxies. If she grabs my hand or if we're close to each other, at least, we tend to always end up in the same place. She must not be too far away. It might take years. Centuries. But I'll wait."

"Why can't you just go home?" I asked. "You can jump there, can't you?"

"No, I can't," he said. "The universe is so big. In space, there is an infinity of directions. I have no idea where home is at this point. Or if it's still there after all this time."

It hit me then how lonely he was. He was used to traveling the universe with his sister, but now, he was truly alone. Stuck on this planet. My planet. And it was my fault.

The doorbell rang, and my heart leaped. You'd think after all the excitement, I would have learned to stay put by this point.

But it was only Marcy. Marcy, who had been waiting for me in the park as I was abducted. Marcy, who was already worried enough about me as it was, whom I had forgotten to text.

"It's my friend Marcy, could you—"

But when I turned around, he wasn't there. He had disappeared once again, leaving me to deal with a livid Marcy, with nothing but sand to support my story.

CHAPTER EIGHT
MESSY THINGS YOU CAN'T CLEAN WITH A SPONGE

Zander had disappeared, again. He was just gone. I guess I was starting to get used to it, but it still hit me like a blast of cold water. He hadn't even said goodbye. And, come on, who leaves a person alone when their world had been turned upside down?

Marcy barged through my door, a bottle of inexpensive Chianti under her arm and a frown the size of the Mississippi river on her face. She brushed past me and through to the living room, depositing the bottle on the kitchen island before I could utter a word.

"Don't," she ordered, grabbing a glass out of the cupboard and pouring me a drink. She held it toward me, indicating I should sit down.

"I'm really sorry, Marce. I've ... I've had an awful few hours."

"You and me both, sister." She scowled. "Why haven't you been picking up your phone? I've been calling and calling. I thought something awful had happened to you."

I pulled my phone out of my pocket—dead. It must have died after I used the map app. I had been very lucky to get Matt's call when I did.

"Something did," I said, before realizing that there was no way I could tell her what happened.

Her eyes widened, her frown inexplicably growing. The Mississippi had breached its banks. "What?"

What, indeed? I had been abducted—then saved—by aliens, and, yes, aliens did exist and were somehow living amongst us, enjoying Starbucks and getting outted on Instagram.

Marcy didn't push. She ran to me, flying around the kitchen counter and wrapping her arms around my shaking body. I hugged her back, my grip tightening as I let the events of the day wash over me.

Oh, Marcy. I don't deserve you.

"You're one of those people that are only supposed to exist in fairy tales, Marce."

"Nope, just a good friend." She forced a smile. "A friend who knows when her bestie isn't being straight with her. So, come on, tell me what's going on. Also, this bottle is all we have. I won't allow any more, all right?"

"Got it." I nodded. "Where'd it come from?"

"Got it for my birthday. Thought you could use it more than me. So, tell me."

"Tell you what?"

"Everything," she said, rolling her eyes. "What happened today?"

I let out a heavy sigh and waved her over to the

sofa; this would take a while. Marcy grabbed the bottle and her glass and sat on the plush armchair while I collapsed on the couch. Her phone buzzed in her pocket, and she slipped it out, placing it on the coffee table next to the bottle without reading the text.

"It started last night," I explained. It was time to get this off my chest. Well, not all of it, but enough so my friend could help me. "I hit a ... a deer or something ... with my car."

"You what?"

"A deer," I repeated, going for a sip. The red liquid tasted strong on my tongue, making me frown. It was hitting me harder than it should have. "I think it was pretty bad, too, but it ran into the woods, so I never got to see it."

"Ouch." Marcy shook her head. "Not good."

"So, today at lunch, I knew I couldn't take the car, so I started walking ..."

"Yeah?"

"And got mugged," I said, putting all the emotional punch into it that I could.

"Holy shit on a crab cake." Marcy flew to my side. "Are you okay? What happened?"

"Don't worry, I'm not hurt or anything," I said. "He had a gun, though, Marcy. I was really shaken up. I kind of, well, I know I should have called you sooner, but I went to the cops."

"Understandable." Marcy nodded, ignoring her buzzing phone. "Are you okay? Did he...?"

"Just my wallet, thank god." I was surprised by how easily the lies spilled. "The cops found it, but they didn't catch the guy."

"Aww, honey." Marcy reached over to give me a tight squeeze. "You going to be all right?"

"I'm fine." I smiled, trying to make the lie the truth and push the real events from my mind. "I love the fact you're here."

"Hey, that's what friends are for. But, um, last night—"

"It's okay, Marcy." I held up a hand. "I get it. And you're right—I need to get out more. Live my life."

"I didn't mean to—"

"I get it. It's fine," I insisted. "I've been in a slump for a little while, and—"

"A little while?" Marcy scoffed and smiled. "It's been two whole years, Sally. Since John ..."

I froze. That was a name I couldn't hear. Not right now, not when everything else was such a mess. Panic rose and I forced myself to remember how to breathe.

Marcy's face paled.

"Don't say his name," I begged, gripping the couch for support.

"Hon, have you taken your meds?"

"Yes." Another lie. With everything going on, I hadn't had time.

"I'm worried about you, Sally Webber," she said, using my whole name like it was a plea. "I don't know how to help."

"It's okay," I said. My panic subsided, which surprised me. It was unusual for it to pass that quickly. Something was different. "Has it really been two years? I guess ... yeah, it has. But I'm ready for a change now, you know?"

"Don't do anything you don't want to do," she

insisted, sneaking a glance at her phone as it buzzed again, but she didn't touch it. "I'm not trying to pressure you into anything, understand? I just hate to see you like this."

I smiled. "All I need is ... a job, a roommate, and, well, a life."

"Take a day off first," said Marcy, glancing around. "And what's with all the sand? When was the last time you went to the beach?"

"Ugh, true," I agreed, trying to brush it off. "But for now—Netflix? We can hit some Firefly eps. I have cake mix in the cupboard. We can make a feast."

"Perfect." Marcy grinned. "And I've got to tell you about Dany."

"From last night?"

"Yes, her," she said, brimming. "We got talking and never really stopped."

As if to agree, the phone buzzed again. This time, she picked it up, read the past few messages, and giggled in an oddly adorable way. I watched her quietly; I hadn't expected my day to get any weirder.

"So, the two of you hit it off then?"

Marcy nodded. "My gosh, yes. I foresee a date in our near future. Many, actually."

"What's she like?"

"She's ... awkward," Marcy answered. "An endearing kind of awkward, if you know what I mean. She's well-traveled but poorly situated. I know it doesn't make much sense, but you'll get it when you talk to her. It's amazing, though, how she listened to me ramble on for hours. I was even naming the best kinds of macaroni and cheese brands, and she was genuinely interested.

Like it was fascinating. I've never had a person treat what I was saying like that before."

"And all this running business?"

"Overbearing father." She shrugged. "Understandable, really."

"Where's she from?"

"Didn't say."

"You spoke for all that time, and she never said where she was from?"

"I did most of the talking," she replied awkwardly. "Hold on, I'll ask her."

Her thumbs flew over the screen, blurring as she typed. Seconds later, the phone buzzed again.

"Small town in Nebraska," she read. "But she spent some time in Nepal because of her dad's job. Odd stuff."

"I dunno, Nebraska isn't the oddest state," I started, but my friend gave me a look that meant I was neither funny nor clever.

"So, Netflix?" I offered.

"No, you shower first." Marcy grinned, turning back to her tiny screen as it chimed again. She laughed and dropped the phone on the armrest beside her.

"Fine, but when I get back, I have to tell you about my own success. Guess who asked me on a date?"

"Seriously?" I didn't think her grin could have gotten any wider, but she proved me wrong. "Wait, who?"

Her phone buzzed again, and this time, she apologized and went for it. She and Dany texted back and forth, making her eyes twinkle. I felt so happy for her.

I stood and walked to the bathroom. There was no way I was going to let Marcy see the mess in there. I closed the bathroom door to inspect the wreckage in peace: it wasn't so bad. There was sand everywhere, of course, but the big issue was the huge canvas sheet soaking in the tub. The blood tinted the water red.

It was grotesque. I did a double take at the sight of it, holding my hand to my mouth to keep my gag reflex under wraps. How on earth would I explain this?

I wouldn't. I grabbed some trash bags from the cleaning cupboard and threw the sodden wrap inside without wringing out the water. I drained the tub, brushing the sand away. I would have to mop and clean tomorrow. Marcy, in the meantime, didn't look up from her phone, asking me if I was all right as she texted her new belle.

I wondered where Zander was. I shouldn't be the one cleaning up after him, though I guessed it was only fair after he saved my life. Neither of us had said goodbye, but maybe that was a good thing. Maybe that was the last time I would see aliens. Maybe I could try to fix my life—the normal way.

The me who's writing this now, the one who's thinking back over these events and trying to piece together those stray thoughts, that me is laughing uncontrollably.

········•••●●●•••········

After a restful Sunday—boring compared to everything else that was going on, so I'll spare you the details—I finally got myself out the door, driving my junker car to the closest garage which, in itself, was miraculous. The mechanic inspected it, scratching his head as I told him the same story about hitting a deer.

I didn't have to fake the tremor in my voice.

"All good?" Marcy asked as I slipped into the passenger seat of her car.

"Should be," I replied, faking my cheer. "Hopefully, it'll be repaired soon. Sorry to make you drive me around like this."

"I offered." Marcy grinned, pulling onto the street. "I told you, I don't mind."

"Still ..." I kept an eye on the street. Ever since that Saturday, anybody remotely glancing in my direction sent shivers up my spine.

"There's one last place I need to go," I said, clutching my purse to my chest. "It shouldn't take long."

"Where's that?"

"I need to find a pawnshop."

"A pawnshop?" said Marcy, "Sally, what—"

"Don't worry. I have some stuff I need to sell. It'll keep me going for the next few months. It won't take a second."

"Then lunch," she urged. "I'm famished. Any preference where we go?"

I grinned. "Your car, your pick."

Marcy pulled up in front of the first pawnshop she saw, a dingy looking place with a pile of odd-looking junk in the window. There was a statue of a clown playing a saxophone, its red hat faded from years in the sun. It was kind of creepy.

Really creepy. Did I mention I wasn't a fan of clowns? Most of my fears were rational: I mean, lots of people are afraid of heights, but when it came to clowns, something inside me just didn't sit right.

"Should we go somewhere else?" she asked. "The

only thing I know about these places comes from Pawn Stars, and I'm not sure how reliable that information is."

"Nah, it won't take long. I'll be right back."

I slipped out the car and into the dark store, gripping my purse. The coins Zander gave me jingled noisily in my pocket as I walked.

The place was full of strange trinkets, antiquities, and gaudy decorations, a patchwork of things that found themselves there by odd circumstance. A foot-tall angel statue glared at me from the top shelf above the counter, its face twisted to the point where it could no longer be called angelic. I glanced down trying to fight the glare of the bronze face, my eyes falling to the contents behind the glass. Instead of the old rings and watches I expected to find, two long cutlasses sat on a velvet cushion, almost as if waiting for a duel. Incredibly old, incredibly ornate; I was shocked to find items like that in this tiny place rather than a museum.

"Beauties, aren't they?" the shopkeeper said, making me jump. I looked up, glad that he stood between the distraught angel and me.

"Incredible," I replied. "How old are they?"

"Not as old as you'd think," he said, shaking his head. "Perfect replicas of a dueling pair from the sixteenth century. They're only a hundred years or so old."

"Seriously?" I looked down at them. They were in surprisingly good condition. The blades looked sharp.

"May I help you with something?" he asked, snapping me out of my reverie.

I nodded. "Yes, um, I'm looking to sell some

things?" I replied, wondering why I felt so nervous. Fact was, Zander had given me these coins as a gift, albeit thinking I could use it as actual currency. Trying to sell them felt wrong.

I dumped the contents of my change purse on the counter. The six tiny gold coins clattered against the glass, rolling every which way. The owner put a firm hand over them then picked one up to inspect it. He held it close to his eye, letting out a low whistle.

"Now where did you get these?" he asked in a soft voice. He put the coin down and picked up another, holding it so close to his eyes I had no idea how he could see anything.

"I was cleaning out my grandmother's attic," I lied. "Are they worth anything?"

He laughed quite suddenly, making me jump for the second time that day.

"Worth anything?" He chuckled. "They're pure gold and date from the last time we had a woman running this country."

"Wait, what now?"

The man leaned back casually, a winning smile plastered his face as he picked up one of the coins again.

"Back in the days before Hamilton," he joked. "These coins were the currency back when Queen Anne was, well, Queen of the colonies."

"You're kidding me!"

"It's no joke," he said, pulling out a small set of scales and dropping the coin on it. He nodded at the numbers, though they meant nothing to me. "These coins are four hundred years old, at least. But ..."

He held it up to the light, frowning slightly.

"What's wrong?" I asked, leaning forward. A small fear grew in the pit of my stomach.

"The coins should be four hundred years old," he muttered, "but the gold has barely aged. There are no wear marks, except for the scratches. Either your grandmother kept them incredibly well ... or, more likely, they're like the cutlasses—replicas."

"Oh," I said. For a second, I felt as if I'd held a piece of history in my hands. "Are they still—"

"Hey, they're still high in gold content," the owner said. "Maybe their historical value has diminished, but the gold is strong. I'll give you $4,000 for the bunch."

I almost fell over with shock. That was more than I had anticipated. It was more than enough to cover the cost of my car's repairs. Heck, it would probably cover my rent for the next few months, with some to spare.

Gone was the worry about bills, the fear of not being to make it through the next month. Just like that.

The check felt heavy in my purse. Marcy picked up on the look on my face the instant I got in the car.

"What happened? You're pale."

"Just a little surprised," I muttered.

"Why is that?" Marcy's stomach grumbled loudly, and I laughed so hard I couldn't see where we were driving. Tears ran down my cheeks as relief washed over me. Maybe, just maybe, I was going to be all right.

But my relief was quickly replaced by guilt. I owed Zander that money, and holding on to it felt dishonest. Sure, he had given the money to me, but he hadn't known the true value of those coins. Keeping the money felt like I stole from him.

After lunch, I asked Marcy to drop me off at home.

This was good for her since she made plans to spend time with Dany that evening. The second she drove off, though, I turned around. Instead of going into my building, I made my way into the park.

I had never been afraid of it before, but I felt like Little Red Riding Hood as she went off-roading on her way to her grandmother's house. The trees seemed closer together and the path thinner and more winding than I remembered. And, worst of all, I felt stalked, as if someone or something were watching me, hidden somewhere in the shadows.

"Zander?" I called out, my stomach twisting in knots. "Zander, are you there?"

No reply. Instead, wind flowed through the tree-tops, rustling the leaves and chilling me to the bone. I wrapped my coat around me.

"Zander, where are you? I've got to talk to you about something?"

Still no answer. Not that I was expecting one. I had only hoped ... no, I was still hoping—hoping for a reply that would not come. I had no idea where he was, if he had a place to stay, if he was even on this planet anymore. Maybe his sister had made it back. Maybe he had moved. Maybe he had been captured. There was no way for me to know.

I wondered, vaguely, why my life was changing so quickly. If it hadn't been for the hot-air balloon, I would still be working the cash register at Price's right now.

The hot-air balloon had changed everything.

I called out again and waited, and waited, and waited. He wasn't going to answer, even if he were here. He had left without saying goodbye. Obviously, that meant he was done talking.

I took that as it being over. All of it. And I turned around, returning quietly to my house.

CHAPTER NINE
LIFE GIVES ME LEMONS

Job-hunting is hard.

Seriously. Though I assume I'm being Captain Obvious here.

I worked on my résumé—plumping out the two-line paper that summarized my adventures in retail—and sent it out as far and wide as I could. So far, no one had called back—even to decline, let alone offer an interview.

Which, of course, made me feel even more lousy. I had thought about re-enrolling in university but couldn't decide what major I wanted. There was nothing I was passionate about, or even interested enough in to lie convincingly on an application. Life just felt like a huge, complicated mess.

And yet, through everything, I felt different somehow, almost like I knew myself better. Not enough to know what I wanted, but it was something. Even so, you can't put 'survived an alien abduction' on your résumé.

So, I did what Matt suggested and sent my résumé to Mr. Grisham. Matt had given me his boss's personal email address, which I found odd, but within two hours, I had a response. My hands flew into the air in victory; I had an interview.

Tomorrow.

A celebration was in order, and while Marcy thought that kind of party deserved to be held at a club with a bottle of who knows what, I was more of the opinion that a Netflix marathon was in order.

I sat down in front of my small TV with a box of chewy chocolate chip cookies from CVS and a bottle of Dr Pepper. I put on an episode of Futurama and grabbed my phone. There was one person I needed to text.

I got an interview with your boss, I typed and sent it to Matt.

He replied in less than a minute. That's fantastic! I knew you would.

Yeah, well, it's just an interview. I don't have the job yet...

You will!

Then came the onslaught of emojis. He was so excited for me, and, man, did it feel good to text back and forth, as if I was back in high school, before everything went down with John the way it had. Eventually, I realized I wasn't even watching the show. The two of us had been texting for so long that it was now dark outside and all my soda was gone.

Ok, Kirk or Picard? Matt had asked. This one took me more than few seconds to respond.

Don't hate, okay? I sent back. Picard all the way for me. Way better diplomat. And French. Space French.

I'd be wary of any Frenchman in space, Matt replied, but he was a force to be reckoned with.

We chatted all night and continued into the morning. By the time I had fished out my best-looking outfit, I knew his entire life story. I knew about him growing up in New York, about his vinyl collection—both what he was proud of and what he was still hunting—and I knew about his taste in movies.

A geek after my own heart.

The conversation moved on to his boss, the mysterious Mr. Grisham. Now, I say mysterious because only a handful of people had ever met him. Members of the press repulsed him, and he only spoke to his employees, whom he treated like family.

Matt said the man was like a father to him and that he had spent all week talking me up in the hopes of bringing me into the fold. He was under the impression I was already hired, talking like I would show up to work on Monday and we'd have lunch together. He even offered to carpool.

I wasn't nearly as confident. My nerves were shot, and my hands trembled as I buttoned my shirt. It was silly. After everything I had been through, there was no way I should be scared of a little job interview. But I was, dangit.

Marcy picked me up outside my apartment, but she wasn't alone. Her new beau, or belle I should say, sat in the passenger seat. Dany looked much less threatening in daylight, though her height and muscles were still intimidating.

"Hey," I said as I climbed in. "Nice to see you again, Dany."

"And the same with you, Sally," she replied, out-standingly courteous.

"You look great, Sal," Marce said. She looked tiny next to Dany. "Let's get your car. Don't want you to be late on your big day."

I groaned. She sounded like my mother.

I was thankful, though. Without her help, I would never have gotten my car back. It looked so much better now the fender wasn't busted. I paid the mechanic and climbed back into the battered chariot, adjusting the mirror the way I liked it and pulling the seat forward.

I watched from the driver's seat as Dany leaned over to kiss Marcy on the cheek, making my friend blush. I had never seen her like this, and I was so incredibly excited for her. I barely knew Dany, but seeing how she made my best friend feel, I was sure I was going to like her.

I shook this out of my head. Time to focus. No relationships on the mind. No aliens trying to ruin my day. I was going to fight for this job, and I wasn't going to mess it up.

The road was newly paved, built expressly for Grisham Corp. The company had been in the news for months, maybe even years, but nothing about the technology was ever released. It was, so they said, quite possibly the best-kept secret in the world.

Outside the fence, people protested, but their signs didn't say very much. I guess they were worried about the environmental impact or maybe the lack of info. The press releases about how it all worked were vague.

People were mad, but many didn't know what they were actually mad about.

Driving up here made me wonder if the rumors were true, not that I particularly cared. Today, somehow, I had incredibly high clearance. I handed my driver's license to the guard on duty, and he checked the list—I was on a list—and let me in.

The parking lot was surprisingly empty but it wasn't scheduled to open for another two weeks. It was a little odd that Grisham was still hiring so close to the opening date though. I thought people would have been in place well ahead of time.

I parked next to the entrance and admired the building. It was fancy, all glass and chrome; it could have passed for an Apple store. For a split second, I remembered thinking that this is what I expected when I had been abducted by aliens. Grisham Corp looked more futuristic than I had imagined. The cooling towers were painted a baby blue, almost blending into the sky. It was kind of cool looking.

I was going to like it here—if I got hired, of course.

I stared at myself in the rearview mirror, happy with what I saw. I looked quite professional with my hair pulled into a tight ponytail and a little natural makeup. I rubbed some moisturizer on my hands. I was nervous, and it was making my palms sweaty and gross.

Walking through the front door, I found myself wondering if I had ended up at the wrong place. The brightly lit room looked more like the entrance to a five-star hotel than a workplace. The marble floors and lush plants made it feel like a palace, and unlike most industrial or commercial buildings, the lights were warm, not harsh and fluorescent.

The only odd thing about the place was how empty it was. Not a soul walked through the marble halls. You could a fly buzzing in a room meters away. There wasn't even a receptionist. I was entirely alone and incredibly nervous.

The place was humming, though. While it hadn't yet opened for business, something must have been running. In the absence of people, you could hear the place thrum with noise.

"Ah, you're here."

I spun on my heels, expecting to see someone standing behind me, but no, the lobby was still empty.

"Hello?" I called out, searching for the source of the voice. "Who's there?"

"Just me," a male voice replied. "Oh, sorry. That probably sounded quite menacing. Believe me, that was not my intention. Look over to the reception desk ... yes, hi, hello, over here."

I did what he asked, looking over at the previously empty desk, which was, unsurprisingly, still empty; however, the large screen on the wall behind it had filled with a close-up of a balding man in glasses wearing a pinstriped suit. He beamed at me with a grin that showed off his teeth.

I recognized him from the news and my research before coming here. My new—potential—boss.

"There we go," he said cheerfully. "Let me introduce myself. I am Ridgell Grisham, the proprietor of this facility. Sophie, the receptionist, is out for the day, so I shall send you up to my office myself. Awkward," he said, imitating an eighth-grade girl. "Anyway, feel free to head on up. Take the elevator to the third floor. I'll meet you there."

With that, the television shut off, leaving me to stand in silence in the empty lobby.

Ping.

The sound echoed through the hall. My heart skipped, but it was only the elevator. The doors slid open with a hiss like the sliding doors in *Star Trek*. The elevator, too, was outlandishly ornate, the brilliant golden interior more suited to a five-star hotel than an electrical plant.

Okay, this was a little unsettling.

For the first time, I wondered if I was walking into a trap. Maybe the events of the past few days were making me paranoid, but nothing here felt right.

The doors closed, and I pressed the button for the third floor and felt the elevator rise. The back wall was a window that looked out over the lush, green landscape outside.

The doors opened on to another upmarket hallway, with polished wood walls and thick carpet. The man who had greeted me on the screen was there, but he was much shorter than I had anticipated, and sitting on a matt black electric scooter.

"Pleasure to make your acquaintance," he said, extending a hand to shake mine with enough enthusiasm to sell me a used car. "You must be Ms. Webber. Matthew has told me so much about you."

"He has?" I shook his hand in return, feeling both nervous and flattered. "All good things, I hope."

"The best." He nodded. "Please, come with me. We have so much to discuss."

He spun around and aimed his scooter along the hallway, going much faster than I'd expected. I had to jog to keep up with him.

"Welcome to the future," he said. "Everything you see is breaking new ground, advancing humanity toward a brighter, cleaner tomorrow. And it's only through the hard work of people like yourself that this tomorrow can be reached. You with me so far?"

He did not wait for an answer. We took a left. Automatic doors whooshed open for us, leading us out to an empty terrace overlooking the sprawling country-side. Small tables and chairs were propped up against the wall. The man led me to the ledge.

"You may have noticed how little this place resembles a power plant."

"Oh, that's for sure," I said, chuckling. Gosh, I was nervous. "This doesn't run on any kind of nuclear energy, right?"

Grisham smiled. "Nope."

"So, where is the energy produced?" I asked. "Oh, sorry, I think you're the one who's supposed to ask the questions. I'm sorry, I'm getting ahead of myself. I'm just curious."

"Stop that right now," he said, sternly. "Not the question asking, that much is great. Stop apologizing, there's no need. I'm not a dictator. Please, treat me like a friend."

"Sure?" It felt like a trick statement, but the guy seemed nice enough.

"To answer your question, the energy is produced right there." He pointed at a large cement cap in the ground, situated right below the terrace we stood on.

It was large and flat and utterly featureless.

"Underground?" I asked, trying not to let my disappointment show.

"Entirely." He grinned. "I found a pocket of natural gas a few years ago. All we had to do was install some turbines, and presto, we have a source of power that rarely depletes. Impressive, is it not?"

"Incredibly so," I said, leaning over the railing to get a better look. The thing didn't look any more interesting close up. "But wouldn't it be incredibly, I don't know, volatile? High-pressured gas, just below the surface and all."

"We have precautions in place." Grisham nodded, backing up his scooter, turning it around, and gesturing for me to follow him back inside.

"Why are you telling me this?" I asked, trotting next to him. "This is more than you've told the media."

"Well, if you want to work here, you ought to know what we do. So, are you interested?"

"In what?"

"Working for me—with me—to make this dream a reality."

"Definitely," I replied, reaching for my purse, "I have my résumé right here, and—"

"No need, no need." The man waved away the paper. "Can you get the door?"

I held the large, oak door open for him to drive through. "Now," Mr. Grisham said, riding his scooter up behind his large wooden desk. He reached into the silver-inlaid antique and pulled out two glasses and a bottle of wine, and poured us both a drink.

This was getting weirder by the minute.

"I'm a people person, and I like you," he said, raising his glass in salute. "You've got an honest face, and having read your application, I think it's safe to say that you're exactly what I need."

Definitely weird.

"And you," he paused to take a sip from his glass, "you, dear girl, have got 'trustworthy' written all over your face. You see, I need people I can trust for this project. It is a revolutionary idea, and I don't want the details to get out before I'm ready. I don't want the world using my technology without me getting the credit. So, what I'm saying is ...." He raised his glass. "I like you, and I want you."

"Um, sir?" I said, taking a step back.

"To work for me, Ms. Webber. To work for me. To run this plant. To make history while creating the future." He downed the rest of his drink in one gulp.

I took a sip of the wine, still trying to figure out if I was supposed to be flattered. by all this. I was, a bit, but I was mostly creeped out. "So, is this when we do the interview?"

"Already done." The man waved away the idea. "You passed with flying colors. I looked you up online, ran a few background checks—nothing invasive—and I know, I just know, I can put my trust in you. Call it my superpower. I can see your potential. It's radiating from you, and I simply must have it—you—here at the plant. So, what do you say? Will you join the Grisham Corp family?"

"I'm not even sure what I'll be doing."

"It's quite easy," he said. "As you can see, walking isn't my forte. I'm going to need someone to do all the running around for me; that's it. Answer the phone and tell people I'm not here, maybe drop off and pick up my dry cleaning, play some Scrabble with me from time to time when things get slow. Oh, and this would be your starting salary."

Just like in the movies, he wrote it down on a small piece of paper and slid it across the table. I looked at the figure, then at him, then at the paper again.

It was like winning the lottery.

"Just like that? No interview or anything?"

"You've had your interview." He chuckled. "I don't need your words to answer my questions; all I needed was your face, and your face shouts honesty. Shake my hand, and embrace the future."

I shook his hand. I embraced the future. After all, the future was full of large paychecks.

And just like that, I was hired. Everything was written down, agreed upon, and signed. I left the office with a job that paid in more zeros than I had seen in my entire life. For a job that was, basically, nothing more than picking up the phone and saying no one was there.

Doesn't this seem a bit weird? I shook the thought away. Not weird, just incredibly lucky. Or highly improbable.

"Before you go, just so you know," Grisham said quietly, leaning forward to press the elevator button for me. "I care a lot about Matthew—call him my protégé if you will—and he thinks very highly of you."

"Oh?" I replied, not sure what to say to that.

"Don't break his heart."

"I wouldn't dare."

That's when I realized, or maybe I had before and put it in the back of my mind but it was incredibly clear now: Matt was the reason I had this job. Not my trusting face or good vibes, but Matthew Daniels.

And I wasn't mad. I swallowed my pride and shook my boss's hand. After all, this job might be one of the best things to ever happen to me.

It could be the worst, too, but that was for time to tell.

CHAPTER TEN
DANG ALIENS, ALWAYS GETTING THEMSELVES ARRESTED

That evening was full of excited texting and phone calls.

First, of course, there was Marcy. She was ecstatic, even before I told her my good news. She posted on my Facebook wall, which led to my mom and dad thinking they needed to check up on me.

Thanks, Marce.

"Why didn't you call us first?" Mom shouted the second I picked up. "And why did you switch jobs? I thought you were happy at the flower shop?"

I hadn't worked in the flower shop for nearly eight months. I didn't interact much with my parents, not since John. Even so, when we did talk, they heard what they wanted to hear. And they hadn't heard much since I told them I was dropping out of college.

"This job is huge, Mom. I'm working in a new company. I mean, this place is space-age. It's super advanced."

"So long as you're not working for the government, I'm happy," Dad said, the most excited of us all. "I've heard about this place. It's been in all the papers. You might actually be able to make a difference in the world, Sal."

"Thanks, Dad," I replied, and I was happy. He wasn't a man who showed his feelings easily. What he was really saying, or at least what I heard, was that he was proud of me. I took it as a compliment. If they could pick and choose what they heard, so could I.

Matt, of course, knew that I had gotten the job the second I had walked out of Grisham Corp. Did Grisham have him on speed dial? From what I could tell, the man really was taking his role as a mentor seriously, involving his student protégé in most of his decisions.

When the phone rang next, I'd expected Matt, but, instead, it was an unknown number.

"Sally Webber?" the voice asked, gruffly, as I picked up.

"Yeah?"

"This is the police department. We've got one of your friends here ..."

"What?" I stood up, wondering who the man could be talking about. I only knew one person in this city who would turn to me in her time of need, and my heart sank. Marcy.

"He got himself in a little trouble. Nothing to worry about, he's not hurt."

"He?" I insisted. "He, who?"

"Oh, sorry; he says his name's Zander," the cop replied.

I felt like taking a drink, just so I could spit it back out.

What. The. Heck.

"What did he do?" I asked, shocked. Yes, what had he done? And why was I, of all people, being called about it?

"It would be easier to explain once you get down here," the man said solemnly. "He needs help getting home, and, well, he needs someone to pay his bail."

"I'll be there in a minute." I put the phone down. This was odd, very odd. Of course, I could probably afford to pay his bail, and I owed him, what with everything Zander had given me. Why would he be in the station? He didn't seem the type to attract undue attention.

Why wouldn't he have jumped out of there?

I looked up the route on Google Maps and hit the road. Man, I was happy to have this baby back. My taxi, so to speak, was out on a date tonight. She was—from what I could tell from the lack of warning texts—having a fantastic time, so I was glad I didn't have to rely on her for such a strange request.

I was surprised at how little time it took me to reach the police station. I went in, and smiled awkwardly on my way to the desk. The place was practically empty. There were only three or four officers inside, one at the desk and others busy with other stuff.

"Um, hi," I said. The receptionist jumped. "Ouch, you almost gave me a heart attack," he said cheerfully. "Didn't hear you come in. Good evening, by the way. What can I help you with?"

"Oh, sorry about that. I'm here for my friend—

Zander."

The man froze, his face dropping into a look of shock. From the back of the station, someone scoffed—loudly.

"Is everything all right?" I asked.

"You're Sally Webber?" one of the officers in the back piped up. I nodded, my worry growing. He sounded familiar, and I assumed he was the one who called me. By the looks of it, he wasn't very happy. I approached him, but he turned away before I reached him and waved me toward the cells.

I had expected much, much worse. Zander sat on the bench in the drunk tank, staring into the distance. And he was shirtless again for some reason, and had a towel wrapped around his shoulders. His hair was still damp too. He didn't look harmed—if he could ever look injured—nor did he seem uncomfortable. He seemed happy.

"Zander, hey," I said, walking to the cell to get a better look. He wasn't alone. A wasted guy slept in the corner. At least, I assumed he was drunk—and I assumed he was sleeping. A man the size of a mountain sat opposite Zander. His shirt said something along the lines of Grace Town bender-bender benders, with a picture of a paper clip. Absolutely no idea what that meant. I thought nothing of it, focusing instead on Zander.

"Stay gold," the big man said as Zander stood up and walked to the door.

"You too, Big Eddy."

"I mean it."

"So do I."

"Open your chakras!"

Zander grinned casually, giving me a small wave that turned into an elaborate move of fingers running through his hair. "Thanks for coming, Sally. I'm really sorry about this."

"What happened to you?" I asked, relief washing over me when I took in the complete lack of blood on him. He hadn't gotten into any fights.

"I was taking a bath," he said with a shrug.

The cop snorted. "He was taking a plunge in a pond—completely nude, I might add. Public indecency."

"It's a free body of water. I should able to bathe in peace." Zander sighed. "Anyway, I had no idea I was doing anything wrong."

"He says he's been living there for a few days," the officer continued, ignoring Zander's eye rolling. "Did you know about this?"

"No," I replied. Zander made an 'I told you so' face at the officer. "In any case, I'll pay the bail. Do you intend to press charges?"

"We can recommend a few hostels for—"

"He's coming to stay with me," I said, making Zander jump in surprise. Ha. Finally, I was the one to surprise him.

Zander tore his eyes off the cop and looked at me, his eyes wide in what I could only assume was fear.

"Well, until he can get back on his feet, that is," I continued, forcing myself to ignore Zander's reaction.

"You all right with this, Mr. Smith?" The officer sighed and unlocked the cell. He let Zander out, who reached over to plant a kiss on both the cop's cheeks, took a step back, gave him a bow, and extended an arm to shake his at the elbow. The police officer shook back, completely befuddled, his eyes wider than dinner plates. I fought the urge to laugh.

I went up to the front desk to pay the fee and fill out the paperwork, while Zander haggled with some of the policemen for the loan of a shirt. They found him one from their last Fun Run Fundraiser, which was far too big for him, but at least it was something he could wear without getting into trouble. Luckily, the jeans Jules had given him were still intact, though stained in places. They returned his small items, which he shoved into his pockets.

"Where's the car?" Zander asked as he trotted down the stairs of the police station.

"The parking lot behind the building," I said. It was cold out, cold enough for me to be more than glad for my coat. Zander appeared comfortable in a t-shirt and jeans, damp hair or not.

"I haven't gotten all the sand out of it yet," I said, getting in the driver's seat. "Sorry. Well, no, I'm not sorry, actually. What's wrong with you?"

"Most places don't have restrictions about swimming. I didn't—"

"I'm not talking about the skinny-dipping in a public park," I snapped. "I'm talking about Saturday. Now, sit down."

"What about Saturday?"

"You left me." I tore off into the night, completely forgetting there were cops watching. "You told me my life was in danger and that you were an alien, and then you just disappeared. Are you kidding me?"

"I promised you were safe," he said and furrowed his brows, "and I meant it. You didn't need me hanging around. You got all the answers you needed."

"Not all of them," I scoffed. "I wasn't done."

"I was."

We drove in silence, but his frown turned into a smile. I avoided his gaze.

"Which reminds me, I was trying to find you earlier. It seems you overpaid for the reparations. By a few thousand dollars, to tell the truth."

Zander smiled. "I'm glad it covered it."

"I need to give you—"

"Keep it." He looked cheerful, even in this cold and after being in jail for an hour or so. "It was a gift. I'm not going to take it back."

"Zander, that's an awful lot of money. A boatload. A shit ton."

"Those aren't recognized units of measurement." He grinned. "And, in any case, it's no use to me. I hope I won't be here long. I'm just glad I had some Earth currency on hand; it's hard to tell with some of the coins I have."

"That currency hadn't been in use for centuries."

"Still, right planet and all." He stuffed a hand into his pocket, pulling out a handful of oddly shaped, glimmering things before putting them back and patting the denim. They were probably worth a lot of money off-world.

He didn't seem aware of the fact that the ones he had given me were replicas.

"You could use it, though," I urged. "They found you bathing in a pond, for goodness sake. In a park.

Why didn't you go to a hotel or something?"

"I don't like hotels. Too many people seeing me come and go. Security cameras in the lobby and so on. Plus, living in the woods is comfortable. Especially here. Nothing wants to eat you. It's soft and predictable. Smells better than most hotels, too."

"What did you do for food?"

"Squirrels are good. And pigeon as long as you know how to cook them."

"Eww." I shuddered. I had seen what pigeons ate and knew what they did all day. Eating them was on the bottom of my to-do list. "Those are the jeans from Saturday, aren't they?"

"Yes." Zander didn't seem in the least bit phased about the damage. He seemed almost proud, running a hand down the length of the denim. "Incredible material. Oh, come on, Sally, don't look so disgusted. They're just pants. Get over it."

"They're still wet."

"Hey, I'm trying to fit in." He chuckled, giving me a playful grin. "I'd rather not be wearing them in the first place, but I think your cops might want to talk to me again if I get rid of them now."

"True."

We drove the rest of the way to my apartment in silence. The gray face of my building stared down at us with a heavy gloom. I parked and got out. Zander led me to the door, presenting it with a flourish and a low bow. I returned the gesture with a curtsey.

"Good night, then," he said, somewhat cheerfully, "and thanks for bailing me out. Thanks again, if I've already thanked you."

130

"Ah, no problem there," I replied. He nodded, smiled, then turned around and walked in the direction of the park.

"Wait," I shouted after him. "Where are you going?"

Zander turned around, a little confused. "I'm going back to the woods. I won't bathe in any ponds again, I promise."

"I meant what I said at the station," I told him. "I can't have you staying in the woods like that."

"The woods are fine. Nice and ... woodsy."

"Zander," I snapped. "Let me ask you one question. Just one. All right?"

"Shoot."

"Why are you staying in this park if there's another closer to where I hit you?" I crossed my arms in front of my chest. "Wouldn't your sister be more likely to find you there?"

"Well, um," he said, "I wanted to make sure nothing else happened to you. Not something I can do from the other park ..."

"Kind of creepy," I pointed out.

"Exactly what I was trying to avoid," he stated with a shrug, "which was why I didn't tell you, which makes it sound even creepier. Yes, I know. But is there any other way to secretly keep an eye on the woman who ran you over because you think her life may still be in danger because of you?"

"You could remove the secretly part and just ask," I said. "And while the whole thing is kind of weird, it's kind of you. But wouldn't it be more efficient if you were staying in the same place as me?"

"I guess so."

"I've got an extra room," I offered. "I've been meaning to find a new roomie, but I haven't had any luck yet. It's got a shower and a washer and dryer, so you won't have to worry about taking baths in a pond anymore. And best of all? Food. Real food. No more squirrels."

"You saw me kill someone," he stated, "practically in front of you. That doesn't bother you?"

"You said it's over, though, right?" I implored. "You said they wouldn't be bothering us again?"

"They won't be, but others ... I need to stick around to make sure."

"Perfect," I replied, "and are you planning on offing anybody else?"

"No."

"Then let me do this for you. No funny business, just a place to stay until you get on your feet."

"Sounds lovely." To my relief, his smile returned. "I'd be honored. But you realize Blayde may be gone for a long time."

"Nothing permanent," I asserted. "By the point I'm ready to move out, I think you'll be well enough settled to get along on this planet alone. It's the least I can do."

"My fault," he said sourly.

"I hit you with the car in the first place."

"We should stop this blame game."

"Yeah."

"Both of us have a part to play," he said, "and I'm pretty sure we agreed we're even."

"Yup," I shrugged. "So, we've both got to work it out."

"I'm going to have to get a job, aren't I?" he said

suddenly, sighing heavily. "That's going to be wonder-ful."

"Hey, don't worry," I said. "I'll help you find one. The whole Earth experience. Wait, have you got any work experience?"

"Nothing that would be applicable here." He took a step closer to the house then paused.

"Well, what are you good at?"

"Travel." He grinned as if it were a joke, but I guess I didn't get it. The grin faded.

"I guess you never held a job for very long," I said.

"Depends on what you mean by 'long,' but no. No career or anything. Not that kind of person."

"Ambitions?"

"Only secret ones."

"Do you do anything other than travel around the universe?"

"I tend to get people in trouble then get them out of it. I'm assuming my special set of skills, if you will, doesn't really get me anywhere on this planet."

"Law enforcement?"

"Yeah, better keep my face away from them. You never know who could recognize me."

"Alien cops?"

"You don't wanna know." Zander shook his head. "In any case, I need a boring office job of some kind. Keep my face hidden in the crowd."

"You seriously want to be an office drone?"

"Does it involve actual drones?"

"Probably not."

"Then that's the best place for me." He sighed heavily. "Look, I could pop over to a university and talk universal theories with people. You don't travel for this long and not pick up a few things—thoughts, questions, ideas—but your planet isn't ready, and I don't know if I'd be able to have an intelligent conversation. So, for now, put me somewhere boring and let me blend in. It's better than throwing your planet into chaos."

"You could probably mess with the heads of some of the local students, or researchers," I offered. "Many of them are studying physics, and I'm pretty sure the school offers courses in cosmology and astrophysics."

"Sounds like a blast." He grinned. "In any case, rule number one, maintain a low profile. I'll become an accountant."

"Zander, the alien accountant," I scoffed. "Absolutely lovely."

"It beats mersation." He chuckled as I let him into the building. I had no idea what he meant, but let it slide. There would be time for questions when my mind wasn't so freaking exhausted. "Is this socially acceptable?"

"What do you mean?"

"Well, I wouldn't want you to get into any trouble with society by living with a man," he said, a note of humor in his voice.

"This is the twenty-first century. I think it's fine," I told him. "But if you're worried, we can pretend you're my cousin or something. No alarm bells there. How does that sound?"

"You're too kind. Are you sure about this?"

"Positive. Now, come on, it's cold out here, and I've got to set up your room. You coming?"

"Yes," he said without hesitation. "But I am

warning you, I don't know much about Earth culture."

"I'll help you," I promised. "Oh, and speaking of which, tomorrow you'll need to get yourself some actual clothes. Those look ragged, and there's a huge stain on that pant leg. Is that ... blood?"

"Squirrel," he said. "But I can see why that could freak someone out."

I opened the door, but he held it for me to enter, smiling. He kept smiling until I wished him goodnight.

CHAPTER ELEVEN
CLOSE ENCOUNTERS OF THE COFFEE KIND

Sleeping in was heavenly.

Having not yet bought a new alarm clock, I allowed myself to fall into a more natural sleep pattern. In just a week, I found myself waking up around ten or eleven, much later than expected. And it was amazing.

I rolled over and checked the clock. The jolt of seeing 4.00 am on its face was enough to shock me awake, even though I remembered a second later that it was still broken. I turned it upside down on the stand. I needed to get new batteries for it eventually.

I heard a noise from outside the room; cabinets opening and closing, feet shuffling on the tiled floor. All right, so now I was wide awake, keenly aware of the fact this was not normal.

There was someone in my house.

Moving as quietly as I could, I slipped out of bed. I reached into the closet to grab the baseball bat I kept for nostalgia's sake, weighing it lightly in my hands. My clammy palms stuck to the wooden handle, making it impossible for me to grip it right.

I made my way into the hallway. The noise was coming from the kitchen, I was sure of that now. The smell of coffee was overwhelming.

There was definitely someone in there.

I pressed against the wall and leaned over the threshold, peeking into the kitchen. The man had his back to me, but to my horror, he wore the flowery dressing gown my mother had given me for Christmas, and he was ... cooking.

He turned around, and I whipped the bat behind my back. Zander. I had forgotten the events of the night before, believing them to be so surreal that they must have been a dream. But there he was, flesh and bone, quietly cooking in my kitchen in my pink, silk dressing gown.

I let out a sigh of relief. It could be worse.

Can't really think how, though.

"The next time you try sneaking up on someone, don't hold your arm out straight like that. It ruins the fact you're trying to hide," he said, turning back to the food.

"How ...?" I asked, balancing the bat against the wall. Wordlessly, he pointed at the stovetop, his finger reflecting in the polished chrome.

"I couldn't remember what Terrans eat for breakfast," he said, changing the subject, "so I cooked what I ate last time I came for a visit." He held up a frying pan with an omelet in it. "You want one?"

"Sure, why not?"

He finished the one he was working on, flipping it

in a way I had only ever seen done in films. He grabbed the plate next to him. He had been expecting me.

"Thanks," I said as he slid it on the table in front of me. It smelled heavenly. "Can I ask you something?"

"Sure," he replied, pulling open the oven door and retrieving a plate stacked with imperfectly formed omelets. He sat down at the table facing me and tore into the top one, downing it in seconds.

"Why are you wearing my dressing gown?"

He looked down at himself then back at me, obviously confused. "What's wrong with it?" His eyes were wide. Too wide. There was something a little off about him this morning, like he was in a daze. "I mean, it's a bit tight, but I thought that was the fit."

"It's a dressing gown," I replied, but he continued to look confused. "One, you can't wear that out of the house. Two, you're stretching it, and most importantly, number three, fuchsia is really not your color. The mall has some gorgeous ivory silk ones that would do wonders for your complexion though."

"It was the only thing that was even close to my size," he sputtered. "I took your advice and threw the jeans in the wash, but the stains are stuck. And I inferred from last night's stay at the police station, that Earth has a few policies on modesty; I needed to wear something."

I rolled my eyes. "I could have found you something a bit better than my gown. You're stretching it," I insisted, my heart sinking. "Seriously, you need more clothes. One pair of jeans won't cut it. So, any plans for the day?"

"I didn't really think about it," he said after he

finished his mouthful. "Not yet, anyway. I made you some coffee."

He pushed a mug in my direction. The room smelled much too strongly of coffee for just one cup, the scent more pungent than the lingering smell of fried eggs. When I turned my head, my eyes fell on the countertop, or the place where it was meant to be. Mug upon mug were lined up, covering the surface until none of it could be seen. I could hardly believe I owned so many mugs.

As I thought about it, I was sure I didn't. I didn't recognize at least half of them.

"Zander, are you all right?" I asked. His dazed look put me on edge.

"I really like your coffee," he said, taking a huge bite of his last omelet.

"What?"

"Earth makes the best stuff to drink," he continued. "I hope you don't mind, but I used your computer this morning. That Internet's the best thing to come from Earth, trust me. Oh, my stars, the cat videos. The worship has gotten way out of control. Anyway, I was trying to learn as much as I could about current events, trying to understand the appeal of the current coffee craze, and realized I wanted some." He paused, looking at the countertop. My worry grew tenfold. "You humans need a reality check. Do you honestly drug yourselves with this?" He pointed at a pack of coffee grounds, which I didn't recognize as belonging to me either. "It's just not right; not right at all. And gah, so bitter. And then, then I had to try some other blends, so I tracked some more down, and—"

"Wait, slow down. How many cups of coffee have you had?"

"Uh ... fifteen? Twenty?" He ran his tongue over his lips. "Does it matter?"

"Yes, it matters." I jumped to my feet. "You're right, too much is not good for you. You're full of caffeine. Can your metabolism even take it?"

"It's taken worse," he replied, making eye contact and staring into my eyes. "Oh, Sally, Sally, Sally. Sally, Sally, Sally ... I'll be—"

And with that, he toppled off the chair, his head hitting the tiled floor with a resounding crack.

Oh, crap.

I ran to his side, feeling my chair topple. I reached for his pulse, feeling nothing. Did he even have a pulse in the first place? I checked his mouth for breath. The man wasn't breathing; he was snoring—snoring very, very loudly.

Great. Freakin' alien can't handle his coffee.

I grabbed his arm and dragged him to the living room. He was heavy, but I couldn't leave him sleeping on the kitchen floor with his legs half stuck in a chair. With a lot of effort and a great deal of difficulty, I managed to hoist him onto the couch, but he was too long so he slept with his head pressed against one armrest and with legs dangling over the other. He almost looked peaceful, if a little uncomfortable. His dangling hand twitched as it hung in the air.

Was there a handbook that could tell me what to do next? While there were thousands of books that taught parenting, I was sure there wasn't a self-help book about alien roommates. If there were, it was

140

probably about abductees, not subletters.

I didn't know if I was supposed to be annoyed or scared. He was only asleep, after all, but he had also drunk what looked like a lethal dose of caffeine, certainly enough to kill someone like me.

Well, he was from another planet. Maybe he could handle it better.

Maybe.

Hopefully.

"Blayde ..." he muttered from the couch.

"She's not here right now, sorry," I replied, sitting on the coffee table. "It's just me."

"Blayde ..." Zander repeated, throwing his arm out and hitting my knee. I shoved it away, but he threw it back, mumbling incoherently. "You're nice," he muttered, the only words that made any sense out of the babble.

"Thanks."

"No, I mean it," he continued, his words coming out garbled. "You're really nice."

"And you need some rest. You've OD'd on coffee. I didn't even think that was possible."

"Everything's possible in an impossible chicken ..." he said, eyes still shut and his voice oddly deep, like it was coming from the bottom of a well. "You're cool, Sally. Really cool."

"Thanks," I replied, getting to my feet. He threw his arm out once more, and finding nothing, moaned quietly in annoyance, letting his hand dangle mid-air.

And with that, the snoring began again, stronger than before. Loud, thunderous roars. Loud enough to shake every wall in the house.

Why had I brought this upon myself?

I got dressed quickly, trying to go through my normal morning routine, with the exception of the loud snores reminding me that this morning was anything but normal. I cleaned the mugs one at a time, splitting the ones I knew I owned—about three—from the rest of the odd assortment. A sinking feeling filled my gut as I wondered where they had come from. One had 'world's best dad' printed on it in bold black letters; definitely not mine.

Unfortunately, getting squirrel blood out of jeans didn't have a Wiki page devoted to it, and I wasn't about to ask Reddit. Now, I wondered how I was going to get Zander out of the house without sending the town into a frenzy. I couldn't bother Jules again, and I couldn't call Marcy since she wouldn't be able to help. She didn't own any men's jeans, and anyone else would ask questions.

Okay, so this was turning out to be much more complicated than I had initially thought. I had hoped that someone who claimed to travel across the universe daily would be able to blend in a little better.

And this was just the simple stuff, like wearing clothes. How would he manage complicated things, like getting a job, or a bank account, or identification?

Talk about an illegal alien.

When I returned from the laundry room with our clothes as clean as I could get them, Zander was gone. The room looked as if he had never been here; even the extra coffee mugs were gone. Zander was nowhere to be seen, which was a frightening thought; an alien doped up on coffee and wearing a flowery dressing gown, possibly commando, would cause widespread panic. Worst case scenario—he'd end up viral on the internet.

So why weren't there any screams outside?

I went to the balcony, scanning the limited view I had of the neighboring buildings and the street below. Nope, no Zander down there, no screams from the passersby, not a sound from anyone anywhere.

He had gone. Again.

"You drop something?"

I spun around, and there he was, leaning against the balcony rail, out of the dressing gown and back in jeans and a t-shirt—except these ones weren't stained.

"Where were you?" I snapped.

"What do you mean?"

"What do you mean, what do I mean? What is with you this morning? You … you … you OD'd—on coffee."

"I did?" Zander asked, confused. "Oh, yeah, I had a little too much to drink, sorry. Out of my system now. Happens pretty quickly with me."

"That's messed up."

He shrugged. "I didn't know it would affect me like that."

"Twenty cups of coffee and you didn't expect that?"

"Twenty bottles of beer didn't give me any problems."

"What?"

"Sorry. It won't happen again."

"If you want to fit in on this planet, stay away from the drinks," I advised. "Just be careful, okay?"

"I am being careful."

"Are you?" I asked. "Because from what you've been telling me, you get out and about a lot. I thought you could handle yourself in the real world."

"I'm sorry, I'm just—" He didn't finish his sentence. I don't think he knew how to.

"Where did those clothes come from?" I asked. "Who—"

"Your other neighbor." His lips spread into a grin. "Jumped onto his terrace, told him I was running from my girlfriend's parents. He tossed me something to wear. Not a perfect fit, but at least I'll look more, well, normal."

"Ingenious," I replied.

Maybe I had misjudged him. Maybe he could make do here. It seemed that the more risk he had to take, the better he was at getting what he wanted. Maybe he had a problem with monotony.

"Thanks." He grinned proudly, handing me the silk gown. "Sorry about the dressing gown."

"It's okay," I replied, closing the terrace door after walking inside. I took the dressing gown, marched to my room, and dropped it in the empty laundry basket.

"We're going to have to buy you some other clothes, though," I said. "One pair of jeans will not hold you over."

"I gathered as much," he said with a curt nod. "If I'm lucky, I still have an account on this planet, maybe even this country. I may have opened one the last time I was here."

"So, we'll go to the bank first," I replied.

"Yeah, but I can't remember which one," he said. "Blayde kept it written in her journal. I've never had to remember the details."

"Well, we should be fine with the money I got for those gold coins of yours," I told him. "You'll need some shirts, and we'll have to find you a suit if you're going to go for job interviews. And a tie."

"Great."

"So what do you wear back on your planet? Togas?" I asked him, trying to make conversation. I was also dying to know more about this guy. "Where did you come from, exactly?" My phone buzzed in my pocket—Matt, probably, keeping up with our conversation from last night, but he could wait a little longer.

"It's complicated," he replied, his face suddenly going cold.

"I've got time." I beamed, but Zander frowned. I felt as if I had touched a nerve.

"It's not that," he replied. "I want to give you answers, Sally, but that question has none. So please, ask me something else."

"Oh, sorry ... you sure you don't mind me asking all these, well, kind of personal questions? I can stop. It's just ..."

"Nah, it's cool. It's been a while since I've had someone to talk to. Ask away."

"All right, then." I grinned. "Stop me if I get too personal. But the desert clothes? And the blood on them? That wasn't from my car or me. Where did you come from? I take it you jumped, but from where? The Sahara Desert?"

He chuckled. "A little further away than that."

"Where?"

"A small military outpost named Gamma—Beta—

4465, in the Quara'tz region, System ZZ—Alpha Singular, in the Keeran Cluster."

I snorted so loudly I felt my breakfast coming up my nose. It was gross.

"Oh, you've been there?" he asked, winking. "Yeah, not a great place."

"So, I take it you weren't on holiday." I wiped my nose with a tissue, stuffing it into my pocket.

"Business," he said, casual-like. "An accidental arrival, but Blayde and I found a reason to stay for a while. That was until they chased us off at gunpoint."

"You say that like it happens to you every day."

"No, not every day." Zander rolled his eyes. "Every other day, maybe."

"What brought you to Earth?"

"An accident, really."

"Another one?"

"Yeah, jumping long distances is pretty awful. We can make all our cells jump simultaneously to any point in the universe. Like, um, Earth thing. Earth thing. Do you guys have paper shredders yet?"

"Yeah, hang on." I ran to one of the closets and pulled out the shredder my dad had gotten me for my last birthday, still in the box. "The government will go through your mail when you're out shopping," he had told me. "Do me a favor and use this. I don't want them reading what I send you." I hadn't used it, considering nobody mails me these days. The Internet is a marvelous invention.

I unpacked it and placed it on the coffee table. "Is this what you're talking about?"

"Yeah, that's it. Well, kind of." He took a piece of

146

paper. "The paper is me. I'm point A. The shredder is the space in between." He passed the paper through the shredder then emptied the container on the table. He found some tape on the countertop and taped the paper strips back together. "Now I've reached point B, safe and sound."

"Looks like you're a puddle of man mush."

"Yeah, it's a bit more complicated than that." He shrugged. "I heal, right? You get the picture?"

"Crystal clear," I said. "So, that's jumping. But when we were in the car, driving away from that ... ship, you disappeared? I thought you said you couldn't control where you went."

"I don't always jump randomly. I can jump to places I can see. But only where I see. I couldn't jump, I dunno, through that wall or anything. But anywhere I can see inside, I could go to, if I wanted."

"Is that all?" I snorted. "I mean, is there anything else you can do? Like, how can you understand what I'm saying right now? I'm assuming not everyone in the universe speaks English."

"Universal translator chip," he said, pointing to the back of his ear. "There was a pretty advanced civilization that figured out how to interpret brain waves and translate any language they were presented with. It's a handy, dandy little gizmo."

"Like Miko's?"

"Miko's was pretty low tech." Zander shrugged. "Just one language to another. Mine doesn't care about that."

"Way cool."

"I know, right?" He grinned from ear to ear. "So,

maybe I can get one of those translatey jobs. Wouldn't require too much work, though, admittedly, my area of expertise is in private security."

"Ha." I let out a short laugh, but let it slide because at that moment my phone chimed. I picked it up and read the new text, which came, surprisingly (or, not so surprisingly) from Matt. Another one to say he was looking forward to our date tonight. So was I.

Zander stared at the device, muttering that he needed to get himself one. He glanced over at me knowingly.

"Who's this?" he asked, but the look on his face said he already knew. Possibly because of how red my face had gotten.

"None of your business."

He waggled his eyebrows at me. "So, what's lover boy saying?"

"Hey," I snapped. "Rude much?"

"You like him?"

"Yeah."

"Good for you." He nodded. "I won't bother you then."

"Thanks," I muttered, reading and rereading the short text. I couldn't help but smile. I hadn't been on a date in ages and had never looked forward to one as much as this. All this chatting by phone made me wonder if we'd have anything to say in person. I sure hoped we would.

"What do the Terrans do on dates?" he asked. "What's the mating ritual like?"

"Excuse me?"

"Does it involve dancing? Food? Breathing into

each other's faces? Or bright outfits?"

"What are you talking about?"

"On Yuhulis, the trick is to make pungent smelling food," Zander continued. "If the date reciprocates the feelings and is down for getting dirty, they rub the food through their ... um ... what do you call it now... ah yes, ridge spikes."

"Why are you telling me this?"

"I assume a similar thing happens on Earth." He grinned. "Well, without the ridge spikes. Or does it involve people playing racket sports in short garments? Or is it as the Internet suggests? Do women claim to be Russian and share under-clad images online while males assert dominance with Yu-Gi-Oh! battles?"

"I am so confused right now. None of those things make sense."

"Love doesn't make any sense."

"You're messing with me, aren't you?"

"If you say so," he replied, giving me a wink. "You go and have fun on your date."

"And you can work on your Earth skills. You may look human, but you don't pass as ... Terran."

He nodded yet again. "I guess it's time for me to learn what it is to be an inhabitant of Earth. Hey, do you guys have anything decent to watch? I need a good laugh."

I slid my computer toward him, though he had made it clear he had already used it.

"Check out Netflix." I showed him where I had bookmarked it. "You'll find everything you need there."

Zander kept grinning. "Well, this is going to be a blast," he said, scrolling through the account.

Yup, it was. With the alien engrossed in the world-wide web, I was free to text Matt and get myself more and more excited for this evening. Though I really hoped Zander wouldn't take our alien tropes too seriously.

CHAPTER TWELVE
SOMEONE CRASHES MY DATE AND THE GLASS CEILING ALL AT ONCE

When the text with a smiley face showed up on my phone to tell me that Matt had arrived downstairs, I was fighting a losing battle with my shoes. The little strappy bits weren't being cooperative. Every time I tried to buckle one up, the other came undone, making me freak out as I tried to rush for the door.

The shoes were new. I had played the good interplanetary host, taking Zander to the mall to find something he could wear that wasn't stolen or covered in nature stains. While he had wrestled with trying to find clothes that not only fit him but pleased him, I had treated myself to a pair of new shoes. I wasn't the kind of person who bought many things for myself, but after the week I'd had, I thought it was worth it.

Treat yourself.

Plus, I was trying to impress Matt, though I doubted a pair of shoes would do it.

The mall had confused Zander, not that he had anything against malls; there were shopping centers on other planets. Apparently, capitalism wasn't unique to Earth. As he strolled around the clothing stores, he kept asking me the oddest questions, like, "how do they expect me to buy their clothes if their models aren't wearing any?"

Not that it had been an unpleasant experience. I had my shoes and Zander had some decent clothes, so I had more reason to push him into getting a job and start paying his half of the rent. Yay, me.

He was binging on Doctor Who, though right now he wasn't watching it. No, he was watching me hop from one foot to the other, desperately trying to attach my feet to my pretty, strappy shoes. "Do you need help with that?"

I glared at him.

"Okay, fine. Well, have fun on your date."

"Thanks," I grumbled. The shoes seemed to be staying on now, which was good timing because I had received a second text. I told Matt I would be down in a second.

The shoes were a killer to walk in, though. I hobbled down the stairs and out the front door to where Matt waited outside his car. His face lit up when he saw me.

I had gone all-out for this date. I had put on a dress, which I rarely wore, and pinned up my hair in a 'do that looked more elaborate than it actually was—thanks, Pinterest. I wore a light layer of makeup, and I managed to craft eyeliner wings, which had taken forever. I had matched the shoes to the dress, a night sky blue a shade darker than the TARDIS.

152

His reaction was the one I'd wanted; he was impressed.

Heck, yes.

"Sally, you look lovely." He stepped forward to give me a hug. He smelled nice, like cinnamon and pine.

"Thanks, Matt," I replied. "You look good too."

We chatted about nothing important as he drove us to the restaurant. The rain was picking up, hinting at on oncoming storm, but I barely noticed. We drove out of the city and into pretty much the middle of nowhere. I realized then where we were going — La Casa Italia, the fanciest restaurant in the county. It sat alone on the top of a beautiful hill in a refurbished observatory that had repeated rave reviews for its gorgeous design and fantastic food. I had never imagined ever going to it; the cost was exorbitant.

As I stepped into the lavish lobby, I wondered how Matt could afford to take me to a place like, what with him being an intern. He didn't look rich. His suit was several years old, slightly faded, and wasn't tailored. Yet he looked incredibly handsome with his chocolate-brown hair tussled around with gel. It brought out the electric blue of his eyes.

The waiter led us to a table in the center of the dining room, underneath the vaulted glass ceiling. The rain pounded the panels hard, but it only served to contrast the warmth of the room, making everything feel cozier.

"Tonight's special is Chicken Parmigianino," the waiter offered as he seated us, "served with a fresh tomato sauce, with a side of hand-cut pasta. I have the wine list right here, sir."

"Are you going to have the Parmigianino, Sally?" Matt asked.

"Sure, it sounds fantastic."

If this place hadn't been so fancy, I wouldn't have worked so hard to keep the drool in. It smelled like heaven, and I couldn't wait to eat. The fact that Matt and I shared a similar taste in food meant this night was starting out great.

"Same here," Matt nodded, turning to the waiter. "Can you recommend a red to go with the meal?"

"Of course," the man replied, pointing to the carte while I admired the room around me. Huge velvet curtains draped from each of the windows, framing the view of the city below. A landscape of tiny yellow and white pinpricks of light in the darkness masked only by the deluge of rain.

Everything about the restaurant screamed regal, from the paintings on the wall to the golden frame around the bar. I had eaten in good restaurants before but never in one as nice. Or even close to this nice.

"This is amazing," I said, completely in awe.

Matt joined me in admiring the room and smiled.

I blushed. "I feel underdressed."

"Compared to you, it's the room that's underdressed. You look absolutely gorgeous."

The way he said it made me feel all warm inside. He meant his words, and I hadn't ever felt a compliment, however light, so deeply.

Gosh, I was feeling things.

The waiter returned and poured our wine, leaving me to rein in my face while Matt looked away. The wine was bitter, but I smiled all the same, using it to mask the red that had been coloring my cheeks.

"So, um, what exactly is it you do for Mr. Grisham?" I asked, trying to sound casual.

He chuckled. "You're trying to figure out how I can afford this place, aren't you?"

"Kind of."

"Well, I'll be honest here—my boss—or should I say, our boss, is paying for it."

"Seriously?"

"Apparently, I've been talking a little too much about you."

"You're kidding me. You only met me a few days ago ..."

"I don't think you realize the effect you've had on me." He smiled. "In any case, it was enough for my—our—boss to offer us this date."

My cheeks burned. "I guess, um, my interview went better than I thought."

Matt grinned. "Grisham was as enamored with you as I am," he said. "Well, not in the same way; that would be weird. But he sees your potential, same way he saw mine."

I snorted, feeling the wine climb up my nostrils. "You're kidding, right? I didn't last a semester in college. I have nothing but retail experience, the last of which I was fired from. What kind of potential is there for him to find?"

"Sally," he said, his face growing serious, "he sees the same thing I do. He sees how much you care. He sees how determined you are. How brilliant you are. How strong you hold on. He sees a brilliant woman with a bright future. So what if life's been trying to shake you off the path you want? You've been forging your own. Grisham can see that."

"He seems like an amazing man," I whispered. I was dumbfounded. No one had ever told me such things, and knowing that he hardly knew me, I wasn't inclined to believe him. Though I wanted to. I desperately wanted to.

"Oh, he is," said Matt. "Only now we're talking about my boss on our date, so that's …"

"Yeah, kind of weird," I said. "But there's one thing that's been bugging me. Then we can change the subject, okay?"

"Shoot."

"Well," I said, trying to make this sound as casual as I could, "Aren't you just an intern?"

"Yeah, I thought so too, but Grisham's taken me under his wing. I was only supposed to be working on PR for him, but he's mentoring me now. What started as a work-study program might just become my life. Between you and me, I think he wants me to run the plant someday."

"And do you like it? I mean, if you're making it a career, you should like it, right? It sounds more like it's his idea than yours."

"Grisham has a way with people." Matt laughed. "A way of getting them to see things his way, and I really do like working for him. You will too. Congrats again on the job, by the way, and, of course, on the impression you made on Grisham. You're going to go far, I know it."

We clinked glasses. It was classy.

"I don't think I could have done it without you."

"Believe me, Sally, it was all you," he replied. "Oh, perfect timing."

The waiter placed the steaming plate in front of me, the smell of hot tomatoes and cheese wafting up my nostrils, setting my brain alight with excitement. It looked amazing, the chicken a picture of beauty. Instagramable. I couldn't wait and dove in immediately. The flavor soaked my tongue, and I felt myself floating to heaven.

"You know, this might sound, well, weird," Matt said awkwardly, "but I've had a crush on you for ages."

"You what?" I stammered, a string of homemade pasta hanging from between my lips.

"You remember that creative writing class we had first semester?" he asked. "Well, I—"

"I did too," I said, quickly swallowing the pasta and giving him a wide smile. "I thought your novellas were great. I kept making weird excuses to sit close to you."

"So did I." He laughed. He was doing a lot of laughing, I realized, but it was quite endearing. "When the semester ended, I tried signing up for the same electives as you, but I stopped seeing you around the campus. Which was, well, kind of heartbreaking."

"Sorry about that. I just ... stopped ... around finals."

"What went wrong?" Matt asked, waving his fork around. "Did something happen?"

"Yeah," I said. "It became a little too much for me."

"Oh?" he said. "May I ask why? Or is that too personal?"

I made the decision right then and there to tell him the truth, as much as it was killing me inside. I liked him, and I think he liked me. Better to get everything out in the open early on, right?

"Well," my voice dropped, but I caught it immediately. "My brother died, right when I was graduating high school. Let's just say I didn't deal with it very well and leave it at that."

Matt nodded slowly, a look of understanding in his fierce, blue eyes. Gosh, I was so glad he didn't push it. Talking about John always raised some dark thoughts.

But the panic didn't rise. Usually at this point, I would have to control my breathing and force myself to focus on my happy place. But right now, my body was calm. For some reason, I was completely fine.

"I lost my parents when was fifteen," Matt said. "I know how much it hurts. I'm so sorry, Sally."

"Oh, Matt, I'm sorry, too," I replied. He extended his hand, and I took it across the table. Which of course meant I had to stop eating.

Poor guy. I had lost a brother; he had lost his entire family. I wanted to ask him how, why, and so much more, but a weight hung in the air between us—the weight of those words made it impossible for me to speak.

My eyes were drawn to the ceiling again, that great glass structure that looked like something out a greenhouse. I couldn't take my eyes off it. The large panels revealed the ferocity of the rain outside, making me feel as if I was in the heart of the storm without having to leave the comfort of the restaurant.

But there was something weird going on, too. A figure interrupted the rain, its black back slamming hard against the glass. I squinted, trying to make it out. It was probably some kind of animal, maybe a wild cat, but it looked too big for that. I returned to my chicken and my date, pushing it out of mind.

"What were you planning to do, before you dropped out?" he asked, between mouthfuls. "Any career plans?"

"Gosh, why does everyone ask that?" I asked. "Sorry, I don't mean that against you. It's just, first, it's what college do you want to go to, then what degree, then what job. Like you can expect an eighteen-year-old who's not legally allowed to drink to be able to map out their entire life plan."

Matt nodded, fully intent.

"I had no idea what I wanted to do," I said. "When John died, everyone told me to go to college, that I was just thinking those things because I was depressed, but I didn't know what I wanted to do even before that. Even my therapist agrees that my brother dying had nothing to do with what happened to me. Everyone around me had dreams, goals ... hell, they were passionate about things. But I didn't know what I wanted from life. From my life. You know?"

"I do," he nodded. "I ended up where I am because a counselor told me I had an aptitude for it. But you know? All I like is a good story."

"A story?"

"Everything has a story," Matt replied. "Shows and movies and books, those are evident. You read them. You hear them. I love something that transports me, you know? You experience them. But food tells us a story, too; you can't limit a good story to which sense it appeals."

"So, what kind of story is your food telling you?"

He smiled. "This chicken tells me about a man—or woman—in Italy, years ago, who decided to cook the poultry that specific way, that specific day. But it also tells me about yesterday, when this unassuming chicken became part of that legacy, becoming the image of what that person imagined before it was even born. To feed us, to make us happy, to give us conversation."

"Wow," I nodded. "That's deep … for a chicken."

"Yeah, that's me." He winked. "Deep chicken. I like good stories and hate the rain. I'm afraid of rodents and large birds, and I dream of being happy."

"Happy?"

He shrugged. "It may not seem glamorous, but it's a good thing to aspire to. Set your goals for happiness because you won't find yourself making decisions that hurt you down the road."

"I guess that would depend on your definition of happy," I pointed out. "If being happy means them being richer than everyone else, or—" I froze, hearing a loud thwomp above my head. I wasn't the only one who heard it either; people around us were staring upwards, some pointed at the glass ceiling, where two figures were desperately clinging to each other in the downpour.

"Can you see …?" I asked, but Matt had fallen silent. As a matter of fact, the entire restaurant had. The pounding on the ceiling was the only noise in the entire room.

The figures appeared to be fighting—if there were two of them, it was hard to tell—rolling and slamming into the glass, finding it hard to keep a grip with the rain pounding down. With a resounding crash, one of them slammed down so hard that cracks appeared in the glass beneath him.

"Everyone move!" Matt was not the only one to scream the words of warning, bounding to his feet along with at least three other patrons. They flew to the tables directly below the growing crack to help people out of harm's way. The ceiling shuddered and collapsed. Glass and water rained through the hole. The deafening shatter made my ears ring. A lone, dark-robed man fell, crashing to the floor in the center of the room, his wail of terror cut short by his landing.

I held my breath—in my mind, there was only one person it could be. No one dared move. They stood in frozen bewilderment, no one wanting to get wet. Eventually, a waiter got up to check for vital signs, and everyone began moving again, chatting in whispered tones. Matt gave me a worried glance before going forward to see if he could be of some assistance. I waited at the table, only feet away from the body. My stomach was in knots, so I took the last bit of chicken off my plate.

Food, the ultimate comfort in my time of need.

"Sally, I need your help."

I jumped. "Chicken?" I held the poultry on my fork in front of my face. "Is that you?"

"Down here." I dropped my gaze to see a hand poking from under the floor-length tablecloth waving at me. It was sopping wet, slightly red from what I could only assume was blood, even though the hand itself was fine.

"Zander?" I gasped so hard I accidentally threw

myself into a coughing fit, which probably covered up the name, in case anyone was listening in.

"Are you all right?" Zander grasped a piece of the tablecloth, pulling it up so he could see my face. He looked as if he had come out of the trenches. His hair was soaking wet, his clothes muddy and brown.

"What are you doing down there? Were you—"

"I'll explain in a sec," he hissed. "I've got a lot of work to do. Please, I need your help."

"With what?"

"Saving the planet." He grimaced. "It involves cunning, deceit, and trickery. You in?"

"I'm on a date."

"Was." He shrugged. "Sorry, that was probably a mood killer."

"By that, you mean the man you tossed through the ceiling?"

"The assassin tasked with killing the Killian prime minister."

"The man you threw through a ceiling."

"Yes, him." Zander rolled his eyes. "So, are you in?"

"Um ..." I glanced at the man in the middle of the room. He was breathing, still alive, but he was in bad shape. People were trickling closer, gushing and worrying. Matt seemed completely wrapped up with helping them.

"Sally, I need you," Zander urged. "I don't have anyone else I can trust. Please?"

"You trust me?"

"One hundred percent." Zander nodded. "Do you trust me?"

I sighed. "Yes, but—it sounds dangerous."

"I'd never willingly put you in harm's way if I couldn't keep you safe. Sally, your entire planet is in danger. I need your help. You're the only one I can count on. Please?"

"You're kidding me," I said, but he shook his head. "If you say so, fine."

"Find an excuse to slip out. I'll meet you in the women's bathroom."

"You—" But it was too late; the second the cloth dropped, he was gone. The space beneath the table was empty once more, leaving me to wonder if I had imagined the whole thing.

I was a woman on a mission now. I strode to Matt's side. He stood a foot away from the man he had been helping, leaving the work to those more adept at handling this kind of situation. He seemed restless and obviously itching to do something, but he refrained.

"Matt, my roommate, Zander, just texted me," I said trying to make it sound as awkward as I could. "The storm has ruptured some pipes at my apartment. I have to go back, catch an Uber, and deal with it."

"Oh ..." he replied, surprised to see me there. "Well, I was kind of hoping we could take the date somewhere else, seeing as someone crashed our dinner, like a movie or something?"

"I'm not trying to make an excuse to slip out." I smiled. "I was having a lovely time before ... I really do have to go back and deal with my flooding apartment, though. Shall we call it a night and try again some other time?"

"This is the oddest conversation to have while a

man is lying unconscious on the floor." He chuckled lightly. "But I would love that."

"I would too," I said, and I meant it.

"I'll call you?" he said, leaning down to give me a peck on the cheek. I felt my face warming, and in a moment of excitement, I kissed him back—a quick peck on the lips. His face turned a light shade of red to match my own.

I seriously liked this guy.

I didn't know why, specifically, but I wanted another date, and soon. If there was going to be another one. After all, Zander had said something about needing to save the planet. Maybe there wasn't going to be a planet to date on after tonight.

CHAPTER THIRTEEN
I GET BEAMED UP TO THE MOTHER SHIP

I slipped into the women's bathroom where Zander stood, suddenly dry, wearing a bright green suit with purple lining.

Holy crap, he looked like the Riddler! Like, 1960s Batman Riddler: all he was missing was the bowler hat.

I stood in the doorway, unsure of how to react to this. It looked as if a lime had granted him until midnight to go to the ball and find Prince Charming.

"What on earth are you wearing?" I said, slightly disgusted.

"It's all about the effect," he replied, holding out a dark black trash bag. "Put these on, and do it quickly. They'll be back in a few minutes."

"Who will?" I asked, stepping into a cubicle so I could get changed in peace. My trembling hands made it tough for me to open the bag. Inside, there were tight silver leggings and a black dress I didn't recognize.

"The Killian soldiers I ran into," he explained, his

voice carrying over the door, "right before I got that assassin out of the way. They insisted on talking to Blayde and me. Wouldn't see me without her."

I froze in the stall, halfway through tugging up the leggings.

"I'm dressing up as her, aren't I?" Things were becoming clearer in my mind. He didn't need me. He needed a stand-in for his sister.

"You catch on fast, good. I'll do the talking, you just scowl at them. They won't know the difference."

"They don't know Blayde?"

"Only by reputation," said Zander. "Hey, I'm going to have to ask you to hurry up a little."

"Going as fast as I can here," I said, tugging on the dress and stepping out of the bathroom. The leggings were too tight, but the dress fit ok, even if it was a little more low-cut than I was used to. Not something I would wear out.

"Shoes?" he asked.

"There were shoes?"

"Oh, sorry." He grabbed a box off the counter and tossed it to me. I threw off the cover and found a pair of black stilettos inside, more lace and strap than actual shoe. "I have a wig for you too."

"A wig?" I scoffed, still inspecting the torture instruments masquerading as shoes. They looked painful. I had never worn anything that high before. "When did you get the time to put all this together?"

"Somewhere between running into the soldiers and taking out the assassin." He shrugged. "You sure you're ready for this?"

"My planet's on the line. I'll make myself ready."

Well, I was terrified. But I'd had half a glass of wine at dinner, which was half a glass more than I was used to, and the looming fear that my planet was on a course toward imminent doom would give me something to say.

I stuffed my clothes into my purse.

"That's the spirit." Zander grinned a wide, cheeky grin, and for a second I could have sworn the two of us were going to a costume party together and not heading off to protect the only planet I'd ever known.

"So how does Blayde talk?" I asked, stumbling as I put on the shoes. I reached for the counter to keep my balance. "How does she act? What's she like?"

"Blayde is ..." he paused then handed me the wig, which looked oddly like a Halloween witch's wig with strands of black color poorly spray-painted on. While the rest of the outfit looked completely credible—not that I knew his sister—the hair was a definite fail. It looked awkward and wrong.

"This looks like crap," I said, not holding back.

"It'll be enough," he replied. "It's not like Killians have great vision. As for Blayde, she's like a ... like an incredibly hot star about to go supernova. I'd say, act as if everyone in the room is out to kill you, but you have a secret weapon that will destroy them and everything you've ever loved. Can you pull that off?"

"She seems like a delight, your sister."

"Just try, okay?" he urged, checking his watch. "All right, they'll be here any moment now. Let me help you with that wig."

I handed him back the wig and pushed my hair into a bun for him to cover with the makeshift bald cap. So much for all that work and hours spent on the Pinterest boards.

"I'm going to have to give you a translator," he said, somewhat awkwardly. "I stole the one from that assassin. He'll wake up sprouting gibberish, and you'll be fully equipped to handle an alien envoy. Here." He showed me the tiny metal washer he held between his thumb and forefinger. "Don't move."

"Wait, what?" I asked, glaring at him. "What are you …?"

"It goes right behind your ear," he said. "Just be glad it wasn't the suppository."

I grimaced but turned my head for him all the same. I would have asked if it was going to hurt, but what was the point? In any case, it didn't. He pressed the metal against the bone, and the skin behind my ear grew warm. He let go and everything went back to normal, leaving a slight bump on the back of my skull, barely noticeable at all.

"Your words will still come out as English," he said, removing his hand, "since you haven't had it in long. But it'll do the trick."

"And what do these Killians want?" I asked, taking out the wig and tugging it into place.

"Oh, you know, incinerate the planet's atmosphere," he replied, completely casual.

"But you attacked the man who wanted to kill their prime minister?"

"It's a little confusing, I know. And it's been a helluva night," Zander said, "but we can't let them burn down the planet."

"No, we most certainly cannot."

A second later, I looked like an entirely different person. I teetered awkwardly on the heels, but a look in the mirror was enough to tell me exactly whom I was supposed to look like.

I was the girl from the park. The one who appeared beside the other Zander and the other me and then disappeared without a trace. So, that had been Blayde. But if she had been on Earth with the other Zander, could it be she didn't know he was missing?

No. That would not explain the other Sally. The healthier, prettier Sally.

I realized then that I should have brought the encounter up with Zander, but what was I to do? We had other problems to deal with. And then a wall exploded. which made things a little trickier.

The cement burst in every direction, with dust spewing to fill up the entire bathroom. I winced, turning from the blast. Zander stood tall, as unperturbed as if he were watching an ant crawl on the pavement.

Two men—if you could call them men—appeared through the dust and the rubble wearing bulky, navy blue uniforms and clutching thick gun-like weapons. If I didn't know what was at stake, I would have been tempted to take off then and there.

The men were aliens.

Not alien in the way Zander was, but fully alien in every sense of the word. They were large-headed, green skinned, bulbous-eyed aliens. Their three-fingered hands drummed on their weapons. It was obvious they did not want to stand around waiting.

Honestly, it was weird. They looked exactly how I expected aliens to look. It was only then I realized my phone was at the bottom of my purse, and there was no chance I'd ever get a picture of this.

Zander let out a loud, high-pitched ululation. The soldiers replied in kind, snapping and shouting in such a way that it was almost impossible to hear my own thoughts.

And yet, there was a layer above the ululating. I heard the sound, and yet, at the same time, I knew what they were trying to say, as if there were a poorly dubbed version of the noise in my head. My translator, I took it, was working now.

"I've made them aware of the fact that your translator's broken," Zander whispered. "Their own devices will allow them to understand English, so I'll speak in English to keep everyone on the same page."

But my translator's working, I wanted to tell him, but he must have known. He probably had a larger plan, so I just nodded.

One of the men made a sound that could have been interpreted as agreement. Then they bowed to us, which was just weird. Zander replied in kind and I followed suit, taking his lead and adopting an expression of both calm acceptance and power. Not an easy feat. It took all my energy just to hide the shock.

Aliens.

In the restroom of an Italian restaurant.

Maybe something had hit my head when the window shattered. Maybe I was out cold, and this was a messed-up dream, making me believe I was doing something important.

Nothing else made any sense.

Well, if this was a dream, I was going to play the

part to the end. The aliens indicated for us to step forward, and I swung the fake hair over my shoulder with a flick of my wrist, keeping my neck poised and stiff. I took a hesitant step on those impossible shoes and found that if I kept my legs tense, I could move without flopping over. I marched over the rubble without a second thought, following the aliens outside.

The aliens. I would never get over that. At least with Zander, you could forget he wasn't human. Same with Miko and Taylor, minus the one reptilian hand. But seeing actual alien aliens—this was unreal.

Once outside, the soldiers led us to the service parking lot where the rain just sort of stopped. It made no sense because I could see it falling in the distance, hear its roar surrounding us.

The aliens stopped in the middle of the near-empty parking lot and looked up. I did the same. Seconds later, we were basked in a warm white glow, and I felt gravity release its grip on me. I floated upward, toward the source of the light.

"Zander?" I hissed, reaching out for his hand. My fingers slid along the sleeve of his suit. The material was cheap and thin, and could not have been comfortable.

"Don't panic," he whispered, giving my fingers a tight, discrete squeeze. "They have a tractor beam. It shouldn't mess with your internal organs very much. I just hope you haven't eaten recently."

"We're at a restaurant," I hissed.

"Then hold it in until this is over. Clench your teeth. It helps."

"You have got to be kidding me."

"Also, breathe," Zander added as the light became

blinding, "Just because the situation looks dire doesn't mean you shouldn't remember to breathe."

"This is dire?"

"Not yet."

"Fantastic."

The light was brighter than anything I could have imagined, making my eyes sting. I didn't notice we'd entered the ship until it finally shut off and I dropped to the floor, landing face first on the cold metal.

Stars flashed before my eyes as they readjusted to the dimmer lighting. Everything rang like the world had replaced birds with church bells. Soon my body adjusted, and the sound reduced to an electric hum.

Truth was, I wanted to let my jaw do its thing and just drop. I was on a spaceship, an actual spaceship, and it was oddly disappointing—again. I was in what looked like a dull gray garage, complete with wires hanging from the ceiling and what could have been a car in one corner, half covered by dark shadows.

Though it probably wasn't a car.

I had expected the grandeur of the Enterprise, or the Heart of Gold, not an imperial trash chute. The place looked dismal for a prime minister's ship.

But it hit me that this was still a life and death situation. This ship had tractor beams and who knew what else. If they wanted to take Earth, I wasn't going to stand for it. If it meant pretending to be a woman I had never met, pretending I wasn't screaming internally, I could do that.

They all want to kill me, I told myself, recalling Zander's words, but I can destroy them.

Oddly enough, it helped. I glowered at the aliens,

172

and they took a step back, remaining silent as I rose to my feet and somehow managed to balance on the stilettos.

A man—an alien man, or at least it appeared to be male, but what would I know—entered through one of the doors, saying a few words in that impossible language of theirs. Words that were somehow making sense to me with that translator sitting on my skull. I was impressed by his stature. While he appeared shorter than I was, he had an imposing stance, doubling his impact by the way he stood, like he was surveying us from the top of a hill. I tried to mimic his effect, moving my arms behind my back and sucking in my gut. I felt a foot taller. Was my posture really that bad?

"All right, asshats," he said, "let's get this show on the road."

"I shall be conversing in a common tongue," Zander said. "My associate has a broken translation device. As such, I shall translate for her."

He turned to me, and I met his gaze. I was taking a bit of creative freedom with Blayde's character, and, for the moment, it was working. Even Zander gave me a curt nod of approval.

"The general offers his greetings to you, Blayde. He has heard much about you and wishes to extend an invitation for you to follow him to the bridge."

"I accept," I said coolly, my words coming out in plain English. Drats, it really wasn't working. Even so, I didn't wait for Zander this time. I followed the man with my chin held high. The alien didn't seem surprised by my reaction—I must have been doing something right—and escorted me down the hallway.

Again, I was disappointed. I thought I would be impressed by the fact I was walking down the length of a spaceship, but it looked like a service tunnel I could have seen anywhere. Were we even moving? I had no way of knowing since there weren't any freaking windows.

I wanted to look back at Zander and find some comfort in his eyes, but knew very well I couldn't. It would have been out of character, that much was clear, so I kept my eyes fixed ahead and told myself I didn't need him.

Doors opened, and I entered a large room full of more of the aliens, the Killians. They froze as they watched us enter. It was obvious Zander was well known to them, and Blayde's reputation preceded me. They did not look happy.

I could have been wrong. Maybe frowning was a sign of good-natured cheer on their home world. In which case, this was the happiest place on earth.

We must have been on the bridge. A taller, older Killian, with skin grayer than the vivid green of the rest, and his uniform beautifully adorned with silver medals, sat in the center. He looked either angry or impressed by Zander's entrance; I couldn't tell. He leaned forward from his higher position, looking down at us with his large, black eyes.

The general who had led us there spoke a few words, relaying the news about my translator. Zander didn't speak up for me, which meant I had a lot of guesswork to do. The man on the pedestal said something in the loud screeching language, which did not register, and his general left quickly after that.

"Blayde," Zander said in a calm, almost musical tone as he leaned closer to me. "Allow me to introduce to you Prime Minister Harbin of the Killi nation."

"It is an honor," I replied, bowing low at the waist as Zander translated. "I assume we need no introduction."

Harbin nodded. Zander continued, his eyes riveted on the prime minister. "I have done my duty as peacekeeper by taking down an assassin intent on ending your life. Do not make a mistake of ignoring our request."

Harbin spoke, staring at me the whole time; he obviously wanted to hear more from Blayde.

"I can't ignore what we're not talking about," the prime minister snapped. "What do you want with me?"

"He says he cannot ignore what is not being discussed," Zander relayed, "and wishes to hear your plea."

Okay, so I had no idea what the plea was. Things I knew? Zander had said they wanted to attack us. Well, not exactly. He said they were going to incinerate us. Not cool. I also knew that Zander was bad at filling in other people on his plans, leaving me to improvise.

Luckily, I was already mad. Call it the good posture that had my blood flowing right or the stilettos that made me feel like a superwoman, but I felt a fire burning inside me that I had never felt before.

"First, I want him to tell me what the hell he thinks he's doing," I snapped, taking a firm step forward. The energy pulsing through me rolled the words off my tongue. "Listen to me, Prime Minister Harbin, and listen well because I know you can understand. I don't know if anyone's told you this before, but you cannot threaten the lives of an entire planet without attempting diplomatic communication with those who care for its well-being. We—they—are a developed race, capable of space flight and communication, choosing to resolve their issues at home before delving into the universe. They can do much more than you assume. So, let me speak for Earth, and say, quite clearly, that we want you out of our airspace—now."

The look on Zander's beaming face said it all. He looked at me like he had recognized a long-lost love, practically falling toward me like a needle to a magnet. The entire room was quiet, the weight of my words heavy on their minds.

Well, I could only assume. Maybe I had said something wrong and they were thinking how much I needed to burn. But I felt good. I hadn't even broken a sweat.

"Shiiiiiit." The prime minister let out a low whistle. "All right, we're listening. Tell your sister she's got our attention."

"We will ..." Zander translated, somehow keeping a straight face. "We will speak with you."

"Then speak," I said, my voice echoing through the silent chamber.

"We are here for our sons and daughters," Harbin said. "The ones who never returned."

"Did they die here? Were they taken by our people?"

"They crashed but still live," Zander relayed. "We do not know where they are, but assume they are held hostage by the Earth government for knowledge and information."

"They are not," I said sternly, though I hadn't the slightest idea. "When did they crash?"

"Three thousand Earth rotations around the star ago," Zander said, mimicking the stern, all-knowing voice of the prime minister.

"Just say year, Zander," I said to him. "Look. Earth humans do not have a long lifespan. Three thousand years is over 10,000 generations ago. Your crashed ship has not been heard of. Are you certain it crashed on this planet?"

"We followed the distress call. It has only recently been shut off, so we know we are in the correct hemisphere."

"Then it is yet to be found," I asserted.

"Then find it."

"We are not your lapdogs," I said. "Send some men down to search. Better yet, convince some humans to do it for you, but don't hold the entire planet to ransom for a reason it is unaware of."

I was on a roll here, and I felt good. Better than I had in ages, in fact. The fear of dying and being surrounded by Roswellian aliens stoked a fire in my gut.

Zander added a few words that made the prime minister angry. He growled while glaring at Zander.

"What's he saying now?" I asked, confused.

"He said if we don't find his people this *grishning* instant, he's going to boil everything on the planet's surface."

"Can we stop them?"

"We do not take threats idly," Zander spat at Harbin. "Leave this planet or face our wrath."

"No."

The voice resonated through the room. This man wanted his people, and he wanted them now. And, although I wasn't this Blayde woman they seemed to fear, I wouldn't stand for my planet being threatened. I took a step toward Harbin, feeling his eyes riveted on me and me alone.

My name is Sally Webber. I'm a human from Earth, a college dropout with no career ambition. I'm wearing a wig, and I really need to sit down; these heels are killing me. And I'm going to save my planet and everyone on it from complete annihilation.

"Give us time, and we will find your people," I asserted. "You know of my power. Trust us."

Zander sighed. "He says he doesn't."

"Either trust us to find your people, or leave and never come back. Either way, you leave this planet now."

"And now he wants you dead."

It was, quite literally, a do-or-die moment.

"Fat chance," I snapped.

Then I caught myself—I had nothing to bargain with. I fell from being Blayde and became Sally in a split second, like waking from a dream, or a deep spell. I almost squeaked with the realization of where I was and what I was doing.

Holy shit. Why for goodness sake? You could see the entire East Coast from the window. We were on a spaceship, hovering high above the planet's surface, and I was trying to parley with a creature I had never even heard of before.

Luckily, Zander kept his promise of keeping me safe. In an instant, he subdued a guard, gotten himself one of the large guns, and had it trained on one of the control panels on the deck.

During the next few seconds—seconds that felt like years—the two aliens argued, speaking too low for me to hear anything. I kept scowling, hoping I hadn't destroyed whatever impression I had made earlier.

And, then, Zander did the only sensible thing, and blew up the control panel.

CHAPTER FOURTEEN
IT'S A LONG WAY DOWN FROM OUTER SPACE, BUT WE'RE ONLY AT LOWER EARTH ORBIT

People scrambled everywhere, screaming, shouting, pressing buttons, but it was too late. The ship hurtled toward Earth at an increasing rate, and it was going down. While everyone on board jumped out of their seats and toward what must have been escape pods, Zander tossed the weapon to the ground and wiped his palms.

Okay, not quite the way I had wanted this to go.

"What the hell did you just do?" I screamed, dropping all pretense of ever having been Blayde. Zander shrugged as a light burst above his head and sending sparks through the room.

I tossed the wig to the ground as it caught fire, my face hot with fury.

"Never fear, sister dear." He winked, sliding to a control panel and typing in an apparently random assortment of numbers. "Ship's going down in the Atlantic. They're taking an escape pod far away from here. Their weapons are useless, and we're free to go. Great performance, by the way. Totally sold the Blayde-itude. I couldn't have done it better myself. Well, I probably could, but I wasn't feeling the dress today. Too bloated. Anyway, shall we?"

He held out his hand, expecting me to take it, but I drew back.

"To go where?" I screamed. "We're crashing, Zander. And guess who has the pods?"

He grinned in response, picking the large weapon up again. "So, we jump."

"Out of the ship?" I sputtered. "Zander, I don't do well with heights."

"Trust me?"

"Not enough to jump out of a spaceship, no."

"You trusted me enough to get on it. I promised to keep you safe, and you are going to be safe."

"By jumping out of a spaceship?" I looked out of the window, and my stomach fell. At least we had artificial gravity. The thought of tumbling around the gigantic room did not sound very pleasant, and by the way the earth spun outside the window, it gave me enough of an impression to last a lifetime.

"Safest way," he replied. "Give me your hand if you're scared."

"Scared?" I shouted. "Of course I'm scared. This is suicide."

"Have I led you wrong?" he asked. "Ever?"

"I've only known you for a week!" I snapped, but I grabbed his hand like it was the last lifeline in the middle of the ocean and closed my eyes.

Seconds later, we were falling.

Plummeting was more like it. The wind ripped the bun away in seconds, my hair pulling itself upwards as I tumbled toward Earth. Zander screamed in excitement, squeezing my hand tightly.

I forced my eyes open, the land rushing toward me at a vertiginous rate. And yet I could see it all, recognize the large cities, the huge hives of light in the middle of the dark expanse. I could see my world beneath me. It was small, and it was huge, and it was incredible.

And then I began to choke.

Falling from near outer space does that to you.

I gasped for air that would not come, for a breath to reach my lungs. My lungs burned, begging me to take a breath, a real breath—

The ground felt soft against my face.

Where it had come from, I didn't know. It was just there. No harsh slap, no crash, no pain—only soft grass caressing my cheek as if I had fallen in a dream but awoke in my bed.

If my bed was a park.

"Sally?" a voice said awkwardly. A hand reached for my hair, trying to move it out of my face.

"I'm fine," I replied. My mouth was still pressed against the earth, so it sounded more like "uh-huh," which worked fine too.

Zander laughed, falling back on the grass with a loud thwomp. I rolled over and found myself laughing too, the rush of endorphins sending me into a fit of giggles that made my abs hurt.

I was alive. Alive.

"How did we ..." I asked, between guffaws of relief.

"We jumped," Zander replied. "We should be close enough to home."

I fell against the grass again staring at the stars above. I was on Earth again.

I stamped my foot, snapping off the stiletto heel. Thwack—the second foot was free as well. I used my toes to slip off the instruments of torture. There—I was free. Alive and free.

"There's just one thing I don't get," I said, sitting bolt upright.

"Shoot," Zander replied, the laughter subsiding.

"If we were falling that fast," I asked, "how come we hit the ground softly? I mean, we didn't hit it. We were just ... here."

"Because I jumped."

"But where did the momentum go?"

"I folded time and space for you, and you're worried about some lost momentum?"

"It has to be conserved," I muttered. "Where did the momentum from our fall go?"

"Wherever we went when we slipped through the fabric of the universe."

"Which is?"

"Nowhere." He shrugged. "Everywhere. Honestly, I've never been bothered by missing momentum before. It's been darn useful."

"We just negotiated with aliens," I pointed out.

"Nice observation skills."

"We saved the planet?"

"You betcha." Zander grinned, throwing himself back down on the grass. "Well, for now."

"Whoever your sister is, they were scared of her," I said, eager to get some answers. "The Killians, I mean. They were terrified of you. No, scratch that. They were scared of you, terrified of me. What can Blayde do? Zap people with lightning bolts or something?"

"No," he replied, suddenly going cool. "My sister can't control the elements."

"But the way they looked at me—"

"Blayde's reputation is built on gossip and legend," Zander said sternly. "Not everything they believe about her is true, which is good when you want to make a power play. By the way, great job. Fantastic performance. It's hard to believe you've never met her."

"I'm kind of wondering if I want to."

"She's a hoot." He chuckled, staring at the stars with a sigh. "She talks big when in truth she's, well, she's Blayde."

"Hope I'm still around when she gets here."

"I hope so, too," he replied. "Thanks for tonight."

"No problem." I lay down on the grass. "So, are we even now?"

"Were we not?"

"I dunno." I shrugged. "I ran you over, you saved my life …"

"Don't keep tabs on life like that," Zander said. "What's a friendship if we don't have each other's backs?"

"So, we're friends?"

"Aren't we?"

"It's kind of hard to know these things when it comes to intergalactic roommates," I pointed out.

"Sally, you're the closest thing I've had to a friend

in years," he said earnestly. "I'm not saying this lightly. I wouldn't have asked just anyone to pretend to be my sister."

"I'm flattered."

"I'm flattered you're flattered," he replied. "Anyway, let's get to some real beds. And let's hope we're in the right park."

We weren't. Not even close.

"Central Park?" I snapped, marching across the asphalt and staring at the sign with wide-eyed amazement. "Central effing Park?"

"So, it's the right one?" Zander glanced in every possible direction, somehow seeing in the near darkness.

"It's not even the right state."

"Right country, though?" He shrugged. "We were falling toward Earth rapidly, I'm amazed I managed to get us to an empty park at all."

"Well, thanks for that," I replied, throwing out my hand for him to take. He stared at it, unsure of how to proceed.

"What's that for?"

"Take us back," I ordered.

"I can't."

"You can fold the universe. Take us home in the blink of an eye."

"Not if I can't see where I'm going," Zander scoffed. "We could end up three solar systems off and three hundred years in your future. We have to go the human way."

"You're kidding me." I rolled my eyes in a wide circle, "This means we're going to have to find a train or a bus and I ... Zander?"

"What?"

"Where's my stuff?"

"In the bathroom at the restaurant? But it's all right, I grabbed your purse for you."

"Well, that's lovely." The wallet had my card and some cash in it, which was a small relief. Zander said nothing. He paced around the small, grassy knoll with his eyes riveted on the stars.

"Where are we, then?" he asked, calm enough for the both of us.

"New York City. A cultural hub. A megacity of a dozen or so million people."

"Oh, cool." He grinned excitedly. "Let's get some dinner. What's this place famous for? Does it have gigantic statues? Does it have museums?"

"We may be a little late for dinner. What time is it?"

"A little past eleven. So, food?"

"How can you think of food at a time like this? We fell out of an alien spaceship."

"Best time for food if there ever was one," he replied. "Come on, let's eat something, then we can worry about getting back to Franklin. You said it yourself, we saved the planet. We deserve some cake. You, especially."

"Me?"

"After that performance, you need a bouquet and an encore." Zander chuckled. "You know what, Sally, I underestimated you. You do amazingly well under pressure."

"Never again." I shook my head, taking hesitant steps on shaky legs, my feet bare after being ripped out of the stiletto heels. Which I then realized I shouldn't have done, seeing as we had a way to go.

"We need to get you some shoes," Zander said. "Would you like me to carry you?"

"I'm fine," I replied, but I did take his arm. "Where would we get shoes at an hour like this?"

"Leave that to me," he answered, guiding us to the grass, which felt much better on my toes.

But cold. Oh, so cold.

"Keep an eye out for dog crap. I don't want to step through that."

"Dog?"

"Furry domesticated animal, common household pet," I replied. "Four legs, tail, panting tongue."

"Oh, those fluffy creatures." He nodded.

"The ones on the leash. The small ones with pointed ears are cats."

"Oh, I'm well acquainted with them," Zander said as we reached the street.

"Right, we'll find some food then we'll get directions to Grand Central Station and ride home. I don't want to spend any more time out than I must. Matt thinks we're fixing pipes, and Marcy might get worried."

"Of course, but first ... wait here."

He took off like a bullet down the street, vanishing from my view. Seconds later, someone yelped.

"Oh, honey, those shoes." The voice didn't even sound like Zander's as it rose through the air, punctuated by a shrill eeek of excitement. "Do you have any idea what you are wearing on your feet? A gold mine. Those are the most dramatic shoes I have ever seen. I simply must have them. Come on, I'll give you anything. Anything."

He had returned with bright pink flats in hand, smiling sheepishly as he handed them over. I was impressed by how well they fit, though they were sweaty and a little gross. It was better than going barefoot.

"How on earth did you pull that off?" I asked, leaning on Zander as I slipped them on.

"Tossed a few crystals at her. Currency on Turbij is worth more here than there. They fit?"

"Perfectly," I grinned. "Let's go."

......•••●●●•••......

"Your shift's up," Zander said with a yawn, stretching in his train seat.

"What shift?"

"You weren't keeping watch?" he said, glancing up and down the empty compartment. "Seriously?"

"For what? We're in an empty train car, and we're not exactly on the run for our lives. Unless there's something you're not telling me?"

"Nope." He shrugged, fully awake now. "I guess old habits die hard."

"You're in the habit of sleeping in shifts?"

"Yes."

"May I ask why?"

"Nope." He paused, just for a second, the tiniest of breaths, then punctuated it with the most awkward of half shrugs. "Did you get any sleep?"

"I hate sleeping on trains," I answered, fully aware that he was trying to change the subject. I let it slide. Sue me, I was tired. "I never manage to zonk out."

"You're not exhausted after all this?"

"Heck, yes," I replied, "but I'd rather sleep when I

188

have a nice bed and a fluffed-up pillow."

"Makes sense. These trains are rather slow, aren't they?"

"Compared to instantaneous teleportation through the universe, I would say so."

"Too bad my navigation is shit," Zander replied, shaking his head in disappointment. "You all right?"

"Somewhat." I shrugged. "I did like those shoes ... the ones I wore to my date? You know, my date with Matt? The one you threw an assassin into?"

"They'll put them in lost and found or something."

"When they find them in the restroom with a missing wall?"

"Um, maybe not, but if they trace it back to you, you can always claim alien abduction."

"Lovely." I snorted, but I was kind of frustrated. "Speaking of aliens, they looked familiar."

"How so?"

"Well, they were the image that pretty much everyone on this planet associates with the word alien, you know. It's as if—have they been here before?"

"I wouldn't know." He shrugged, but leaned in closer, though there was no one nearby to eavesdrop. "But there's no reason for them not to visit. Maybe the crew that crashed three-thousand years ago was seen by humans and—oh, shit. They're Killians."

"So?"

"So, they're an empathic race." He shuddered. "And they've been sending out a distress call for generations. Their faces are soaking into your dreams, Sally."

"That would make sense," I agreed, though honestly, it didn't. "But if that were so, wouldn't we have some idea where the crash site was?"

"Did anyone chronicle any crashes?"

"I don't know. But if we want to get to the bottom of this, we need to talk to them."

Zander's grin broadened exponentially. "You sound like you're in."

"In what?"

"In on the mission." Zander could barely hide his excitement. "Finding these aliens, getting them back to their families before the rest of the fleet arrives."

"Finding these ... hold on ..." I froze. "What fleet?"

"You don't think a ship that size could stand around making threats to a planet this big, do you?" Zander asked, shaking his head. "They sent their prime minister with the ultimatum and negotiating chips. The rest of the fleet will get here in a few months, and they're not going to be happy if they don't find the crew. Usually, Killians are a gentle race, so something has got them seriously pissed. I suspect there was someone rather important on board."

"How in the hell are you so calm about this?" I practically shouted. "They're on their way to destroy the planet, and you're talking like they're bringing us pizza."

"Because we'll have the crew back before they show up," he said, still with the same calm demeanor. "And the Killians are—or were, last I dealt with them—a very agreeable race."

"We'll?"

"You'll help me, right?"

"Dude, I'm not a planet saving person," I replied. "And how can you be so sure they're even alive? They could have died in the crash. They could have died since."

"A few reasons," he explained. "Firstly, the Killians have an incredible life support system. It runs off the life force of the crew. They're an empathic species, which means their connection with their ship runs deeper than just handheld controls. In the case of a crash, their lives keep the ship alive, and, in return, the ship keeps them alive. Neither can die while the other survives. It's pretty freaking cool."

"But if they both were destroyed?"

"That's point two, I'm getting to that." Zander poked his tongue out like a child. "When the ship crashes, it uses a special form of force field to move through the earth, like cutting through butter. Great for not destroying ships, terrible for getting out afterwards. Usually, they had someone come and pull them out quickly, but they might have gotten too deep to save themselves. My theory is that they're in a near hibernation state in a ship-sized crevasse, somewhere on this continent."

"This is insane." I would have laughed, if I still could.

"Logical." He shrugged. "Screw insanity. At this point, everything in the universe is messed up, so we should agree that there simply is no baseline sane. Insanity is the new logical—nothing's impossible. Everything's just got screwed up probability ratios."

"You seem pretty all right with all that."

"I live off improbability."

"But it makes no sense. You can't transfer energy through empathy."

"Says who?"

"Science," I scoffed. "Think about it, there will always be a loss when energy is transferred back and forth, there's no avoiding it."

"Says the planet who hasn't even got a warp drive."

"Oh, come on, we're getting there."

Zander smiled. "That's what I love about you, Sally. You see something you've never imagined, and the first thing out of your mouth isn't a scream but a stream of questions about the conservation of energy."

"Nobody asks you about that?"

"No one. They're more concerned with the why than the how. As in 'why are you standing in that sandbox? Why are you holding that flowerpot?' The real questions, though—"

"Do you know?"

"Come again?"

"Do you know how your jumping thing works?"

"The last time someone asked me that, they were holding my liver in their hands and spouting some nonsense about super soldiers."

"Of course they were."

"Told them I didn't want the liver back."

"I bet you did."

"Got away using a belt, a thumbtack, and an empty key ring."

"You're not making any sense."

"Sorry." He shook his head slowly. "Truthfully? No clue how I do what I do. I just can. And no, I've no idea what happens to the momentum."

"It's really messing with my brain. I'm trying to wrap my head around it. It's as if you momentarily become massless ... but you can't, can you? That would mean the velocity would somehow have to become—"

"Yeah, I know what science says, but here I am, living proof that no one has any idea what they're talking about."

"We've got a pretty good idea," I insisted, annoyed. "Come on. We're just starting out. You said it yourself; we don't even have a warp drive yet. Or any kind of space drive thingy. Yet we've put men on the moon and robot cars on other planets. We have people living in space 24-7 for months on end, and all this only a hundred years after we put men in the air. So, we're getting there."

"I never said you weren't." Zander smiled awkwardly. "I'm impressed. Earth is doing quite well, and ... look, do you want to see for yourself?"

"See what?"

"What happens to the momentum when I jump," he said, slipping out of his chair. "This is your fault. It's bothering me now, and I never used to care."

"What do you want me to do?"

"Just watch, I guess." He swung his shoulders and kicked his legs as if preparing for an Olympic event.

"What am I supposed to see?"

"Um ..." Zander looked around, making sure we really were alone in the car. "So, the current theory is that my momentum reverts to zero when I reappear, correct?"

"Yup."

"So, I'll jump to a spot a little above the ground over there. If that's correct, I won't be going at the same speed as the train, so I'll crash into the wall."

"But the planet has—"

He didn't wait for me to finish. He pelted down the empty row, determination carved into his face, leapt into the air, and blipped out of existence.

I had never watched it head-on before. Seeing a man disappear in front of your eyes has a strange effect on people. He reappeared instantly, without a second lost, at the opposite end of the carriage, standing on the carpeted floor as easily as if he had been standing there for hours.

"So …?" I asked.

"Kept the momentum of the train but not the run," he said, confused, "which doesn't make any sense."

"Why is that?"

"Because, when I do this"—he spun in the air, kicking his leg out and flickering from existence halfway through the move, only to reappear mid-kick on the other side of the train car, finishing the jump smoothly, his leg colliding with one of the chairs with a resounding thwack—"It remains effective. No momentum lost, see?"

I could feel my eyes getting wider. "Zander, you said anything that touches your skin comes with you in the jump?"

"Yes?"

"What if you're cuffed? Can you jump out of them?"

"Sure."

"You can decide what you bring along on a jump?"

"Seems that way. I don't have to bring anyone along if I don't want to."

"Including momentum." I grinned. "You can pick and choose if and how much of your momentum to bring with you. This is freaking awesome. You can actually manipulate the fabric of the universe."

"And you're making my head spin," he said, throwing himself across the row of empty chairs across from me. "Not an easy feat, I can assure you."

"But haven't you ever been curious?"

"Sure, but you know; you get curious, you get answers. Accept, forget, and move on. Momentum is the least of my problems."

"I just find it odd that someone would live their life with such a gift without questioning it."

"Sure, I question it, but I've just learned to accept that I'm not going to get any answers. That seems to be the only way to exist in this universe without losing one's mind."

I didn't say anything. My own existence had become so inherently bizarre over the past week that I was having trouble making sense of any of it. Thanks, Universe.

"You still awake over there?" Zander asked.

"Yup."

"Thanks."

"For what?"

"Not freaking out," he replied. "It's nice to be treated like a person. Most of the time it's pitchforks or golden crowns."

"Golden crowns?"

Zander chuckled. "They're not as comfortable as you'd think."

He shared silly anecdotes until we reached the end of the line a few hours later, and he kept them going as we walked home. It kept me from noticing how tired I was until I had returned to the comfort of my own room. It was as effective as carrying me the whole way home.

CHAPTER FIFTEEN
ZANDER SEEMS TO WORK HERE, NOW

I had not expected the fanfare. The quite literal fanfare. As in, the brass band playing as it paraded around the power plant. I had expected none of this. Grisham had warned me today was going to be big, but he hadn't specified how big. The front parking lot looked like a fairground—there was a bounce house, people spinning cotton candy, a ring toss, even a mechanical bull.

Most of the people enjoying the celebrations were employees of Grisham Corp and some singular VIPs. And by VIPs, I mean some of the biggest faces in our country. I'm sure there was even a mention of the vice president showing up, though I wasn't sure if that was true. Though Sophie, the plant's receptionist, claimed to have seen the man take off his shoes and slip into the bouncy castle.

It was surreal. All this for the first official day the plant was operational.

"So, how was the date?" Marcy asked, taking a large

bite out of a caramel apple. No, she didn't work here, but like most of the people in the city she had turned up for the big event. As the CEO's personal assistant, neither of us were bothered in the VIP section. Marcy's familiar smile was twice as large as normal. She had rapidly switched the conversation to her relationship with Dany, which, it seemed, was more serious than I had anticipated.

"It was fantastic," I replied, trying to keep an eye on the proceedings. "Matt is a real gentleman. It was a great evening until … well, you know."

"The drunk guy came crashing in?" Marcy giggled. "Yeah, I bet that's enough to ruin an evening."

"Well, not ruin, per se," I said. "I mean, the date part was great, so that's something. So, some guy comes crashing through the ceiling, and someone else blows up the wall in the women's restroom. I feel bad for the owners. they're going to be in some pretty deep shit after all this."

"That's insane," Marcy scoffed. "All this happened on your date?"

"I still can't believe it." I shook my head. "It's either a sign of good things to come or a catastrophic relation-ship."

"At least you won't be bored," Marcy pointed out as she turned around the bend.

"True."

"Is there going to be another one?"

"Another date? I sure hope so."

"Maybe we can double up," Marcy suggested. "You, Matt, Dany and me. We hit the town, eat out, go to Scintillance or something. I dunno. When's the last time we double dated?"

"Junior prom?"

"It'll be fantastic then." Marcy's excitement was somehow, impossibly growing. "Wait, hold on, I think you're up. I'll get out of your hair."

She slipped into the crowd as I took my place, making my way to Grisham's side as he took to the podium. A stage had been erected at the far end of the lot, close to the lobby entrance. A huge sign above us held the logo, an oversized tree, as well as the company slogan: For a cleaner, greener tomorrow.

"May I have your attention, please," Matt said into the microphone. Grisham had wanted him, specifically, to introduce him.

The crowd gathered around the stage. It was odd seeing the faces in the crowd. They looked as young as I did, either fresh out of, or even still in, college. There were a few faces that didn't fit in. Many people had cameras or were taking notes. Others had cotton candy or caramel apples.

"Thank you all for coming here today," Matt continued. "We're so excited to be able to open our doors to you on this momentous occasion. But enough from me. Let's hear from the man of the hour, the one and only, Ridgell Grisham ..."

The crowd erupted into cheers, which I imagined was quite difficult with all the sticky desserts in hand. Still, they were loud. The thunder swept over us as Grisham rolled toward the mike, which Matt had politely lowered.

"Yes, yes. Thank you all so much," he said, beaming. "I am so excited that this day is finally here. I have been planning this for years, and today, my dreams have become a reality. We're finally working on progressing onto a new and cleaner future. For our children and our children's children. They're going to look back on today and be very proud of us. Of all of us: you should all be very proud of yourselves, for today, you make history."

There was applause once more, and nobody wanted to stop. The charismatic Mr. Grisham was tearing up from his own words. People in the audience were feeling it too.

It probably helped that a string quartet was playing some very dramatic, very powerful music to accompany his words.

"My friends," Grisham continued, "I can't tell you how happy I am to see each and every one of you. For you to be here as this plant joins the grid. Within hours, this plant will take on every single one of our city's needs. Within a week, it will power the entire state, and together, we will work to increase that efficiency, and bring this technology to the world. We're going to bring a new meaning to the words 'power plant'."

If I had thought the applause was thunderous before, I was wrong. It sounded like the Earth itself was rumbling. The cheering was so great, so loud, that Grisham waved frantically to calm everyone down. I tried to cover my ears without drawing attention to myself.

"All right. Let's get this party started. After we join the grid, we'll be hosting a few tours of the plant, specially tailored for our curious reporters. Yes, I see you. We'll also be having a barbecue—with vegetarian and vegan options—for you all. Feel free to post or tweet or snap all of this. It would be a shame for anyone to miss out." He got a few laughs from this. "All right, then. Who has the ceremonial button?"

It looked like a religious procession. Four men and women approached the stage holding a giant, and I mean humongous, red button. It was the size of a manhole cover. The guy in the back was threading the extension cord.

"Right, everybody ready?" he asked. "Oh, come on, for once someone of my generation wants you to hold up your phones, and you have them all tucked away in your pockets. That won't do at all. Come on now, this moment is historic. Capture it."

Once he was certain that everyone was photographing or filming, while completely ignoring the film crew that was trying to get by, he pressed the button. The band played louder and with more enthusiasm as confetti erupted from cannons strategically placed around the parking lot.

The crowd went wild.

"All right. Let's party," Grisham shouted, gesturing for me to follow him off the stage. The band played an upbeat melody.

"That was amazing, sir," I said earnestly. Matt was close behind us.

"You're all amazing," he replied. "There's no way I could be here without you. Come here."

He wrapped the two of us in a big hug, squeezing us against his large chest.

"The three of us are going to change the world," he announced, his eyes tearing up again.

"Oh, here you go," I said, pulling out of the hug

and handing him a tissue. "You want to look good for the cameras!"

"That's right, Sally, I do," he said, taking the tissue and wiping the tears away. "I'm so glad I hired you. You keep me in the green."

I blushed: even though I knew very well he was exaggerating, it still felt good to get a compliment like that.

"Sir, NBC calls dibs on an interview," Matt said, awkwardly. "They actually shouted dibs from the audience. It's weird. Do we run by the rules of dibs?"

"I guess we should respect them," he said, sighing heavily. "Right. They'll only get until the first tour. Then we must go. I want to make sure our plant is being properly represented. Not that I don't trust our guides, I just want to be there."

"Say no more, sir," Matt replied. "You're the boss."

"Indeed, I am." Grisham grinned. "Now, let's put on a show."

While Grisham drove away toward NBC, Matt reached out to give my hand a tight squeeze. I smiled at him.

"You good?" he asked.

"Yup," I replied. "Pretty exciting day, huh?"

"You bet. Everything go okay with the pipes?"

"Yeah, got there right in time," I lied. "We managed to save the place. Got a plumber and everything."

"Fantastic," he said. "Listen, I'm sorry our first date failed. Do you want a do-over?"

"I'd love one," I replied, "but we don't have to do anything fancy. I'd be perfectly happy with pizza and some TV, honestly."

"That sounds great," said Matt. "Hey, I've got to go with Grisham. We'll catch up after this is over? Work something out?"

"Right!" I said. He leaned forward and planted a small, sweet kiss on my cheek, smiling as he left. My heart was pounding, and this time it wasn't out of fear: I was so happy. It was as if nothing could possibly go wrong.

Of course, then it did.

As he turned to stride away, my heart sank. Because that's when I caught sight of him, there, in the crowd, wearing a blue button-down shirt and chatting with Sophie. A man whose face I would recognize anywhere.

What in the holy heck was Zander doing here? Was there nowhere he wouldn't show up?

I could have ignored him. I should have. I wasn't going to let him ruin another aspect of my life. But I didn't. I stormed right over to him, all steam and fury.

He saw me coming and smiled, like it was the most natural thing in the world, and said three words that would completely set me off. "Oh, hey, Sally!"

I would have exploded if I hadn't been surrounded by co-workers. He obviously noticed I was holding back because the smile vanished off his smug face.

"Is … everything okay?" he asked, confused.

I glared at him. "What are you doing here?" My hands were clenched into fists by my sides. By this point, I knew that every time he showed up something alien was about to go down. I couldn't have this happening. Not at work. Not in front of my boss. My boyfriend. The newscasters of the entire East Coast.

Hurricane Sally should be a storm, not a person.

"I work here," he said, still looking like a dejected puppy.

"You? Work here?"

"What is so hard to believe about that? You're the one who wanted me to get a job!"

"Yeah but … how?" My fists shook. "And why here?"

"What? We can't both take advantage of a great job opportunity because they happen to be in the same place?"

"Look, Zander," I said. "This is just weird. You said the danger has passed. Why do you insist on following me around?

His expression fell. "Sally, I just wanted a job. I'm trying to help with the rent, and I apologized about stomping in on your date, I mean—"

"You're right, you're right. I didn't mean to say that." I sighed, pinching the bridge of my nose between my thumb and index finger. I could feel parts of my mind not cooperating, and I couldn't remember if I had taken my meds this morning. Boy, I was tired. "You're just soaking into every aspect of my life. I thought work could be free of aliens, at least."

He grinned. "Don't worry, you won't see me."

"How did you even get here? You don't drive."

"No, but it's flat, and I can jump." He shrugged. "I didn't want to bother you for a ride."

"But how long have you even been working here? Why didn't you tell me? What do you do here? How—"

"I have my ways." He chuckled. "I'm Lysander Smith, a twenty-two-year-old University of Maryland graduate from Tennessee. My Tinder profile says I like hiking and laser tag. I've never done the latter, but it sounds like fun."

"You have a Tinder profile."

"I was told it would help me meet people." He shrugged. "Anyway, I'm an accountant, as per the plan."

"Let me guess, you hacked their servers, created an identity, and gave yourself a job?"

"Hack them?" Zander scoffed. "Look, I may get the gist of coding, but I don't know Earth's systems. No, I hired someone to make me a fake ID, just like the rest of you do. Heck, I have a birth certificate and everything."

"And you picked the name Lysander?"

"Lysander, Zander, it's close enough that I'll get used to it," he said, proudly, handing me the small plastic card. It looked incredibly legit. "I read it in a book. Anyway, I thought you would be proud of me. I'm human now. At least, legally."

"Tour group one, we're starting in five minutes. Please meet by the stage."

The voice snapped our conversation in half. I realized I was staring at Zander with my mouth agape and closed it quickly. He pulled out an iPhone and snapped a picture of me, mid-mouth closing, grinning as he did.

"I guess you're fitting in quite well," I said, handing back his ID and crossing my arms across my chest. "Nice tie, by the way."

"Thank you, but I don't really get the point of it," he said, touching the thing. "It's like wearing a decorative noose."

We shuffled toward the stage, and I shoved my

hands in my pockets to stop my fingers from fidgeting. "Hey, I hope this isn't too personal, but how old are you really?"

"By your standards?" He shrugged. "No idea. It gets confusing when you switch units of time across the universe. Does it matter?"

"Not really." His new identity claimed he was twenty-two, which was fitting, but still, he looked ageless and it was messing with my head.

"All right, tour time," he announced. "Let's go see what this place has in store for us."

We gathered at the foot of the stage where Grisham waited with a smile. He had attached a ridiculous flag to his scooter so we'd all be able to see him, though it looked more like a bumper car now.

"Is that everyone?" he asked. There were about fifty of us, and I only recognized half the people as employees. The rest were reporters and journalists with a few cameramen coming along for the ride.

"Hey, Sally," Matt said as he approached us. "Who's this?"

"Zander," I replied quickly. "My roommate."

"Lysander Smith," Zander piped up, stepping forward to kiss the man on his cheeks. "It is a pleasure to be acquainted with you. May our meeting promise many years of smiling friendship and success."

"Sure, nice to meet you too," Matt said, turning cold. His expression was foreign, but then again, I hadn't seen him frown in all the time I'd known him.

"Sally?" He took me aside. "I didn't know your roommate was a guy."

"I told you at the Casa," I said, a little weirded out

206

by his reaction. I didn't really like this side of him, this weird, moody, jealous side.

"I thought you said Sandra."

"He's just a friend if that's what you're asking," I said, slipping his hand from my shoulder. When had it gotten there?

"Sally ..."

"He's a cousin!"

He loosened up a bit but was still very stiff. I loved how quickly my good days slipped into being lame. I hadn't pegged Matt for a guy who'd be bothered by that sort of thing, and it was disappointing to find out otherwise.

"All right, everyone, follow me for the tour," Grisham said, waving us along.

A young man pushed through the crowd, huffing and puffing. "But, sir, did you forget—?"

"Oh, right, yes." He grinned. "Everyone, this is Germaine. Germaine is going to show you around. Don't mind me, I'm just here for the ride. But bear in mind, I will quiz you at the end."

The tour group laughed. I joined in, though it wasn't all that funny. There was a certain charm to the man, though, an energy that made you wanted to please him, even if that meant laughing at a stupid joke.

Germaine led us through the lobby and through the parts of the plant I already knew: the office spaces, the administrative wing, the cafeteria, all that fun stuff. He pointed out the ergonomic shape of the cubicles and desks, the amount of natural lighting, and the recycling rooms on every floor.

All the while, I stood by Matt, who stood by

Grisham, and walked with them like I was running the place as well. Grisham sure did act like it. He was the head honcho, but the respect and drive he had for the two of us made it sound like we were right up there with him. It was incredibly weird.

Then again, maybe he saw something in me that I couldn't see myself. Maybe I did have a future. Was he going to groom me for great things, too? The way he was doing with Matt? With everyone here? The man knew every employee by name as well as most of their life plans and career goals.

He had a cult of personality going here. Everybody loved him. They had pictures of him in every room—pictures of him building the plant or standing in front of sunsets, though the jury was still out on whether that last one was actually him. They were there because the employees wanted them there. If people waved and cheered when he passed their cubicles, it was because they were happy to see him. That, or they were alerting the others so they could tab out and wipe their browser history.

He was our Obi-wan, our Yoda. Matt and I were his Padawans and proud of it.

"And this," he said as we reached the elevator, speaking before Germaine could open his mouth, "this is the only time this floor will be open to the public. On most days, it is very dangerous. I only allow a few people down there. But today, just today, we're going to the turbine room."

"We are?" Germaine asked. It seemed even he wasn't in the loop about this.

"Yes." Grisham pulled a key card from his pocket,

inserting it into a slot in the elevator I had never noticed before. "Now, this elevator will get very crowded, so we'll be going down in small groups. Let's see how many can fit in here with me?"

We were only about a dozen, but boy, we were crammed. The elevator wasn't industrial sized, and Grisham's scooter took up most of the space. Luckily, the ride underground was short. As soon as the little ding sounded, we rushed out as quickly as we could, peeling away from each other.

We emerged into a small gray room with a tall ceiling and bare walls. A large metal archway sat in the middle, next to two guards at their desks, one with his feet up on an X-ray machine. I had never seen them before, let alone suspected them of working under the power plant.

"Ah, welcome," said one of the guards. The other took his feet off the machine. "Could you pass your bags through the X-ray and walk through the arch for us? Thank you."

We did as we were told, though Grisham rode around the side without a second glance from the men. Once we were all on the other side of the arch, he led us to another door, gesturing for Germaine to open it for us.

We entered another gray room. This one had a screen, dials, and controls; it looked like an observation station. A stack of new hard hats with small cave lights sat by the door. They looked like mining equipment.

But the main attraction was the huge board of controls. Two more men in security uniforms sat at the table, working the dials and buttons, men I had never seen before today.

"This is where the magic happens," Grisham explained, gesturing to the back wall, "Right outside this door, we have large turbines running 24-7. You can see them through this small window here. Unfortunately, that part of the tour is off-limits due to security concerns. The gas outside this room is highly volatile."

"Wouldn't that make the premises unsafe?" asked a reporter, the first question he had dared to ask all day. "Like working above a tinderbox?"

"No, everything is strictly regulated by these competent young men, so please, don't sensationalize this for your report. It's perfectly safe. This room is one of the safest in the building. It has reinforced walls and bulletproof glass, and it is the first line of defense if the worst were to happen—which it will not."

The employees clapped at this, and Matt and I cheered along with him. Grisham was good to us. He protected us. He kept us safe. And he was making the planet better, too.

What was there to worry about?

CHAPTER SIXTEEN
A TOAST TO MAKING AN ACTUAL EFFORT

"To new beginnings!"

The light clink of glass gently rang through the restaurant. The wine was sweet and slightly fizzy, perfect for the evening.

This was the first time the four of us had been together since Marcy's birthday, the double date she had been so excited about. She sat next to Dany with a huge smile, the two of them glued at the shoulder with a shared flatbread pizza in front them. They looked as if they had been together for years.

I happily ate my pasta, sharing some occasionally with Matt, who had gotten chicken I did not recognize.

"So, what are you doing now?" Dany asked.

"She's one of those fancy PAs," Marcy answered for me.

"A PA? What does that mean?"

"It means I handle Mr. Grisham's schedule, make sure he has coffee, make his appointments, all that general riff." I grinned. "Not fancy work, for sure, not career-making work either—but it's good work, and it pays well."

"She says that," Matt added, "but she's pretty much running the show."

"Nah, I'm not," I shook my head, blushing.

"You do, though. You make sure the boss sticks to his schedule, keep him fueled … you're practically, um, what … his handler. That's it."

"If you say so." I laughed. "It sounds more important than it is when you put it like that."

"It's super important," Matt insisted. "All hail the mighty PA."

I laughed at this. Matt took me into a side hug. It was nice to laugh, effortless now. I was having dinner, surrounded by great friends, and I could not be happier. It was odd how a single hot-air balloon had changed my life. I had a boyfriend, a job, a roommate, and a best friend who was madly in love, though that last bit wasn't due to the balloon fiasco.

I also knew the truth about the universe, or part of it. Which was pretty cool.

And speaking of the truth about the universe, here he was in the flesh.

"Ah, wow, fancy seeing you here." Zander grinned, standing at the end of the table, smiling from ear to ear. He was dressed in what appeared to be suit pants, matched with a button-down shirt. "Mind if I join you?"

"I, um …" I sputtered. What was he doing here?

"Oh, wait, is this him?" Marcy asked. "Hey, hi, I'm Marcy."

But Zander wasn't looking at Marcy. No, his eyes

were locked on Dany's. The way their eyes shot ice beams at each other, it was as if winter had come into the restaurant.

"Do I—?" Dany asked.

"No," Zander snapped, "you don't."

"I do."

"You think you do, but you don't."

"Dany, sweetie," Marcy said calmly. "Do you know him?"

"Know him?" she scoffed. "Know him, I—"

And she stopped. Zander shook his head, slowly.

"No. I've never met him before," Dany said and laughed. "But, wow, you look really familiar. Hi, I'm Dany."

"Zander," he replied, shaking her hand. "So? May I join you?"

"This is a double date," Dany said coolly. "It may be a little awkward for you."

"Oh, I have a date." He smiled, waving someone over. "Everyone, meet Luna."

"Hey," she said, her voice sweet and melodious, like honey.

Luna was tall.

Luna was skinny.

Luna was one of those women who could walk into a room and take your breath away. She was drop-dead gorgeous, wearing a tight, elegant dress that slipped over her frame like liquid gold. I felt my heart weaken. Zander grinned as she waved at the table.

"Wassap?" the woman asked, sliding into the booth beside Marcy, pushing her out of the way. Zander joined her, still smiling.

"Luna and I are on a date," he persisted.

"Oh, well, um..." Marcy looked uncomfortable, shooting me glances to try and get me to convince them to go away. I guess I was a little too shocked to act.

"And how did you two meet, Zander?" Dany said eagerly, avoiding the spun-silk hair as the woman spun her head.

"It's the craziest thing," he replied. "I was walking outside, and she asked me out."

Marcy nodded. "That is crazy."

She turned to me and lifted her eyebrows knowingly. I said nothing. Luna had a phone in her hand. She wasn't paying any attention to Zander, her so-called date.

"Well, we were just about to leave," Matt interjected. "We've finished our meals, haven't we?"

"Yes, yes, all done," Dany added, "Just about to pay. We were, um …"

"Going clubbing next," Marcy sputtered. "At, um, Scintillance. Would you care to join us?"

"What do you think, Luna?" Zander asked pleasantly. "Would you like to go dancing?"

"That'll be extra," she said gruffly, and he laughed.

"I'll go pay." Matt, closest to the edge of the booth, rose to his feet and slipped his wallet out of his pocket. "We'll divvy it up later."

"Sounds good," Dany replied, obviously none too eager to try and push past the goddess beside her. "So, how are you and Zander related again?"

"Funny story, really," Zander said. "My aunt's husband's brother's cousin's son. On my mom's side," I explained. "His sister is on a trip around the world, and she was worried he wouldn't be able to live on his own. You know how older sisters are, super protective and all. She tracked me down and asked if he could stay with me. Said it would be a good experience for him to live in the US for a while."

"He can't live on his own?" Confusion riddled Marcy's face. "You're kidding me, right?"

"I am right here, you know."

"Sounds way weird." Dany rolled her eyes. "I've never heard of a sister being that controlling." It sounded like she knew this from experience.

"Oh, I'm helpless," Zander muttered in a silly falsetto, putting a hand up to pretend to faint. "No, really, I am."

Luna sighed and scratched her head, reached over to grab the bottle of wine on the table, and poured it into the glass next to her—probably Marcy's—and took a long swig from it. Zander, following her example, replicated her actions, grabbed my glass and filled it up for himself.

"His sister is really controlling," I explained, trying to ignore him. "I had a free room, so it was no trouble. I think she just wants someone to keep an eye on him."

"Yeah, great influence you are," Marcy said jokingly, giving me a wink.

"Believe what you want." Zander took a long chug of wine, emptying the glass in one gulp. "Man, what is this, wine? It's incredible. Incredible," he repeated, glancing over at me to emphasize the word. "What kind is it?"

"The cheap stuff?" Marcy snorted. "I can see why his sister wants him safe. If he thinks this stuff is good—"

"Hey, I think it's good," I scoffed.

"Yeah, it's real high end," Luna added, rolling her eyes and taking another swig.

"Bill's covered, let's go." Matt extended his hand to me. I loved the feel of his hands, strong and soft and always smelling slightly of lilac. I squeezed it tightly. "Have we decided on the next stop?"

"We're hitting up Scintillance? It's right across the street," Marcy replied. "Let's get going."

The six of us left the restaurant in good spirits, following Marcy across the street to the small, black door that led to her favorite place in town. The line was short, and we got in quickly and were soon bathing in music and light, losing ourselves in sound. Marcy rushed to the dance floor as Dany took care of her coat, leaving us to start dancing. The room was flushed in a deep shade of silver with whites and blues and purples flashing everywhere. The music was loud and all bass, almost unrecognizable with the extent of the DJ's remix.

"Right, drinks?" Matt said and counted the hands. "I'll be right back."

"I need to light one," Luna said suddenly. "Heading out. Z'mander, I'm not sure what—"

"I do not smoke, no. Thank you," he replied, unable to tear his eyes off the hypnotizing lights of the dance floor.

Luna glared at him. "Okay, is this happening tonight or what?"

"Is what happening?"

"Look, man, usually people who come up to me on the street have an actual thing in mind," she explained, nicely, "you've been ignoring me all night. Do you actually want me here?"

"Yeah, I like your company," he said sheepishly, "Sorry if I'm a little confused, I'm... foreign."

"Ok, well I don't usually do dates, not with this crowd," she said, "but I guess we can go $60 and hour, if that works for you."

"Wait, hold on," he shook his head like a cartoon character, "is that how dating works here? You rent a date by the hour?"

"I'm not sure what part of this has you confused, man. Usually this sort of stuff costs extra."

"Extra?" he asked, "like, if I wanted to try this karaoke thing, it's more expensive?"

"Oh," she said, her face falling, "this is a prank. I get it. You want to mess with me because of my job, how mature. Thanks for wasting my time."

"No! Wait!" Zander reached into his pocket and pulled out his wallet, a brand new leather billfold stuffed full of small bills. Instead of cards, the pockets held thick stacks of coupons. "I'm sorry. As I said, I'm new here. I needed a date, and... well, here, I hope this makes up for the trouble I've caused."

He handed her a nice wad of cash, mostly ones and fives, along with a coupon for a free steak at some popular chain restaurant. The woman looked up, confused, but smiling.

"Ok, so not a prank. You're just weird."

"Very."

And with that, she walked off, stuffing the bills into her purse, leaving us watching her leave in silence.

I lifted and eyebrow. "You seriously took the offer

of a date from the street?"

"I needed a date, she was there, and it was working out..." He sighed heavily. "Wow. I really failed that one."

"Wait, why were you out looking for a date?"

"That's what people do on Friday nights, from what I can tell." He shrugged. "I mean, that was your plan, and I learn by imitation."

"So, you grabbed a hooker and thought she wanted to date you."

"Why not? I am a suave, up-and-coming go-getter with nothing to lose, at least according to a BuzzFeed quiz." Zander chuckled, leaning back on his legs as if suspended by strings from the ceiling. "I am also what one would refer to as a Charlotte."

In that moment, he really did look alien.

Zander was not a man who fit in with the crowd. He looked uncomfortable, his hand clenched around his sleeve in an odd way as if ready to pull out a hidden knife in a split second. It was as if someone had plucked him out of a war zone and flung him into normalcy without any time for transition.

"Zander," I said slowly, taking a step closer to him. The man radiated danger, even when he was standing still and smiling. And yes, even while he was my friend, moments like these scared me.

"Yup?"

"You all right?"

"Perfectly hunky-dory," he said. "Why?"

"You look tense. You can relax, you know; there's no reason to be anxious."

"I know." Zander nodded. "But I haven't solved our Killian problem yet, and that means these people

218

here will probably be dead within a few months. And here I am, trying to fit in, get a job, lead a normal life—if you can call it that—when I should be out working."

"You're not the only hope for planet Earth, you know. I'm sure that ship didn't go unnoticed by the planet's officials and stuff. They're probably finding ways to deal with it as we speak."

"Yeah, like that's comforting," he snorted. "I'll be out of town this weekend anyway, chasing down a lead."

I smiled. "You need a hand?"

"I have it covered." Zander's grin seemed genuine. "Thanks, but it's not the place for you. A whole lot of running, sleeping in the dirt, and doing things that you wouldn't exactly call legal. And we're going to make sure to keep your record clean, got it?"

"Have you seen Marcy?" Dany interrupted, popping up beside us.

"Yeah, she's dancing," I replied. "Look, Dany, I've got something you need to know. And trust me, I'm only telling you this because I like you, all right?"

"Is something wrong?" she asked, taking a step back. "She's not dying, is she?"

"No faster than the rest of us."

"Oh, maybe it's you, then, who has the cancer?"

"I don't have cancer, Dany," I sputtered. "Though, I guess that is my star sign. No, Dany, it's just that I think you're a good match for her, so I'm going to tell you a huge secret. The thing that'll win her heart forever."

Dany grinned. "This conversation just went from grim to heart palpitating."

"This is going to sound odd," I explained, "but Marcy thinks that if she can go to a club and find someone that will waltz with her, then and there, that she'll have found the perfect partner."

"Oh, lord." Dany grinned. "I think I love this woman."

With that, she ran into the crowd of people. I watched as they engulfed her, wondering if she knew how to dance. I wouldn't have put it past her.

"Is that true?" Zander asked.

"Is what true?"

"The thing about waltzing." He nodded in the direction of the dance floor. "Or were you messing with her?"

"Marcy let it slip when she was wasted once." I smiled. "Huge secret. I don't think she knows she told me."

Zander grinned. "Well, if anyone knows about secrets, it's Dany."

"What do you mean?"

"Hey." Matt handed me a glass of something fizzy. "Where'd Luna go?"

"It didn't work out," Zander muttered.

"Sorry, man." Matt patted his back apologetically. "You all right?"

"Completely fine," he replied, staring intently at the dancers who were moving out of the way of something. They were stepping back, expanding to give them the widest floor space possible.

I downed my drink and put the glass down, pushing my way through the barrier of people without really knowing what compelled me to do so. As I broke through the crowd, I emerged in a hollow circle where two figures twirled as if this were the turn of the last century rather than the new millennium. The crowd watched as two figures waltzed around the dance floor; all eyes trained on them as they spun together.

"Know any other dances?" Marcy giggled, as they slowed.

The DJ changed the music to some remixed version of a classic song I had never taken the time to learn by name, and we watched, astounded, as Dany led her through the paces of an amazingly complex dance as simple to her as breathing. The way she led Marcy made it seem as though she knew the dance already, as if she were as talented as Dany. All the while, Marcy brimmed, glowing with joy, her grip tight on the woman's shoulder.

"Can you dance?" I whispered to Matt, caught in a trance. "Not like that, but ... can you?"

He shook his head, equally awed by the spectacle. They looked otherworldly on the floor, as if they belonged in a realm much higher than this.

"Wait a minute," Zander said slowly, his eyes glued to the figures before him. The intensity of his stare was impossible to measure.

He took a step forward, reaching a hand toward me. I didn't think. I took it, and suddenly we were whizzing across the floor, the dance complex and fast paced.

At first, it seemed as if Zander were copying Dany's footsteps, his feet barely half a second behind hers, twirling me and continuing with the movements. Slowly, the steps became more intricate, building off the base Dany had built as she glided across the floor with Marcy.

My feet were flying, working without my mind having time to think. I followed as the dance shifted from ballroom to something entirely new. Zander seemed to know what he was doing. Even in the sudden, improvised dance, he never misstepped, the dance perfect yet new.

I suddenly realized that Dany and Marcy had stopped dancing and everyone was watching us, their eyes larger than I'd seen on a human being. I spun around and saw the whole crowd before me.

"Zander," I whispered. He didn't seem to take notice. "Zander," I said in a sharper tone. He threw me over his arm, catching and swinging me around before stopping, suddenly noticing, as I did, the look on the faces of those watching.

"Not normal?" he whispered.

"Not in the slightest."

And Matt stood, glaring at us. His eyes shot daggers, cutting and tearing where they touched me. I pulled away from Zander, still out of breath, but Matt was already pushing through the crowd and away from the dance floor.

"Matt, hey, wait up," I shouted, racing after him. I shoved people out of the way to follow him, but the crowd closed in on me, and I couldn't see where he was going.

I could guess, though.

I darted outside, the cold slapping my face. Matt wasn't there. He must have taken the back exit. I made my way around the building as quickly as I could, rubbing my hands over my arms to keep warm. Nights were frosty this time of year.

I found him standing in the back, leaning against the brick wall. He looked up, saw me, then put his head down again. He twisted a cigarette between his fingers.

"You smoke?" I asked, calmly.

"We all have our vices," he said, his voice sharp, "though I have been trying to quit. Which is why I don't have a lighter."

"Oh," I replied.

We stood there in silence for a bit. He twiddled the stick between his thumb and index finger, staring at it with sullen eyes.

"What's going on between you two?" he asked.

"Nothing," I insisted, glad this wasn't a lie.

"It doesn't look like nothing."

"Well, it isn't," I said. "Wait, no. It is nothing. It isn't anything. Ugh, this is confusing."

"Tell me about it," Matt said, taking the cigarette and placing it between his lips.

"Come on, Matt, I really like you. There's nothing between Zander and me. Honestly."

"But he's always there."

More than you know. "I'll have a word with him when I get home tonight. He needs to learn to respect boundaries, that's all."

"You sound like you're talking about a child."

"Like you said, we all have our vices."

"I guess so." He extended a hand, lazily, to take mine. I grabbed it, intertwining my fingers with his, feeling the softness of his skin against my own. The touch warmed me inside, and I was beginning to forget it was cold out.

"Look, Matt," I said, insistently. "For me, there's only you who matters. I know this is only our second date and all, but I really, really like you, and I want this to work."

"I do, too," he replied, giving my hand a tight squeeze. He removed the cigarette from his mouth, putting it back in his pocket, "Could you just ... have him less involved in your life? Ask him to keep a bit of distance?"

"If that will make you more comfortable, sure." I nodded. "But he's still my friend. He might be clingy, but I worry about him. You can't ask me to cut him out completely."

"No, of course not," he sputtered, like it was impossible for me to even suggest it. "I'm not going to be that guy. But if you want this to work, I'd love it if we gave it a chance without him always in the background."

"I'll talk to him," I promised.

He leaned forward, and he smelled of sweet, fresh flowers. Our faces edged closer. I felt a buzz around us, an electricity in the air, the anticipation rising.

Oh, what the heck. Our lips touched, and I moved mine against his, beckoning for him to respond, to join in the silent conversation.

My heart didn't join in, but who cared? I kissed him harder, running my tongue against his teeth, urging my body to feel him, to feel something. His free hand pulled me closer, and I fell into the kiss, into him, feeling myself melt in his arms.

It felt good. It felt gentle.

It just didn't feel right.

CHAPTER SEVENTEEN
IT'S NOT A DRINKING PROBLEM IF ALIENS ARE INVOLVED

As it turned out, all I needed to do was sit Zander down and tell him I didn't need him constantly on my back. Apparently, he had no idea that this was odd: perhaps television wasn't the best way to teach him about life here. While our relationship stayed the same, he stopped popping up in weird areas or in the places I was at. I ran into him at work from time to time. Sometimes we'd carpool, me driving as he blasted tunes and sang along to practically every song, his repertoire growing daily. Other days, he'd sleep in longer and jump all the way to work—though I never got to carpool jump.

And time went on, for once, completely normal. Except for one thing—I was happy. I liked my life. I liked it a lot. Matt and I were good, our relationship was growing stronger by the day, and I could feel myself falling in love with him.

Work was amazing, my only job being to answer the phone. If it rang, I would pick it up, invent an excuse as to why my boss was not available, and hang up. This is what I had been hired to do—keep Mr. Grisham from ever having to deal with phones. Or people in general.

Mr. Grisham always seemed too excited for the work he did. He always wore a grin, as if he was born with it baked into his features. When talking to his employees, he'd wave his hands in a grandiose sweep and shout whatever sentence sounded like it could be printed on a poster. Some eventually were.

I made coffee for the man a few times a day and, as promised, played Scrabble with him every once in a while. During these hours, he would talk about his plans to expand the plant and ask my opinion when it came to dealing with random situations.

Some days, I was instructed not to pick up the phone at all. I would jot down the messages left on the machine and bring them to my boss, who promptly ate them; Grisham had some odd habits. The part of my job that did not consist of answering phones revolved around making sure the world didn't learn about those quirks.

Zander was on a quest to solve all of Earth's problems, though he was currently focused on finding the Killians and setting everything right with them. Every week, he was off on a research project, sometimes asking if I wanted to join him and smiling when I said no. I was done being a part of his messy, alien life. I wasn't a superhero; I was only me. And Zander could handle saving the world by himself, even if it looked like he wasn't making much progress.

So, time went on. Until everything, like it usually does in my life, came crashing down.

It was the night of our two-month anniversary. Matt and I had planned a night in. Serenity was cued up on the TV, and he drove us home while the fresh pizza sat on my lap. Zander had told me that morning he would be out doing research and the apartment would be mine, so it was perfect.

Only it wasn't.

"Ugh, what is he watching in there?" Matt asked, leaning against the banister as I fiddled for my apartment key. I heard a jumbled mush of voices coming from inside. Zander wasn't out, as he had claimed he would be.

"Hang onto the pizza while I clear this up?" I asked, and Matt nodded.

I touched the door handle, and it glided open. Strange, it wasn't locked in the first place. I pushed it open.

"Close it!"

My mouth snapped shut when I saw the room before me. Zander sat in the armchair clasping a huge parchment, blinking ferociously in the near darkness as if I had just shined a flashlight right into his eyes. In front of him on the table, rolls of parchment and foreign gizmos were strewn about. A lone eyestalk swiveled and fell upon me, the alien to which it belonged bellowed a shriek that resembled the bleat of a goat. Its face was short and flat with a single round hole in the middle that could have been a mouth or a nose or both. It wore jeans and a surfer's t-shirt. Discarded on the sofa beside him were a latex mask and sunglasses. He threw up an arm to block the light.

"The door, Sally," Zander insisted. "Please. Barcheens are sensitive to fluorescent light bulbs."

I shut the door hastily, trying not to gawk at the very alien alien in the living room. As the door slammed, the room filled with hovering stars, each one annotated with red figures that could have been numbers or letters; I couldn't tell. A blue giant floated past my nose, a large, fully detailed star in brilliant, burning 3D. I stepped through it.

"Thank you," Zander said, returning to his parchment. How he could see, I didn't know.

"What's going on?" I snapped. "Who's he?"

"Dru, meet Sally, my Earth friend." Zander waved his hand in the guise of an introduction. "Sally, this is Dru. Dru has been helping me figure out where we fit in on the grand scale of things."

Dru waved his orange hand, each of the twelve fingers jittering. I waved back awkwardly.

"What's he doing here?"

"Showing me his maps."

"Yeah, I get that," I replied, "but what's he doing here?"

"We needed a place to talk."

"Zander, Matt is standing outside that door," I scoffed. "You can't bring aliens into the apartment willy-nilly. What if he finds out?"

"Look," he said, standing up. "I get that. But we've been careful."

"Careful? The door wasn't even locked."

"Oh." He grinned. "They don't lock automatically? My bad."

"You've been living here for months," I continued. "You have to take this seriously. Be more careful."

"Sure," he replied. "Have you seen this, though? Look, here's your sun, here's where Earth is." He pointed at a star floating above his left shoulder. "I bet you've never seen a map this detailed before."

"Nope."

"You don't sound impressed?"

"Zander," I growled, "you brought an alien into my home to look at stars. Matt is outside. And you are in here ... with an alien."

"So, no care for the map then?" He sighed. "Haven't you ever contemplated your cosmic purpose before? Where you fit in? Where you—"

"Shut up with the pretentious crap," I ordered. "Can you even hear yourself? Zander, these are maps, not an answer to the meaning of life. Now turn it off, clean up your mess, and get that alien out of here."

"Sally," he snapped. "I live here too. I pay my share, and if I want to figure where I am in the cosmos in the living room, I have a right to. I am not endangering anyone, certainly not you. This is important to me."

"Fine." I spun around, grabbing the door handle with angry ferocity. "Take your time, but I want this gone by the time I get back."

"Where are you going?"

"Out," I growled and slammed the door shut as I left.

"What's going on?" Matt asked. "I thought I heard my name."

"We have to go," I snapped, storming down the stairs. "Zander's got company."

"Seriously?" He glared at my door. "I'm going up there."

"No!" He froze, looking back down at me.

"Why not?"

"Because—and let's just leave it at that."

"Why are you defending him?" Matt asked, taking a step down the stairs toward me. "Come on, Sally, he's walking all over you."

"Do I need a reason?"

"What aren't you telling me?" he urged, his frown growing.

I took a step back. "Nothing."

"I don't believe you."

"Come on, Matt, trust me. It's nothing."

"No, it's definitely something." He scowled. "What's going on? And don't say nothing."

"Look, it's personal, okay? Can't you just leave it at that?"

"No, I can't just leave it at that." He shoved the pizza into my hands and marched past me down the stairs. "You're hiding something. Something to do with that Zander, and I don't know what to think. But until you get him out of your life, the two of us won't work out, all right?"

"Where is this coming from?" I could feel my eyes getting heavy, the wetness of tears piling under the lids.

"I need some space."

And, just like that, he took off.

I stumbled and grabbed the banister for support. I could not even begin to comprehend what had just happened. Had I been dumped? How could a conversation turn to a fight and an exit so quickly?

Somehow, I ended up behind the wheel of my car with no destination in mind. My vision blurred as my eyes filled with tears. I felt full of rage—rage at my regular life being replaced with insane, backwards nonsense. How it had turned from being at the peak of normalcy to being filled with alien-explosion-and-assassin regularity completely escaped me.

It was out of control.

Then I saw a light. Unsure of how much I could trust myself behind the wheel, I parked the car and stepped outside. It was pouring—when had it started raining? —and the storm dumped buckets on my head. I dashed to the closest doorway, hoping it was a place I could get a drink.

I was in luck. It was Scintillance.

The music inside was invigorating. I could feel it thrum with the rhythm of my heart, swinging it back and forth. Times like these, I needed a drink and cut loose on the dance floor until I couldn't hear my thoughts or even feel my legs.

I collapsed in a stool. The bartender, a gorgeous young woman in her late twenties, gave me a sad look.

"Looks like you could use a drink," she said kindly, over the beat of the music. "What's your poison?"

"What's the strongest stuff you've got?"

"Polish vodka?"

"Can I afford it?"

"Probably."

"Then give me some of that."

"A shot?"

"Three, and we'll go from there."

The woman checked my ID—I felt no guilt handing

her the fake—then poured out three shots and turned to her other customers. I downed the first one, gasping for air as I put it down. It burned my throat like hot lava, grabbing my mind and giving it a tight squeeze before releasing me back into the wild.

It was glorious. I was starting to feel better already, or worse, I couldn't really tell.

The bartender was fuzzy looking, and it made me laugh.

I took the second shot, chuckling. Down the hatch. At this point, my tongue was completely numb, my teeth tingly, and my stomach out for the count.

"Did you fall from—"

"Move along," I snapped. Though it sounded more like nouanhanhan, it was effective all the same. The man slipped away without another word.

Now I wanted to dance. Shame there was no music. Or was there? Was it in my head or out in the world? I wanted to let loose, spin around in circles with my hands in the air, screaming at the top of my lungs. Not that I couldn't scream without music. I tried, but it came out in a low hiss.

I downed the last shot. Time stood still. I giggled as I watched everyone freeze in place, in mid-move-ment, and start to move in slow motion. I marveled at the essence of time, which, in my current state, seemed completely linear and obvious.

I held up three fingers.

"Shit, girl," the bartender said, coming into my field of vision. "You're cut off. This stuff hit you a lot stronger than it should have."

"More," I hissed, shoving the empty shots at the

woman. "I need—"

"Sally?"

The voice sounded familiar, yet I couldn't place it. But it sounded worried, that much made sense. I threw out a hand to slap him away but missed. The swing almost pulled me from my chair, but he grabbed my arm and helped me regain my balance.

"How much has she had?" he asked the bartender, keeping a steady hand on my shoulder.

"Three shots of this Polish stuff," the woman replied. She stared at me. "Do you know this guy?"

"It's Zaaaaander. Zandy Zander Zand Zanderton."

"I'm a friend," Zander said, shoving the glasses away from my twitching fingers. "I'll get her home."

The bartender gave him a heavy look.

"Oh, her phone," he leaned over to pick it up, awkwardly, as he was still keeping me perched on the stool. "I'll call her friend Marcy."

The bartender nodded coolly. I was having trouble seeing what was going on around me; my blinking became sporadic. Zander scrolled through the phone, searching for numbers. I leaned on his hand supporting me, happy for the arm.

It was hairy, and it was fun to play with. He didn't seem to mind.

"Marcy?" Zander said, readjusting his arm to hold me up better. "Yeah, it's Zander. I found Sally. She's in a rough state. I'm going to drive her home. No, I'll be fine; I'll be there in five. Wait, hold on, I'll put you on speaker."

"Sally?" Marcy's voice rang through the phone. "Is everything okay?"

"Everything's sunshine and daisies," I replied, but with a thickness in my throat. I sounded like a talking gravel grinder.

"You sure?"

"Life is hunky-dory," I slurred. "Or it will be after I give this alien some grief. Come dance with me!"

"I'm coming over," Marcy said. "I'll be at your place in ten minutes, okay?"

"I said I don't—"

He hung up, and, with a nod of approval from the bartender, helped me off the stool and onto my feet. My legs flopped forward like a game of QWOP, every subsequent step as awkward as my first.

The storm was still raging outside, and I slipped as I tried to walk. Zander helped me into my car, talking all the way in a reassuring voice, but I could barely make out the words. I was more impressed by the family of little green men across the street. They stood on the lawn in front of their saucer, and I waved back at them, smiling.

He drove us back home and parked in the driveway. My mind cleared slowly; parts of it were beginning to respond while others were shutting down completely. Zander opened the passenger door, reaching forward to help me out, but I held up a hand.

"I've got this," I asserted, keeping my finger pointed at the sky. "Just tell me where the lava is."

"There's no lava, Sally." He let me hold his arm for balance as I slipped off the seat and onto solid ground. "Only rain and puddles."

"How can I trust you if you can't see it?"

He said nothing and led me toward the door

instead. I pushed against the doorknob, shouted at the immovable door, and pushed again. Then I remembered I needed keys. I reached into my purse, grabbed them, and struggled to fit them in the lock.

"Keys go in doors," Zander pointed out. "Gum doesn't tend to be that effective."

"Sure it does," I insisted. "It worked before."

The stairs were the next hurdle. I grabbed the banister and pulled myself up, one step at a time like I was climbing a wall. It took three times longer than usual, but I reached the top, proud and apparently clear-minded. I pummeled my fists on the door, pounding hard enough that the sound echoed through the hallway. It flew open, and my fists landed on Zander, who had somehow opened the apartment from the inside.

"You all right there?" he asked as he moved my fists away from his chest.

"No, I am not all right," I snapped, glaring at him.

He nodded his head and slowly walked to the kitchen, so I would not be spooked. But I was beyond getting spooked. Even as he filled the glass with water from the sink, he maintained eye contact. I glared at him with a fury hot enough to ignite a thousand stars.

"Drink," he said, extending the glass. I swatted it away, but he caught it before it spilled.

"I'm not taking anything from you," I growled as he helped me to the sofa. "Ever since you jumped in front of my car, my life has been absurd beyond belief. And not the good kind of absurd—the kind that nearly gets me killed. I have been abducted, almost killed, thrown out of a spaceship, and now my relationship is

STARSTRUCK

crumbling. And it's your fault. You ruined my life."

It was obvious my words impacted him. His mouth opened and closed, as if he couldn't find the words to express himself. He handed me the water again. This time I drank it, shoving the empty glass back to him. Only then did he speak.

"I'm sorry. I never meant to come into your life and impose myself on your routine. I can leave anytime you want me to. Just say the word, and I'll go."

"But you can't, can you?" I snapped. "Because if you leave, who's going to stop the planet from being destroyed? You've thrown me into your world. You can't expect to walk out of mine."

"Then what do you want?" Zander replied, his voice escalating. "I'm a teleporter, not a telepath."

"And the pretentiousness." I laughed. "What with your 'Look at me, I know the answers to the universe,' and your 'Come over here. I'm thinking deeper thoughts than you can even conceive.'"

"Well, I'm sorry if I wanted an intelligent conversation on this planet of ape—"

The buzzer shrilled. I snapped my head back to Zander, glaring. "I want you," I growled, "to flibble the flots."

"To do what now?"

"To flibble. The Flots."

"Excuse me?"

"Flots."

Marcy burst into the room, ripping off her coat and tossing it on the sofa in one stride, her face stern and worried. Before I could react, Marcy grabbed me around the waist, and squeezed me for a long time before she let go.

"What on earth happened to you?" she asked.

"I went for a drink."

"You don't drink anymore," Marcy pointed out.

"And you," I chuckled, "don't usually have two noses. I guess we both went for something new today."

"I found her like this," Zander piped up as he shut the door behind her. "Well, more out for the count than ... this. I don't know what happened since we left the car. Does she have a drinking problem?"

"I don't have a problem," I hissed. "Well, not a drinking problem. I have a problem with you, though."

"With me?" Marcy asked.

"Not you," I snapped. "I like you. You're cute and nice and thoughtful and all that shit which makes you awesome. No, my biff is with you, Zander."

"You mean beef," Marcy suggested. "Biff's the bully from Back to the Future."

"You just don't know when to stop, do you?" I glared at him. He stepped forward but kept a safe distance from me. "Maybe it's an alien thing, but you are such a hypocrite." I lowered my voice to match Zander's. "Oh. Sally, we must be careful. Can't let anyone know I'm here. Why don't I invite other aliens into the house for a tea party? Let's all have biscuits and cake and wait for your boyfriend to walk in on us." I rolled my eyes. "Yeah, Zander, really sounds like you're staying safe."

"Alien?" Marcy asked.

"Illegal." Zander hung his head in convincing mock shame. "I have a few—uh— paper troubles. I cleared that up, Sally, don't worry. None of this will happen again."

"None of this?" I snapped. "So, you mean I'm finally free of men falling through ceilings and walls blowing up? Of middle-of-the-night tractor beams and falling into the wrong park in the wrong state? Oh, bless my soul, it's all over now. I feel free. And all because Mr. Zander the Alien told me so, and this time, he's assured me he really means it."

I stopped, finally breathless. I bent over to calm my racing heart but found myself searching for the closest trashcan instead.

"What is she talking about?" Marcy muttered.

"She's delirious," Zander replied under his breath. "She doesn't know what she's saying. Associating past annoyances with current ones, connecting me to the event at the Casa because she's frustrated with both."

"Oh?" Marcy gave me an awkward look. "What do you do in this kind of situation?"

"I have no idea." He shuddered. "I don't usually deal with hysterical women; drunk—she's drunk if I'm reading this right?—and hysterical ones, even less."

"You have a sister, though, don't you? The one who left you here? What do you do when she loses it?"

"She doesn't lose it." Zander shook his head. "But when she gets angry like this, I usually give her a sword and let her at me."

"Does it work?"

"Always."

"Do you have a sword?"

"That's not Sally's type." He shook his head. "That much I do know. Plus, I'd be too scared to be on the receiving end. I think she needs you, honestly."

238

"I think she just needs to sleep," Marcy said. "Look, her eyes are closing. If she's really got a problem with you, you can talk it over tomorrow when she's lucid."

"Good plan," Zander replied. "I've got this. You go home, and I'll call you in the morning with a full report. Don't worry about Sally, seriously; the only thing she'll have to deal with in the morning is a hangover."

"You sure?" Marcy asked. "I'll stay a little longer, though. Until we're sure she's asleep."

"Positive," Zander replied. "I need to figure out how to flibble flots, and I don't have much time."

Marcy was right, and I nodded off as the wave of fury wore off. I felt myself being lifted into the air in arms I recognized as Zander's. He carried me to my bed, placing me gently on top of the covers. Someone else, Marcy most likely, pried off my shoes, placing them in the closet with the rest of them.

"You're so good with her," Zander said.

"I've been her support, you know, since John's death."

"John?" Zander enquired.

He doesn't need another reason to pity me right now, the rational part of my brain screamed, but I couldn't open my mouth to speak.

"Her brother." Marcy sat down on the bed beside me and stroked my hair. I leaned into her touch, not listening to her words. "Absolutely horrible. The family was on vacation and stopped at one of those scenic overlooks for a photo. You know, the ones where you stand and contemplate the meaning of life, get a picture, and leave? Well, a car swerved around the bend and slammed John through the fence and off the cliff. It punched Sally in the gut. But she never cried; at least, not in front of me. You know that dark look people get when their heart breaks?"

"The one where their face drains?" Zander said. "Where any expression is plastered on top. Where you float through …"

"She suffered a sort of depression after the accident. And then one day, she just … disappeared. Everyone was looking for her, fearing an attempt on her own life. They searched everywhere, and I mean everywhere. But then, as suddenly as she left, she came back three days later with that fake smile we've been living with for almost two years."

Zander said nothing. I mean, I probably wouldn't have said anything either in his place. There wasn't much to be said.

"But in any case, Zander, she's been healing—since she met you. She's been getting more confident. I think she's getting better. I think—you might have saved her."

"No, no, I have nothing to do with it," he insisted, and I could feel him smile as he stared at me. "She's been getting better since she started doing the saving herself."

CHAPTER EIGHTEEN
SHAKING IT OFF MIGHT NOT BE SO EASY

The next morning, a ray of sunlight forced me to wake. I groaned and reached out to slap the heat away, my head pounding like there was a drum circle in there. Every muscle hurt. Every sound scorched my ears. There was something going on in the living room producing a loud and shrill noise, with clapping involved. A song was playing. I hummed a few bars, wondering what it was, my mind unable to place it. With a groan, I fell back on the bed, staring up at the ceiling. The words I had said, the things I had shouted...

But I also felt lighter somehow. Everything was finally off my chest, laid on the table for all to see. It was liberating. At the same time, I felt guilt burning through me as I recalled what I had said.

I shuddered. Marcy had witnessed everything. She would think I was crazy now. And Zander ... he hadn't raised his voice once. Alien calmness, perhaps? No, probably not. Maybe he was used to that kind of outburst. In any case, I hoped he was as forgiving as he was calm.

Time to face the hangman.

I rose to my feet and shuffled across the floor to the hallway. The noise in the living room hit me like a brick wall, my mind reeling from the barrage of sound.

I was shocked to see it wasn't an entire orchestra playing accompanied by a dozen jet planes. There was only my TV, playing a rerun of an old episode of Friends. Zander stood in front of the screen watching it quietly. Well, stood was a broad term, seeing as how he was balancing on one hand, the rest of his body held up as if gravity were pulling his limbs toward the ceiling. As the laugh track ran, he repeated the joke, internalizing it as he absorbed the actors before him.

"You sleep all right?" he asked, turning his head to smile as he noticed me enter. I smiled back awkwardly, clenching my eyelids shut. The world was too bright this morning. "Hold on, I found the Internet again. I think we can safely assume you were drunk last night. Well, from the symptoms, I figured that's how Earth humans look … when they're drunk. Lucky for you, I've been around drunks a few times. Well, more than a few. A couple. Well, more than a couple. Well, that's not the point. The point is—" He somehow managed to turn what looked like a cartwheel—though I could only make out fuzzy shapes as I squinted, so he could have just fallen over for all I knew—and landed on his feet. He strode to the kitchen, grabbed a glass of purplish-brown muck from the fridge, and extended it to me. "The point is, I know how to cure it. A simple blend, but I had to substitute some of the ingredients

242

for things I could find in your fridge. Drink up."

Nothing could have made me feel any worse than I did at that moment, so with a deep breath, I took the glass and weighed it in my hands. Admiring the bubbling mixture within, I tilted my head back and drank it.

It tasted terrible, but it was as if someone had taken the rave out of my head.

"Better?"

"Much better," I replied. "Though my mouth tastes worse."

"I can only do so much with my mystical alien ways," he said, taking the glass and rinsing it in the sink.

"Oh," my heart sank. Oh, crap. The memory was incredibly embarrassing. "Zander, I am so—"

"No need to apologize." Zander held up a hand to stop me. "No feelings hurt, though I'm willing to talk if you are."

"About which aspect of last night's rant in particular?" I slid onto one of the stools at the island, watching him. He washed the dishes as if it was the most casual thing in the world.

"For starters, I need to apologize now you're sober enough for it to sink in," he said, "for bringing an alien into the apartment. It was an emergency, but it won't happen again. I swear it."

"Thanks," I replied.

"In good news, I now have parents," Zander grinned. "Dru helps the unground illegal alien network get settled here. I have people willing to vouch for having raised me. Hear that? I have parents now. How charming!"

He seemed incredibly excited at this, and for the first time, I wondered where the rest of his family was. Were there parents waiting for him back home? Aunts and uncles and embarrassing family reunions?

I nodded slowly. "Impressive."

"The real reason I had him over was to figure out more about the Killians," he said. "He's mobilizing his people to help us. I've gotten the possible landing sites down to about eight hundred possibilities, but these people will help me cut it to half that, and then some. A few have been here since before the ship was meant to have landed."

"What, they're over three-thousand years old?"

"And then some." He grinned. "But anyway, I've been saving up for some time, and they'll be able to help me, so if you want me to leave ..."

My heart sank. Ugh, I couldn't believe I had told him to go. As much as I denied it when Matt was around, I liked Zander as a person.

"You don't need to go," I said finally. "And I'm the one who needs to apologize, and, no, don't stop me again. I'm sorry, okay? I said some things last night I'd rather take back. You haven't ruined my life, and you're no burden. In fact, you're one of the nicest people I've ever met. It's an honor to have you as a friend. I hope last night didn't change that."

Zander smiled. "I wouldn't dream of it."

"And the things I said to you in front of Marcy ..." I shuddered. "Anyway, we'll be late for work. Thanks again for saving me from that hangover."

······•••●●●••······

"Anytime," he replied, and while it looked like he had some questions for me, he said absolutely nothing.

You know how sometimes when you feel bad, you feel like the weather mirrors your feelings? Pathetic fallacy and all that? That's what today was. It was gloomy and overcast like it could burst and rain at any second.

And I was fuming. Fuming and pretty sad.

I wanted to sneak to my desk as quietly as possible: I knew that once I was there, no one would bother me and I could wait the day out. But the second I set foot in the lobby, Sophie waved me over. "You look awful," she blurted out.

"Well, thanks for that, Sophie. Nice to see you too."

"Oh, I didn't mean it like that," she backpeddled. "I just mean—are you ok?"

"Just dandy."

"Hey, do you know if Zander is seeing anyone?" she asked, running a hand through her hair. Holy crap, was she attracted to him? Well, a lot of people were, but come on.

"Not currently, no. Though I don't think he's looking."

"Bad breakup?"

"You could say that. But, hey, I need to go. Do you have any messages for Grisham?"

"Nothing new." She checked the empty notepad before her. "People have stopped trying. I guess they get tired of all the noes, eventually."

"I guess that means less work for us."

"Or nothing at all for me," Sophie intoned. "I've become so good at Minesweeper you'd think the CIA would hire me. Oh, Grisham's nine thirty appointment is here, by the way. I sent her up to the office."

I froze. "What are you talking about?"

This had never happened before. I knew the man's schedule inside and out. He didn't have any appointments. Not today, not ever. And yet …

"She showed me her credentials. They're all good," Sophie assured me, though fear blossomed on her face. "She's some kind of investigative reporter."

I ran.

I pounded the elevator button repeatedly, but it didn't respond quickly enough. I bolted up the stairs instead, taking them two, three at a time, throwing the door open and dashing for Grisham's office.

"This is abuse!" Grisham's door was already ajar, and his voice echoed through the hallway. I tossed my purse on my desk without breaking my stride and rushed into the office.

A woman wearing a scarlet red pantsuit faced him, her back to me, as I entered. A river of bright, blond curls rushed down her back. "Abuse is what you are doing to your workers," she said, "not what I am doing here today. I want to talk to you about the secrets you've been keeping." She was calm and composed, but there was an undercurrent of anger.

Grisham sat bolt upright, glowering at the woman. As he rose, sitting taller in his chair, he looked as if he had grown twice in height. In all the time I had known him, Grisham had never lost his temper. This woman gave him every reason to be angry.

"I'm sorry," he said, his tone calm though he snarled, "but the only thing we're hiding is the secret to an effective workforce. That is not something I want to share with the press, thank you."

"I'm not talking about your efficiency," she spat, pronouncing every syllable. "I'm talking about exploitation of a workforce."

"Really? Ask anybody here, and they'll attest that their work conditions are incredible." He waved his arm in my direction. "Sally, do you enjoy working for Grisham Corp?"

"Immensely, sir."

"Any signs of abuse of my workers?"

"None."

The reporter turned and glowered at me. Her pale, heart-shaped face contorted in a mask of rage. The corners of her lips rose to reveal pearly white teeth. They looked sharp.

Her blonde curls bounced as she whipped her head back around, striding to the desk and leaning in closer, splitting the distance between her and my boss in a way I had only ever seen Zander pull off.

"I'm talking about the workers on the turbine floor. Or, should I say, the lack of."

"The lack of turbines?" Grisham scoffed. "Trust me, we have turbines. A whole lot of them."

"No, the lack of workers," she said. "Engineers. Mechanics. Janitors, even. No one is on the roster, Mr. Grisham. I've had people monitoring this plant for a while now. Every single person that works here is in the administration department. You have no scientists, no labor force. Your plant is running on autopilot. At least, that's how it seems to everyone else. It looks to me as if you've got your workers trapped."

"My workers live on-site, young lady," Grisham snapped. "And they have first-rate facilities. We don't want reporters—like you—snooping around. Our methods for success are bound to create waves. We don't want anyone to know how it operates because we are still in the process of working on its completion. We're already producing more than most of the plants on this planet—and with a method people would kill to learn."

"The global community would like to know more."

"And they will get their answers—once I perfect the process."

"Isn't it dangerous to work on a power source that isn't already perfected?"

He leaned back in his chair. "We have to take risks to advance our planet. We have the full support of the community. Our permits are in order. Nothing can go wrong."

"Until it does," the woman said. "The only information you have given us is that the plant is situated on a gas patch. It could easily ignite."

"You think we haven't considered that?" His anger flared, his face splotchy and red. "We've covered this extensively."

"You haven't given anyone anything except a report written by a scientist who is now living in the Bahamas," she said. "I know you don't want to talk to me, but you will after I tell you this," she said, breathing lightly. Her anger changed to a snicker of pride. She leaned in closer, the sneer on her face growing.

"Tell me what?" His face paled as he shrank into his seat.

She drummed his desk with her fingernails. "I recognize this wood."

She spoke slowly, every syllable rolling off her tongue like a terrifying symphony. All at once, the color drained from Grisham's face, leaving him paler than the walls of his office. His hands shook.

"Please," he said in a whisper so light, so low that it was barely audible. He grasped the armrests of his scooter and, with a deep breath, puffed his chest and let out a long, angry bellow. "Get out of my office—now. You have no idea what you're talking about or who you're dealing with. Leave this plant and never come back."

The woman grinned, grabbing her documents from the desk. "Think about what I said, Mr. Grisham. I'll be in touch."

With that, she spun on her heels, gave me a quick grin, and marched out of the room on her five-inch stilettos.

"Is there anything I can get you, sir?" I trembled.

"How did she get in here? I must be out of my mind keeping you after you let that happen. She's dangerous. I need a word with security—now!"

He rode his scooter toward the door, paused, and retreated.

"She's still here," he spat, incredulous. "Fix this."

I ran out of the office, closing the double doors behind me.

My heart raced. Every word the woman had said rang in my ears. Everything she had yelled at my boss, I had considered asking him myself. I wouldn't have used that tone, though.

Breathe in, breathe out. That was brutal. Just awful. The shaking in my knees still hadn't subsided. But now it was my turn to face the woman in red.

I had stood up to worse already, though. I'd had a gun held to my head, been abducted, and escaped. I had stood in front of an alien prime minister and yelled at him to leave my planet. I squared my shoulders and strode to my desk.

The woman terrified me more than the other three things combined.

"So, can I get an appointment?" she waited for me with a snarky grin, her sharp, red nails drumming my desk.

"Mr. Grisham will be free next Thursday at two o'clock in the afternoon," I offered, flipping through the datebook, acting as if she were taking up a coveted last spot, when in fact, she was the first appointment I would schedule. "How's that?"

"Fine." The stranger wasn't shaken in the least. There was ferocity in her eyes. A fire. As if she were ready to ignite at any second. But even so, her voice carried none of the cold anger she had shown in the office. She sounded sweet, though a little patronizing. "Does he get like that often?"

"Never," I answered. And it was true. I had never seen him like that.

"He must really have something about those workers then," she said, waving her hands by her face as if she were a fortune-teller.

"Yeah, they were here before I was hired."

"Really?" she asked, intrigued, leaning in. I felt like she was trying to x-ray me. I had said too much.

"Look, ma'am. Come back next Thursday, and Mr. Grisham will give you his full attention."

"I'm sure he will."

She spun around, waltzing out of the door with her files tucked under her arm and her blond curls bouncing.

I shuddered.

Five o'clock could not have come sooner. Grisham stayed in his office all day, his doors sealed. He communicated with me through vague texts, asking me to cancel everything he had planned for the day—which wasn't much to begin with. When the clock struck five, I picked up my stuff, issued a quick "goodbye" through the door, and took the elevator down to the accounting department. Zander was supposed to be waiting for me, but he wasn't in his cubicle.

He was standing at the window in the break room staring at the parking lot. I tapped him on the shoulder. The light touch didn't have him spinning on his heels and reaching for knives. Instead, he turned calmly, a sign of his progress on becoming Terran.

"You all right?"

"Fine. I thought I saw … it doesn't matter." He sighed. "What about you? You look a little off."

"It's been a long day." I shrugged. "Let's get going."

We walked to the car in silence. He sat on the passenger side, taking off his tie instantly. He hated ties.

"What kind of music are you in the mood for?" I asked, reaching for the radio.

"Something uplifting?" he suggested. "I think we both need something like that right now."

I took out my iPod and put it on a dancing mix, handing him the small device in case he wanted to change the music. Taylor Swift's Shake It Off came on, and I smiled—perfect.

Zander chanted the lyrics with less enthusiasm, though louder, than usual, as if one somehow made up for the other.

I pulled out of the parking lot, noticing a blur moving through the forest. Weird. I urged the car to drive faster.

The blur burst out of the trees, all scarlet pantsuit and blonde curls. The reporter from this morning sprinted, arms pumping as she chased after my car. Branches and leaves flew off her body as she gathered speed.

"What the frak?" I swore, watching her in the rearview mirror.

Zander looked at me then followed my gaze in the mirror. He did a double take, losing track of the lyrics, then stared into his own mirror. He shot upright. "Holy shit!"

I pressed my foot on the gas, but the woman still chased us, somehow running faster now. She was a machine, a bullet. We were going sixty miles per hour now, and she wasn't breaking a sweat. She still clutched her files close to her chest.

"Stop the car!" Zander shouted.

"What?" I said, "No way! She's insane! She barged into Grisham's office this morning!"

"I know!" He was smiling. Laughing, even. "I can't believe it! Stop the car!"

"Hell, no. She's dangerous!" I shouted and spun the wheel, taking off on a dirt road, trying to shake her off our tail. She was undeterred. Her grin grew tenfold, and she increased in speed, almost right upon us.

"Sally, stop the car!" Zander laughed maniacally.

"Are you crazy?"

Before he could reply, she was there. In my car. Sitting in my backseat, her grin stretching from ear to ear. I slammed my feet on the brakes, lurching everyone forward, but she kept her balance and stared, at Zander.

"Sally," he said, awed, staring back at the woman and keeping the eye contact, "I want you to meet my sister."

"Hello again," She gave me a snide grin and extended a hand. "I'm Blayde. Pleasure. Good to see you again, brother of mine."

CHAPTER NINETEEN
THE SISTER I NEVER HAD NOR WANTED

I tried not to let my embarrassment show as I drove us home, but, boy, was I fuming. My face was hot and probably quite red by now, but I avoided looking in the mirror because that would mean seeing her.

The second we pulled out from the back road, the woman had ripped off the blonde locks, and her black hair flecked with strands of red and purples and pinks and blues tumbled out. She crammed the wig into one of the files she was carrying, none of which held any of the incriminating documents she had been going on about.

The wig was only the first part of her costume to come off. She stripped off her shirt, too. As Zander blathered on in the front seat, she changed her costume effortlessly, replacing the blouse with a dark, form-fitting tunic. She stripped her pants and covered her muscular legs with what looked like leggings made of liquid silver, folding the clothes in silence and placing them in their specific folders. I caught myself watching all this through the rearview mirror. Dammit, I hadn't realized I had given in. I just couldn't help it; she looked so much more unearthly than her brother ever had. Her skin was a mixture of rich caramel tones, the likes of which Earth had never seen; her face thin and angular, chin pointed; her features soft and delicate, yet sharp enough to slice through you like butter. And though she looked like a young, twenty-something-year-old woman from Earth, it was painfully obvious that she wasn't a local.

She was stunning. She was haunting. She was terrifying.

I felt a primal urge to run and hide. This woman was a predator, and I could easily become her prey.

So why did I want her to like me?

Zander chatted with her comfortably, so happy to have her back that he couldn't contain himself. His words spilled out with such enthusiasm that he didn't seem to realize I was still there. Talk about word vomit.

"And to think it only took you two months of Earth time to catch up with me," Zander said. "I thought I was going to be here for years. Luckily, it's a planet I like, I mean, Earth people are cool, and I don't have to deal with the whole issue of me not looking like the locals, so I fit in well. It's been nice. I got myself a job, have a nice place to stay, and I've even made a few friends."

I said nothing and tried to concentrate on the road. Just as I had gotten used to my life the way it was, the universe threw yet another alien at me. It was getting tedious.

And then Blayde blew up.

"Two thousand four hundred and seventy-three nights, Zander," she said, her voice cold as ice. "And you're telling me you spent two months mingling with natives, making friends, and living it up in some cozy veeishing home? You have got to be kidding me."

"Ten years?" he asked.

"I jumped from that desert to Elyssus a decade ago, only I find you missing, so I think, oh well, he'll have ended up somewhere. I combed every inch of that planet. Then I go back, and you're not at the outpost either. Hydra, Julka, Veen, I searched every corner of those planets and didn't find a hair off your janeering head. I do all this and what do I find? You, just sitting there, waiting, playing house with an Earthling who doesn't know a rocket from a toothpick. You tell her our life story, and now she's your personal chauffeur. Probably more, knowing you, bro. Just your type: young, pretty, and empty-headed."

"Hey," I sputtered. "I'm not driving just so you can insult me. Feel free to walk if you've got more to say."

"Oh, the Earthling speaks," Blayde hissed.

"Ignore her. She's angry at me. She doesn't mean it." Zander put a hand on my shoulder. "Nice one, Blayde, space travel's first rule is to insult the locals of foreign planets as soon as you get there."

"And we're humans, not Earthlings," I said. "I'm not going to have my entire race insulted, either."

"I wasn't insulting humans," Blayde sneered. "It's an insult putting them and Earthlings in the same category."

I slammed my foot on the brake, pitching us all

forward.

"Blayde, apologize to Sally right now, or so help me—"

"Fine." The woman rolled her eyes. "I'm sorry. I didn't mean any of it. You'd be touchy if you'd been split up for ten years."

"Accepted," I scoffed, putting the car back in drive.

"I thought you were right behind me," Zander continued. "I figured waiting would be easier than running around. Look, I was scared and—"

"You're an accountant," Blayde scoffed, "at a power plant. I don't know if I should be proud of my little bro, or disgusted. I'm surprised you managed to get anything done without me. So how did you get the Earthling on your side?"

"Earthling has a name, you know," I said. "It's Sally, in case you've forgotten."

"I know." Blayde was obviously more intent on her brother than she was on me.

To make matters worse, we were stuck in rush hour traffic. This day obviously wasn't going to get any better any time soon.

"You don't look as if you've spent ten years traveling around the universe," I said. "What are you, twenty?"

The woman gave Zander a questioning look. An angry, questioning look. Seemed very much like a glare from all the way up here.

"How much does the Earthling know, Zan?" Blayde asked coolly, pausing, testing the water. "I mean, how much did you tell her about you? About us?"

"She knows we're not from here," he said sourly. "And she knows we've been here before, oh, and about jumping. Useless trying to hide that."

"Why?" Blayde snarled. "How many times has your life been in jeopardy? How many times have these humans tried to kill you? Did she try? Was it before or after you told her what you are?"

"Hey! He jumped in front of my car. It wasn't as if either of us had much time—"

"So she did try to kill you." Her gaze fell on me now, and it felt like pinpricks of ice flying straight at me. "He just happened to jump in front of your car, did he?" The eyes rolled again. "Or maybe, and more likely, you saw him appear out of nowhere, and like all Earthlings you were gripped with terror and tried to run him over. Savages, brutes, the lot of them."

"Oy," Zander growled. "I happen to like the people here. They've been nothing but nice. Sally took me in. She helped me make some friends and has been exemplary in helping me with other things."

"What? Like sex?"

"No," he replied, trying to hide his discomfort. "We dealt with a slight alien incursion. She did great; she made a great you."

That was the worst thing he could have said. Blayde's face in the rearview mirror was red and hot, burning like the sun, a ball of quiet rage.

Oh please, please, please, let the traffic move forward.

"So, what you're saying is that it took less than two months to find yourself a replacement for me?"

"No, of course not," Zander sputtered. "She only dressed up as you so the Killians would take us seriously."

258

"She dressed up like me?" Blayde spat. "For what? Veesh. Killians are passive, Zander. What kind of a game are you playing here?"

"They're pissed at Earth, and that's not the issue here anyway. I didn't go out to replace you. Let me get some stuff in order, and we'll be off. Okay?"

"We can't. Not yet." All signs of fury dissolved from her face. Calm and serenity had returned at last. "We've got business to attend to."

She grinned the Grinchiest grin. I shuddered, but Zander didn't look shaken. He almost looked excited.

"Really?" he asked. "Where?"

"That plant of yours is hiding something. I'm certain of it."

" That wasn't a ploy earlier?" I asked. "You weren't using that to get in and look for Zander?"

"Look for Zander?" the woman scoffed. "I had no idea he was working there. That really was me looking for answers. I've been on this dump of a planet for two or three days—found myself in some place called Texas." She spat the name, as if it were bitter. "I checked my phone, found your message, and hopped on a plane to wherever we are now. Then I heard about the plant and got distracted. I wondered if you Ter-rans—see Zander, I can be polite—had the brain cells to reach the next stage in development. The more I heard about it, the more I grew concerned, so I got myself a costume and went on a little adventure."

"And?" Zander asked, "Did you find anything?"

"Of course I did." She grinned. "I know a shifty business enterprise when I see one. Then there's the fact that Grisham isn't human, so, of course, you have ulterior motives and—"

"My boss is an alien?" I slapped the steering wheel. "Well, of course, who in my life isn't from outer space?"

"Marcy, probably." Zander chuckled, but his smile faded when he saw my expression. "Sally, it's normal. Loads of people on this planet aren't actually from it."

"Have you seen this place?" Blayde scoffed. "It's so … outback. Middle of nowhere. It's hard to believe you lot got around to inventing computers. Of course you have off-worlders living here. It's out of the way."

"How many?"

She shrugged. "No idea, but I don't see you complaining about the fact that your roommate is one of them. But that's beside the point, your extraterrestrial—that's what kids are calling them these days, right? Your boss is running a shady business, and none of you even noticed?"

She waited for a response, but got none. A smile crept on her lips; she liked showing off.

"I talked to a few people today," she explained, "and let me guess, your interviews consisted of Grisham looking you up online, placing a few calls, telling you about your potential, and practically throwing money at you?" She looked at Zander, then at me, then back at Zander again, a smirk growing on her tight lips. "And neither of you found this weird?"

I sighed. "Unconventional methods don't mean he's from a different planet."

Zander shrugged. "I was investigating the place as well, you know."

"Wait, what?" I said.

She didn't seem to care. "Have either of you seen

the manual workforce? A single worker? Have you met one? Find it weird they were hired before anyone else? That they never come in or out? That you're all sworn to secrecy? And here's the kicker; didn't either of you find it strange that anyone would hire Zander as an accountant?"

"Exactly. I just waltzed in," he said, "And as I was saying, I only did it so I could investigate."

"Brother of mine, I got further in a few hours than you have in two months," she scoffed.

"I was playing a long game," he muttered.

"And the desk thing?" I asked. "You said something about his desk, and he was livid. What's up with that?"

"The wood is from a Lithorn tree," she said. "They only grow on the sixth planet around a tiny, yellow star. Most people call it Orion Six, but I'm pretty sure the locals call it Glenn."

"Ah," I nodded, pretending it made sense. "So, that means he knows you're not from Earth either, right? Wait, let me get this straight, if the two of you know the other is alien, why don't you … I dunno, is there some kind of community here? Like when people meet up in a new country and find out they're from the same place and get all friendly?"

Blayde laughed, a high-pitched, snort-and-giggle. The sort of laugh that made good super villains.

Zander glared at her before turning his head back to me. "Most do," he explained while trying to shut his sister up with a free hand. "But on a planet so far from most planetary unions? It's like Blayde said, Earth is outback. If you're not touring, you're probably here for illegal business if you're not already running from the law. Something universally illegal. Grisham's probably hiding something drastic."

"And I intend to figure out what it is," Blayde said, wiping tears from the side of her eyes, "and put an end to it before it goes any further."

"Under whose authority?" I asked. "I mean, you can't just show up on a planet, accuse people of being aliens, take matters into your own hands, and—"

"Who says I can't?"

"You do this kind of thing often then?"

"Zander didn't tell you?" She smirked. "It's all we do."

"Um, no, sis," Zander snarled. "I'm sorry to say that I didn't tell my friend that we defend the universe. It's not exactly something I want to brag about."

"Wait, you're hiding things from me?" I sputtered. "After—"

"Running him over with your car?" Blayde spat. "This car, I assume? Or like getting him stuck in this dump?"

"Earth is not a dump!" My anger bubbled to the surface.

"We've been sitting in traffic for twenty minutes," Blayde hissed. "All these cars running, spitting out their fumes, and—"

"Shut up."

But she was right: we were sitting in traffic. With everything going on, I hadn't noticed how unusual that was. We had been at a standstill for quite some time. There shouldn't have been traffic at all; there never was. The sky began to darken, too, and we hadn't made it halfway back to the apartment yet.

"I'm going to check this out," I said and slipped out of the car before either of them could say anything. I needed to clear my head.

Zander muttered something about knowing how to pilot a night wing, whatever that was, as I slammed the door shut. My patience had worn thin; I already looked forward to Blayde going.

The cold was intense and cruel. The chill nipped at my fingers and ears, trying to seep through my coat. I zipped it and wrapped my arms around myself.

My teeth chattered as I pushed my way forward. The line of cars was shorter than I expected, and it was easy to see where the jam started. The twilight made it difficult to make out what was happening, but as the cops set up flashlights, people mulled around, speaking in low, hushed tones.

The driver at the head of traffic switched his headlights on, and I recoiled in horror.

A body was splayed in the middle of the road, her dead, pleading eyes wide. Blood ran down her face like tears and trickled out of her ears, nose, and mouth. It stained her platinum blonde hair and the oh-so-familiar clothes.

If Blayde wasn't sitting in the back of my car, I could easily have mistaken her for the journalist. Blonde curls, stiletto heels, every aspect of her attire, right down to the red suit , was identical.

I shuddered and returned to my car in a trance. Throwing the door open, I slipped into the driver's seat. My head fell against the steering wheel with a dull thud. I didn't notice I was hyperventilating until Zander put his arm on my shoulder.

Before I knew what was happening, I broke into pained sobs and buried my head against his chest. He wrapped his arms around me, holding me close.

"Did I offend you that badly?" Blayde asked. She sighed. "Look, I'm sorry. All right? I'm having a bit of a tough time here. I didn't mean it. Or was it the alien thing?"

"It has nothing to do with you," I snapped.

"Oh?"

"I don't really care about you, Blayde, sorry. You made a shit first impression, congrats. No—after all this time, after all the work and effort I put into my job, all the good times I had being Mr. Grisham's assistant, I never thought he was capable of murder."

"Murder?" Blayde sat up, excited now.

"Someone's been murdered?" Zander asked. "Who? Do we know them?"

"A young woman." I wiped my tears away, surprised to find I was calm. "She looked like ... well, she looked like you did earlier. Her hair and clothes were almost exactly the same. The blood, though ... I've never seen blood seeping out of eyes before."

"The eyes?" Zander's brows furrowed. "Crap. Let me guess—ears, nose, fingers, mouth, every orifice, right?"

I nodded.

"This is worse than I thought. Grisham's got specters," said Blayde.

"Specters?"

But the two were already throwing their hands around their heads, slapping the air as if trying to snag a pesky mosquito.

"They're not pretty," Zander said as his hands flew around his face. "You don't want to know."

"Why? What do they do?"

"They shred you from the inside," Blayde said.

Zander scowled at her. "Thanks for that," he snapped. "Anyway, yeah, that's basically what they do. It's a nanobot swarm. They swim in and reduce your organs to mush faster than you can ask what's going on. It's a quick and painless death, but it's disturbing nonetheless. You can't see the things coming."

"You can hear them sometimes, though," Blayde amended. "If you disrupt their path you can hear them move. That's when you know you're doomed."

"Well, that's dark and menacing," Zander growled.

"There's a dead woman up the street. I don't see how we can get any less morbid." Blayde slumped in the seat, seemingly unperturbed by the turn of events. "At least he thinks I'm dead."

"Specters are like your postal system," Zander explained. "If you don't give them the right address, they still try and deliver the mail. He tells the swarm to find a blonde woman resembling the picture on the security camera and—I think this is how you say it—bingo, the target is dead."

"But can't he just target the alien?"

"Haven't you been listening?" Blayde scoffed. "There are loads of aliens on this planet. Loads and loads and loads."

"There can't be that many if we're so far from that Alliance thing, right? Or those unions?"

"The UPA is still the closest," she explained, ignoring me as I muttered that I had in fact heard about them. "You're about fifteen light years from their core system, so even for them you're—you know how you have to cross the desert to get to an oasis, right? Well, Earth is pretty much that. For tourists, I mean. Personally, I think it's a dump, but some of them like the rustic, underdeveloped world experience. Like humans visiting ... um ..." Blayde obviously hadn't been on Earth enough and struggled to find a good example. "Australia!"

I rolled my eyes, done with trying to correct the woman. Then again, when was the last time Blayde was on this planet? For all I knew, Australia could have been a penal colony back then. Though she had been here somewhat recently what with having a phone, maybe she just didn't care.

"Anyway, none of them settle down," she continued. "They enjoy a bit of culture, see the sights, and leave. Setting a swarm of specters on tourists, well, someone's gonna get hurt and someone else sued. Earth would have a premature first-contact, and the guy responsible would weasel out of it. Trust me, I've seen this before. And don't worry, I've stopped it from happening on more than one occasion."

"I'm still a little unclear on what it is you do, exactly."

"So am I." Blayde grinned. "Oh, look, the coroner's coming to pick her up. We can move—finally. I'm starving. What are we doing for dinner?" Blayde leaned back in her seat again, acting like everything was all right and that we were not currently parked close to a murder victim. I rubbed the back of my neck, feeling the raised hairs. They still hadn't gone flat.

CHAPTER TWENTY
WHEN BLAYDE CAME TO STAY

Blayde made herself at home instantly.

The second I had the door unlocked, she slid past me into the living room and dumped her stack of files on the coffee table. She collapsed onto the sofa and flicked her boots off with her toes, letting them lay where they fell. Zander gave me an apologetic smile before following her, kicking his shoes off his feet and adjusting the files.

I closed the door behind them, trying to hide my annoyance. It wasn't going to be for long. As soon as the question of the planet's safety was resolved, Blayde would be gone, taking Zander with her.

I wasn't sure how I felt about that last part.

"Oy, food," Blayde shouted from the sofa, ripping me out of my daze.

Then again, I would be so happy when this one was gone.

Zander opened the freezer and held up a frozen

pizza. I nodded. Perfect. That would be easy and hopefully, appease the couch warrior.

I turned on the oven. "It'll take about twenty minutes."

The woman sighed. "Fine. Mind if I get cleaned up? I haven't had soap for a few months."

"Explains a lot," Zander snickered. She shot him a quick glare. She clasped something concealed in her sleeve and paused before relaxing. "I'll get you a towel," I offered. Blayde nodded and followed me to the bathroom. She inspected the shower before stripping her clothes, ignoring me completely. "The temperature's a little fidgety," I explained, politely averting my eyes and trying not to think about her perfect body—all high muscles and curves. "I hope—"

"I'll be fine," she snapped, grabbing a bottle of soap and scanning it quickly. "I've toppled empires. I can figure out how to get water to the right temperature."

I left as quickly as I could, my heart racing. There was something about just being in the same room as that woman. Heck, even though I was sure she was shorter than me, she always seemed to be looking down at me when talking.

Not to mention she was drop-dead gorgeous.

"So, you survived my sister," Zander said cheerfully. "Here, have some tea."

"What do you mean survived her?" The tea was incredibly soothing, more than I expected it to be. I sat in the armchair, glad to be out of Blayde's presence.

"She likes you." He grinned. "Trust me, that's huge."

"Likes me?" I snorted. "You have got to be kidding me."

"She's tolerating you, which means she likes you," Zander smiled. "Congrats."

"It doesn't seem that way."

"She hasn't threatened your death." He chuckled. "Yet."

I picked up my phone, half expecting Matt to have texted to try to make things better between us, but there was nothing. I sighed and tucked it away. I would work things out with him when this ordeal was over.

"Is your sister always that irritable? You'd think she'd be more excited to see you after, what was it, ten years? How does that even work?"

"Like I told you, it's a fluke of instantaneous travel." He shrugged. "Relativity means my time was different from hers. I could show you the math but—"

"But she hasn't aged."

"We age differently," Zander replied. "A lot slower than you Terrans. She's much older than she looks."

"So it seems." I nodded. I would have guessed he was older and had been wondering about it for a while, but he hadn't given me a good answer yet. Both seemed to refer to the other as if they were the younger one, anyway.

"You'd be cranky if you'd wandered the universe for ten years by yourself. Her patience is thinner than paper as it is. Monsters, murders, plots, schemes—that's her world. Not plain, old, or boring mundane life."

"You find it boring here?"

"No, of course not." He smiled. "Earth is a fantastically vibrant planet. Amazing people. I can't tell you how much I've loved my time here. I was surprised, actually. When I arrived, I expected to be miserable, but

I adjusted. You know, we travel more than you could ever imagine, and wherever we go stuff happens. Things go wrong. Shit hits the fan. We help, we fix, but we can never stay. And the universe … Sally, you have no idea, it's like a … a drug. The way it pulls you in. Once you taste it, see it, realize its immensity, you just can't stop. So, we keep traveling, and we keep going. We've never had anything close to what you would call a normal life, and we don't expect one anytime soon. Blayde's seen too much, she's done —well, she would never be able to slow down, not for a second. Normal isn't her reality anymore. I guess it was never really mine."

Zander stopped suddenly, taking his tea and drinking it slowly. I waited for him to continue, but it seemed his spiel was over. Sometimes he would say things like that and then remember how inhuman he was. He and his sister were so different, and yet they were the same—misfits, outcasts wherever they went, unable to settle down or fit in. Alienated. With their extended lifespans, it was no surprise they would turn cold or calloused to the ways of the world.

Maybe Zander tried more. Or maybe he was just good at faking it. But Blayde made no effort whatsoever, and it showed. She was done trying. She had accepted the fact that there was no stopping, and it ended there.

And they would be leaving soon. Zander was transparent about his plans. This was temporary; they needed to keep going.

And where would that leave me?

"You all right?" he asked, studying me as he put his mug down. I nodded. "Come on, be honest. Is it

Blayde? Is it the murder?"

"Trying not to think about either of them, thanks." I shuddered. "Though I guess they're part of the problem. So much has changed since you got here, Zander. My world is upside down."

"Sorry about that."

"No, don't apologize," I said. "It just makes me wonder what life will be like when you leave."

"How so?"

"Well, for starters, I doubt I'll find a roommate who matches your standards," I joked. "But what will happen to me when you go?"

"Back to being normal, I expect." He grinned. "You can forget about hitting an alien with your car, about the, um, near-death experiences."

"That's what I'm afraid of."

"Isn't that what you want?"

"It may have been what I wanted before my world grew. Before I got my own taste of the universe. Part of the cosmos has been living in my spare room for the past two months, and returning to such a small, closed normality just ... it just doesn't fit anymore."

"Well, I could offer you a few solutions," he said, calmly—nervously.

"Such as?"

"Well, we could wipe your memory of us. You won't feel the loss that way. You'll return to normal without feeling as if something is missing."

"Wait, you could do that?"

"If you wanted us to." He nodded. "We could track down the right tech. Blayde is particularly good at that kind of stuff."

"I don't want that, though. It would be living a lie. And I think I would know."

"Well, option two would be, well"—he shifted nervously in the chair, leaning forward slowly—"that you would … come with us."

"What?"

"Come with us. See a little of the universe. I'm a poor piece of it."

"Really?" I sputtered. "You'd let me come with you?"

"Of course." He smiled gently, holding back his excitement. "Blayde gets annoying after a few centuries. It'll be nice to have the extra company. You're really great and—well, that is, if you want to."

"I want to!"

His smile broadened.

Was this really happening?

I was going to leave the planet—go to space—see the universe?

I hadn't realized how much I wanted it before that moment, but now, it was as if the veil had been lifted, and I heard my heart scream louder than before.

The oven beeped, followed by an angry shout. A small, black blur flew at the appliance, shouting a war cry that would chill an advancing army.

Zander, up in a flash, grabbed the woman before she could reach the oven, insisting it was nothing but a heating machine. Blayde scoffed, complaining about Earthlings installing the same alarms on our ovens as a G1337 bomb alert. She fired a few more vulgarities aimed at my home planet, which I ignored. Instead, I grabbed the pizza from the oven before it got any crispier.

Before I could get plates, Blayde—wrapped only in her towel and dripping water on my floor—was tucking into the pizza, ignoring the heat and saying nothing about the food. From what I could tell, she liked it.

"So, plan of attack?" Zander asked, slipping a plate in under his sister.

"No attack yet," Blayde said between blissful bites. "Recon only, and I'd like to sleep on it before I assert anything. And no, Zander, you are not making the plan. Your plans suck. They involve over the top fanfare. Not what we need. As a matter of fact, I can probably do this myself. You two can return to your posts as if nothing is happening."

"You don't want my help?" Zander asked, surprised.

"I've gotten used to solo missions, Zan. It's all right. If anything is amiss, you'll be the first to know."

They said nothing more all dinner. Once the pizza was finished, I set up the couch bed for the new arrival. Blayde sat on the mattress and stared as if daring us to fall asleep first. I backed out of the room, relieved to get away from her terrifying gaze.

I was going to space.

I ran the idea over and over in my mind. I couldn't believe it.

And then another thought interrupted me—Matt. What would I do about him? Would I be willing to leave the planet without him?

The fact he hadn't crossed my mind until now was more worrying to me than my actual answer.

There was a smell in the air … a pleasant smell, surprisingly. The aroma of eggs and toast and bacon. It was nice to wake up to it.

I trudged to the living room, limbs still stiff from sleep. I hadn't expected to see people in the kitchen, but there they were—two intergalactic siblings cooking breakfast. Blayde the Warrior at the stove and Zander the Fighter setting the table.

Blayde flipped the pans as if they were feathers. She played with the heat of each of the burners individually, swinging the pans back and forth in an elegant dance.

It smelled like heaven.

She hadn't noticed me yet and was chatting loudly and excitedly with her brother, never stopping to breathe. Zander listened intently, occasionally sipping his coffee.

"… And that thing was after me like you wouldn't believe. I ran for days. You have no idea. I thought I knew huge teeth, but trill it all if I'm going to see anything larger. And I was still clinging to the hope you were on that planet somewhere, so I had to keep going, you know?"

Her brother nodded. "Uh-huh."

"Anyway, when I realized the creature wasn't going to slow down, I changed tactics. I swung by the closest inn and got myself a room. I thought it would keep running through town. Boy, was I wrong. It must have sniffed me out because the next morning I see it sitting in front of the inn, patient as a pup, so I closed those blinds and waited. It had to give up eventually, right?"

"Sure," Zander agreed.

"Yeah, well, it didn't. So, change of tactics again. I

stormed out and gave it a talking to, hoping we spoke the same language. It asked me to hand over the fugitive, as calm as anything, and then this beetle clambered out of my ear and tried to make a run for it. The creature snatched it out of mid-air, and flung it in a tiny cage."

"No way!"

"I kid you not. A few drinks later with the large fellow, and I learned the insect had been using me as a getaway vehicle for weeks. Turns out my pursuer was a federal agent. We bonded, talked a little about scare tactics, and that was the end of that. Only—"

"Hold on ... huge beasts? Huge beast cops? Cop beasts?"

"Yeah?"

"Like in the journal?"

"Exactly like in the journal," she replied, taking a pause from cooking breakfast to give him a telling look. "I found Meegra. Of course, no one remembered us. I don't remember them much either, but I'm certain we'd been there before. The feeling I had about you being there with me, it was old."

"Well, we can check that one off the list, then." He shrugged, trying to hide his disappointment. "How many left to—"

"Don't worry about the numbers," Blayde replied. "Now, how much filling do you want on your checheque?"

"I trust you."

She said nothing, reaching her hand into the bowl at her side and tossing a heaped handful into the pan. It sizzled and popped as she shook the pan back and forth.

"So, no Haaq here?" she asked.

Zander sighed. "Not on this side of the galaxy. No Troq planets, no trade, no Haaq."

"Dammit, this place is even more back-system than I thought," sputtered Blayde. "Shame. I miss Haaq. Haven't had any for a long while."

"Same."

"Probably not as long as me."

"Sorry."

She slid the final product onto a plate. The steaming mountain of curled potatoes and golden eggs sent heavenly breakfast smells into the air. Spinning on her heels, she flicked the plate at the kitchen table. It landed right in front of Zander, his outstretched hand stopping it from rattling.

"Yup, still got it." She snickered, her eyes flicking upward and growing twofold as she caught sight of me. Shock quickly gave way to anger. She snatched a haggard-looking book off the counter and put it in her pocket. Her face flushed a shade of purple so deep it would have made a violet cry in shame.

"How long have you been standing there?" Blayde asked, hiding her annoyance under a thick coat of surprise.

"I just woke up," I lied. "That smells absolutely amazing."

"It's checheque," explained Zander gleefully, his mouth full of the steaming breakfast. "Personal favorite. Earthified. Blayde's a fantastic chef."

"When I'm not busy saving this guy's ass," she muttered, turning back to the stove. "And it's nowhere near its usual quality, seeing as I had to make do with Terran ingredients. I suppose I have to offer you some."

"Um … sure," I replied, taking a seat across from Zander. He winked at me and smiled, a reassuring reminder that his weird sister meant me no harm.

"Seriously, don't let me get in the way," I said. "I didn't mean to interrupt your conversation. I'm sure you have a lot of catching up to do."

"I've been up since three," Blayde replied. "We've been talking for a while now. Maybe we should take a break."

"Now come on, Blayde," snapped Zander. "Don't be rude."

"I'm not," she said. "I'm … focused."

The room fell silent. Zander rolled his eyes. "So, how do we find out what's going on at the plant?"

He wiped his fingers on the napkin, staring at his sister's back. She didn't turn around.

"You're the one who works there," she muttered. "Why don't you tell me?"

"I don't have clearance."

"Tell me again why you decided to work for an obviously fraudulent employer." Blayde turned her head ever so slightly to stare at him. "It wasn't so that you could investigate him."

"I was investigating!"

"The awesome health benefits, sure," she scoffed, "as if you need them. Shut up and tell me the truth, Zander."

"How can I tell you the truth if I have to shut up?"

"Shut up!"

"Sure," Zander said. "Anyway, I needed a job so I

could take some time to investigate the Killian problem."

"And how's that going?"

"Lousy. I don't have any leads."

"You're useless without me, aren't you?" she said, placing a plate of checheque in front of me while keeping her focus on Zander. I wondered if she had done something to it. Poison? Maybe. Zander nodded as if to give the all clear.

The first bite was magical. The blend of spices was so different to what I was used to, fully alien without being from anywhere but Earth. It was warm and flavorful, salty and crunchy. I could feel myself packing on the pounds with every mouthful.

"So, what's the security like on the turbine floor?" Blayde asked, still avoiding eye contact, although she was directing her question toward me.

"Me?" I asked. "Um, well, I only saw it once. There's a separate elevator down to that level, and you need a key to call the thing up. Mr. Grisham is the only one who holds it."

"Of course," Blayde scoffed.

"And all the files about that floor are encrypted, you know, to stop them from getting into the wrong hands."

"Or the right ones," Blayde pointed out. "Seriously, neither of you found any of this troubling?"

"Just a smidge," replied Zander.

"The pay is really, really good," I added.

Blayde let out an incredibly long, incredibly loud sigh. I kept my eyes down and worked at finishing my plate.

"Well, it's more than we usually have when we pick

278

up a case."

"Case?" My ears perked up. "You make it sound as if this is a frequent activity, storming people's employment and accusing their bosses of being aliens."

"That's only part of it," Blayde explained, reaching into the fridge and pulling out whipped cream. She slid onto the kitchen counter, swinging her legs, throwing her head back and spilling the contents into her mouth.

"It's a hobby of ours," he explained. "One of the perks of traveling so much. We've gotten pretty good at it."

"And yet there's an alien armada coming to my home planet, and we haven't found their people yet," I said, a little harsher than I should have. Blayde was a bad influence.

"Yeah, well, we'll deal with them too," Zander said. "Jeez, you two need to stop all this finger pointing. You're making me look bad."

"You're doing great without us," Blayde replied, shaking the whipped cream can and helping herself to another serving.

"Fine, be that way."

"Anyway, we need to get into the heart of the plant," Blayde continued, placing the can next to her knee. "See what's going on down there, down where the turbines are. Or where they should be. We'll need weapons in case it gets hairy. Zander?"

"Stunner. The one I snagged off Jeetle." He grinned. "Works fine. I haven't had to use it while I've been here."

"A stunner?" I asked. All the time we had been living in this apartment, and he had never given any indication that he had that kind of weapon lying around.

"A stun gun," he explained.

"I gathered as much," I said. "But, wait, you have a stun gun?"

"Yeah."

"I have some EM pallets, won them in a game of cards," Blayde reached into her pocket to pull out a tiny velvet pouch. "Should knock out any computer system in a room. Got the laser pointer, too."

"A laser pointer," I said.

She grinned. "My laser pointer,"

"As in, for PowerPoint?"

"I do a lot of power pointing with it, sure." Blayde shrugged. "So, human, got any savage weaponry we can use on this incredibly dangerous mission?"

Zander's palm slammed the table, making every-thing, and everyone jump. "We're not bringing Sally into this."

"It's just recon," Blayde said. "Plus, she wants to help. Why stop her?"

"It's dangerous."

"She can handle it, from what I hear. Danger didn't bother you with the Killians, did it?"

His hands formed into trembling fists. "I'm not going to put her in harm's way. Once was enough."

"It's not up to you," I said. "It's my decision."

"No—it's not," he replied. "We've had training. If we must worry about your safety, we could get dis-tracted. Everyone could get hurt."

"It's just a recon," Blayde repeated, "and Sally's the only one with unquestioned access to Grisham. I say we take her along. It's easier than the usual method."

"I won't like it," he muttered.

"You don't have to," Blayde snarled. "Sally, you in?"

"Definitely," I replied. "Let's find out what my murderous alien boss has been hiding."

CHAPTER TWENTY-ONE
HOW NOT TO BEHAVE IN THE WORKPLACE

The car wasn't getting warm, even with the radiator on full blast.

Zander and Blayde sat in the backseat together, their shoulders overlapping. Of course, they weren't saying anything, making the ride more awkward than it should have been.

The three of us were on our way to figure out what made my workplace tick. I guess we were trying to unearth the best-kept secret on Earth—or one of them—armed with nothing but—

Well, nothing really.

And not much of a plan to speak of, either. We were three against ... whom? My boss? The nicest guy in the world, who apparently had tried to have Blayde killed. Three against one sounded like good enough odds, but if Grisham had something nefarious going on, he probably had backup too. And there was the fact I was putting my life on the line. Oh, and my job too, but that didn't bother me so much. Death kind of ended it all, anyway; unemployment could go on forever.

I parked in my usual spot and walked into the lobby. The only unusual thing was that I was bringing not one but two aliens to work. Gotta love that.

Was Grisham really that bad? Whatever his methods, whatever his end, they were producing clean energy, something the planet sorely needed. What were we expecting to find as the power source, other than some clean alien tech? Why had Zander and Blayde jumped to the immediate conclusion that it was alien, so it had to be evil?

Murder. It was probably the attempted murder that had them like this.

But this was all word of mouth. Could I really trust these people? How much did I know about Blayde, anyway? Or Zander, for that matter?

Well, I trusted Zander with my life. I couldn't trust Blayde with my oven.

Today, she wore a smart suit with a sharp bob and glasses. Completely unrecognizable. She had used her makeup to change the angles of her face, making her look twice her age. Somehow, she exuded an air of savvy confidence as she walked, almost as if it were her perfume. Although she didn't look like an inspector as she had intended, she was still too intimidating for people to do anything more than just glance at her.

"And Sophie's lifting her phone," Zander said, the first words he'd uttered since breakfast. "I'll distract her."

"Let me," Blayde offered, slipping her glasses down her nose to get a better look. Sophie froze mid-motion, staring at the three of us. "I'll buy Sally some time. You go and act normal, all right?"

With that, she waltzed toward the desk, maintaining eye contact with Sophie. She wanted to make sure Grisham would not know about the surprise inspector until, well, until after I had dealt with him.

I went straight to the coffee machine and began my work. Zander shadowed my every move.

"You don't have to follow me around, you know," I said. "I'm fine on my own. Nothing's changed."

"Except that it has," he replied. "Look, your boss knows Blayde is after him. Well, he knows someone is after him. He's going to be a little more tightly strung. A little more careful."

"And I don't know that." I tried to avoid eye contact. "I'm just the PA. I see nothing. I suspect nothing. Everything is as it should be."

"It scares me how fine you are with all this." Zander leaned back against the doorframe. "Do you do this often?"

"Oh," said Gerald, bringing his wide frame into the executive break room. "Oh!"

"Get out, Gerald," I snapped, throwing him a glare. The man, however, brimmed.

"You two?" He chuckled. "The two of you?"

"Gerald, the lady asked you to leave," Zander insisted, a grim look on his face. "Please."

"I would never have suspected," Gerald continued, wagging a pudgy finger in the air before us. "Inner office drama. Gossip. Romance."

"Oh, grow up." I rolled my eyes. I so didn't need this. No one needed this.

I took the steaming cup of coffee into both hands, "As I was saying, Zander, Mr. Grisham is impressed with your proposals for increased profitability. He'll want to see you later today. There was a hint of some opportunities, if you know what I mean."

"What, for him?" Gerald scoffed.

"Anyway, I'll let you know when Grisham has time to see you," I said to Zander then scowled at Gerald. "Good day."

I left the executive break room and made my way to Grisham's office. To my doom, my subconscious said. The coffee shook in the mug, or maybe it was me. I forced myself to hold the cup steady, placed it delicately on the small wooden tray on my desk, and added the day's paper and a fresh Danish pastry next to it.

Then I took a deep breath, gathered my wits, and knocked on the large wooden door.

"Come in," Grisham called from the office beyond. I pushed my way in, gripping the tray.

Just a normal day, I repeated on a loop in my head. A completely and utterly normal day.

"Ah, Sally," my boss said. He had a wide grin, somehow cheerful amidst all this. It was as if the events of the previous day had never happened.

It's weird how one day you think you know someone completely, and then you see them again and think you're meeting them for the first time. The boss I had known for the past two months was a humanitarian, a philanthropist—not an alien and a murderer.

I tried not to think that aloud, but nothing seemed real anymore.

"How are you feeling today, sir?" I asked, placing the tray on the cleared spot, covering the spirals of the otherworldly wood.

"Magnificent, Sally, magnificent," Grisham replied, leaning back into his chair. "And you?"

"Well, I ..."

I reached for the newspaper, eager to show him the report about the murdered woman, when my hand slipped, knocking the mug off and throwing scorching coffee over the front of Grisham's coat. My breath caught as the dark liquid stained the gray fabric.

"I-I am so sorry. A-are you all right, sir?" I stammered. I threw the cloth napkin at him. Surprisingly, the man barely reacted. The smile neutralized, and. he glanced down then back up, unsure of how to react.

"I have your dry cleaning in your private bathroom," I said, rushing to the somewhat hidden door and springing it open. "I'll rush your coat to the cleaners so the stains don't set. I am so sorry, sir. I don't know how that happened."

"Ah, no harm done," he said, backing up his scooter and driving it down the ramp toward me. "Is everything all right, Sally?"

"Yes. Yes, sorry," I replied. "The holidays are coming up, Mr. Grisham. My head is a little bit of everywhere else at the moment."

"Understandable." He tossed his coat, catching me across the face. "Just keep it at home, you get me?"

"Of course, sir." I tugged the coat from my eyes, peeling it off like one would remove an alien face hugger.

I waited for him to change, taking his clothes wordlessly from his hands as he exited his bathroom, clean and fresh. As I closed the doors of the office behind me, a weight lifted off my chest.

"How did it go?" Zander asked, gazing at the pile of clothes in my hands.

"Easier than anticipated." I handed him the key card I had taken from Grisham's coat pocket during the confusion.

"Good luck with the dry cleaning," Zander said. "Looks like a serious mess."

I ripped the key card back. "You don't get rid of me that easily. You said I could come, and I'm coming."

"It's dangerous—"

"I was Blayde, once," I insisted, "and we fell out of a spaceship together. I'm pretty sure a recon under my office won't be any harder than that."

Zander didn't say anything, and I knew I had won. He stood in the corner of the elevator, staring at the balled suit in my hands as if staring at it would make it turn into something more interesting.

The second the doors slid open, Blayde slipped into the elevator along with us. "So?" she asked.

"Got it," I said. "Ready for the tour, inspector?"

"Intently."

I stepped aside to let her through, and she stood next to her brother.

I dropped off the clothes at Sophie's desk, spewing out a sob story about Grisham needing me to stay here but the stain setting in, and just like that, I had cleared the lobby of a receptionist and delegated my laundry duty. Score!

I started thinking of myself as a sort of top-level secret agent, slipping around undercover like a chameleon, changing my identity to fit any situation. I felt a surge of power rushing through me, adrenaline maybe, as I found myself becoming comfortable with the deception.

All I had to do was believe what I was saying. After all, I did work here. I would only look out of place if I started acting shifty, and I wasn't going to fall into that trap.

"Gotta admit, the Terran isn't bad," Blayde muttered to her brother, just loud enough for me to hear. "It's nice to know you've thrown your lot in with the only person on this planet who can lie as effortlessly as you."

I ignored the last remark, turning around in the elevator to find the keypad on the wall. I slid the card over the black panel. The familiar blinking red light turning a vivid shade of green. I gave myself an imagined pat on the back, watching the doors slide shut—

—A hand came between them, and the doors slid back with a ding. My heart skipped as he appeared— Matt. Where had he come from? Somehow, it was as if his existence had paused since Blayde arrival. But now he was here, and we were still mad at each other.

I hadn't texted him in almost two days and hadn't been on the Internet. So when he shoved a bouquet of flowers into my hands, I was both flattered and terrified.

"Zander, mind if I borrow Sally for a minute?" he asked, then added his familiar good-natured smile, the edges unnaturally cold. I clutched the flowers, overwhelmed by the fresh scent of lilies in December.

"As a matter of fact, we do."

I barely recognized Blayde's voice. Her tone had changed, and the words came out an octave lower, making her sound like the stern headmistress students loved to hate.

"And you are …?" Matt asked, squinting.

Blayde stepped forward, extending a hand. "Francine Hartwell, health and safety," she proclaimed, shaking his hand in greeting. "I am a power plant inspector, here to inspect your plant. We need Ms. Webber to show us the way."

"Why wasn't I informed?" sputtered Matt, his eyes darting from me to Zander then back to me. "Where's Mr. Grisham? Or Sophie?"

"Grisham asked me to show Mrs. Hartwell around," I blurted out, looking to Blayde for advice.

"Nice flowers," pointed out Zander from the back of the elevator.

"Ah, yes," he said. "Um, Sally, they're for you."

"I assumed as much when you handed them to me," I replied, though it came out wrong, harsh and hurried and sarcastic. "Thank you, Matt, they're lovely."

"Do you mind if we talk? I want to—"

Blayde let out a loud sigh. She threw a hand out to hold the elevator doors from closing, glaring openly at Matt. "Well, this is sweet and all, and I'm sure you'll be able to joke about it over lunch," she snapped, "but right now, I need to inspect this plant. So please, save it for later."

"Of course, of course," Matt stammered as if suddenly realizing he was holding up a very important woman. "Wait, why is Mr. Smith going with you?"

"Mr. Grisham asked him to join us," said Blayde.

"Now, please—"

"But I know the plant better than anyone," Matt said. "Are you sure you wouldn't rather have me come along? I'd be happy to show you around."

"That's not necessary," she continued. "I would much rather Ms. Webber gave me the tour. I want to see what I see, not what I am told to see."

"May I at least make sure Sally is keeping the facts straight?" he practically begged. My own eyes pleaded for the opposite: keep him out of this, Blayde, keep him safe.

"So, are you familiar with the lower floors?" she asked.

"Um …"

"Then I'd rather you not. Good day, sir." She threw her hand upward, out of the way of the door, ripping the bouquet from my hands and shoving it back at Matt. "Keep these on water until lunchtime."

"But—" Matt looked like a dejected puppy as the doors shut in his face. Blayde wiped her hands palm against palm, loud, with the same stern look on her face.

"And now Matt is probably going to be asking questions," Zander interjected. "We should have dealt with that another way."

"Because answering his questions about his boss being an alien is much easier than dealing with the boss in question," scoffed Blayde. "Yeah. That would have gone over well. Sally, text him something sexy. I dunno, distract him."

I'm so sorry, I was already spelling out on the keypad. We really should do lunch though. Talk this out.

I knew Matt would know better than to barge up to Grisham to demand explanations, so I wasn't worried about him interfering with the recon, but I was incredibly worried about the conversation we were going to have later.

As if I needed something else to stress about. My stomach was already in knots as it was.

Ping. The elevator doors slid open to reveal the small security checkpoint I had seen during the short plant tour. The same security guards stood there—well, sat. They looked surprised to see us.

"What's this now?" The security guard with his feet on the machine straightened up, grabbing a clipboard from the desk his associate sat on. The latter slammed his book down. "We don't have anyone scheduled to be down here today. So, who are you?"

"I'm the inspector," Blayde proclaimed, striding forward, the heels of her stilettos sending shock waves through the air with every step.

"Not on the list," the guard said, jamming a thick finger on the clipboard. "Turn around and go back."

"Really? What's the point of a surprise inspection if everyone knows you're coming?" Blayde sighed. "Look, would I be down here if I wasn't supposed to be?"

The men pondered this for a minute. The first one stood up, sighing heavily. Blayde waved the key card in the air. When had she gotten a hold of that?

More to the point, how hadn't I noticed?

"Reception's not answering," the second guard muttered, looking to his partner for support. "Should I call Grisham?"

"No need," I said, taking a tentative step forward. "He sent me down with them. He's incredibly busy. There's a reporter snooping around upstairs. He's been trying to get rid of her since yesterday."

The first guard nudged the other. "That's his PA," he muttered in tones he probably assumed no one could hear. "Remember? The one you—"

"Shut up and call Grisham," his partner hissed.

"He really should not be interrupted right now," I snapped. "You don't want to get on his bad side, do you?"

"Just let them through, Hal. I'm sure the inspector is eager to get going."

Hal nodded his head. "Sure, there's nothing to see here anyway. Come on through, one at a time. Thank you."

Blayde strode through first, the detector silent as she walked to the other side. I followed close behind, saying nothing, feeling vulnerable under the arch. Again, silence. Hal nodded.

The second Zander stepped through, the arch beeped wildly, red lights flashing. He sighed as if bored.

The guard ordered him back. "Please empty your pockets first, sir."

"Sure. Sorry," said Zander, reaching into his pocket to retrieve a pack of gum, and some scraps of paper with numbers scrawled on them. The second pocket contained the crappy cell phone. He dropped them into the little plastic bowl.

Free of the contents of his pockets, he walked through again. The arch went wild, but before the men had a chance to react, they hit the floor. Zander clutched the stunner to his side, eyeing his handiwork with a smile. The men hadn't even blinked.

"See?" He grinned, taking back the burner and slipping in into his pocket. "Not altogether useless."

"Slower than you should be," Blayde snapped. "He's got his hand on his sidearm."

"Or, you know, he just fell like that," muttered Zander. "They'll be out for ten minutes or so. Not sure how it'll affect their nervous system. Let's get going."

I checked the unnamed guard's pulse, amazed to feel the heart pumping steadily, his breath slow and even. The man was asleep, comfortably so. It was much more effective than simply knocking him out.

"You coming?" asked Zander. His sister had already disappeared through the white door.

"Yeah, sorry," I replied, getting up and trying to put the stunned guards out of my mind. If there had ever been a chance to turn back, it was gone now.

CHAPTER TWENTY-TWO
I ACTUALLY CAN'T HANDLE THE TRUTH

"I thought this was just supposed to be recon," I muttered as I stepped out of one gray room into another. Zander pointed at his sister, as if to say, tell her that.

"What's this place supposed to be, again?" Blayde asked as we joined her, unaware of our side conversation, if you could call it that.

She checked a map pinned to the side of the wall, which showed the entire layout to the subterranean facility. The place was entirely empty. Gone were the two men who had been working the controls when we had come through on the tour. The entire desk was unmanned, if it even was supposed to be controlling things in the first place. Spelunking equipment still hung on the walls, and the buttons still flickered and flashed.

"So, this is the primary control room," Zander said, running a hand over the large blue panel. "Who's monitoring this place? You'd think there'd be someone down here. There was last time."

"You'd think, yes," Blayde agreed. "Grab a hard hat, and let's get going. Sally, you sure you're up for this?"

"Positive," I replied.

"Really? Because whatever's on the other side of that room could mean you've been part of some seriously illegal activity. Also, it could be terrible. No promises, though."

"What are you expecting to find?"

"If we find a gas chamber and turbines, then everything is fine, we go home, but go after Grisham for that woman's murder. We find anything else, anything at all, and we've got him dead to rights."

"So long as we can get the American justice system to deal with this," Zander added. "Chances are, it's out of their jurisdiction."

"Yeah, again, big ifs." His sister shrugged.

"What would happen if it's beyond anyone's control?"

"We handle it," Zander said, sternly.

There was a lull as if they were waiting for me to say something, but I had nothing to contribute. I would join them in opening that door. What happened next would depend entirely on what we found.

"So, if the place is legit," I said, "wouldn't that mean the gas beyond this point is incredibly volatile, like the man said?"

"Oh, yeah, that's always a possibility." Blayde grinned. "So, ready?"

I swallowed hard. "Ready."

"Want to do the honors, Sally?" Zander offered.

"Hell, no," Blayde snapped. "If you wanted the honors, you would have come down here months ago when you were supposed to be examining this place."

Before anyone could object, she stormed to the door, grabbed the handle, and pushed it open, throwing it against the wall and striding into a large, cathedral-like room.

"I see a cavern," she said, pointing at the rocky walls. "No gas, though. Unless it's odorless. It could very well be. But, hey, check out these turbines."

"They're not running," Zander said as he tapped one with his fist. You could hear an echo; it was entirely hollow. "We wouldn't be able to speak if they were turning."

I stepped onto the metal grate and froze. The platform extended across a huge cavern, so wide and high you could probably play Quidditch here. The fake floor had been hastily added, and the ground beneath me was a long, long way down.

Lights turned on automatically when the door had opened, flicking on one by one, and they still hadn't reached the bottom. Maybe it went to the center of the earth?

Or maybe there was something down there we shouldn't see.

My heels slipped through the grating, making me feel like I was tripping and falling every time I tried to take a step, not helped by the fact I could see right through the floor. The memory of falling out of that ship, the earth rising to meet me, rushing to kiss my face overwhelmed me. The wind burned against my eyes, my cheeks, not letting me breathe …

I forced myself to take a breath. You see? You can breathe. You can breathe just fine.

Unless this was noxious gas and breathing faster would kill me at a faster pace.

"So, what kind of gas did Grisham claim to use?" I asked.

"You're the one who worked for him," Blayde pointed out. "Seriously, think back. We're trying to save millions of lives here."

"He claimed it was hydrogen," Zander jumped in, "or at least, a hydrogen-like gas. I think."

"You think?" his sister replied. "You have to stop thinking and start asserting. Veesh, you have gotten so slow. Haven't you been training?"

"As much as one can," said Zander.

"I have a question," I said, making both their heads turn. "If there are no turbines, how come there's a ... a hum?"

Neither of them answered, looking instead at each other. Blayde pointed past her feet to the gorge below.

"I think we'd better find out," she replied, her voice high and eager. She pointed to a metal cage along the side of the cavern; a mineshaft elevator.

I didn't realize I would have cell phone reception so far down, but the cavern echoed the chime of a text notification. I pulled my phone out gingerly, surprised to see the first text I had received from Matt in days.

"He says 'the inspector's a fake,'" I said, surprised that he had found out so quickly, "and to 'get away from her now.' His words, not mine."

"We'd better pick up the pace, then," Blayde said, marching to the elevator. How she walked so effortlessly across the grating in stilettos, I would never know. "Zander?"

"On it," he replied, slamming the door shut. His sister tossed him the tiny laser pointer. He caught it and hacked the door we had just come through. The laser was somehow hot enough to weld the fixings together.

"Oy, you, get over here!" Blayde ordered, waving me over to the elevator. I raced to her side, my mind stuck on the pinky-sized laser.

I wanted one so badly.

Zander caught up with me, closing the elevator door behind us. I clutched the metal bars as it lurched down. The three of us said nothing as the cavern filled with the sound of the metal winch lowering us to the floor of the chasm. I felt sick to my stomach, closing my eyes to avoid thinking about the fall over New York, lungs choking as the thin air failed to feed them…

The elevator lurched to a standstill and I rushed outside, glad to have my feet on solid ground. I slapped the headlamp and illuminated the chasm walls. Zander found an extra light and hit the switch, allowing pale yellow light to replace the darkness. The air was stale and bitter, smelling like salt and sweat and rusted metal, a thick odor that turned my stomach. I glanced at Zander for an indication of what we were looking for. My eyes fell on a large metal structure jutting from the dirt, its curved shell so foreign, yet familiar too. It looked exactly how I imagined a flying saucer should look, exactly how I knew it would look.

"Oh, shit." Zander scanned the craft up and down in awe, scratching the back of his head. "Are you seeing this?"

"I should laugh at you, you know," Blayde said, punching him on the shoulder.

"What's this?" I sputtered, shocked, staring at the machine in awe. What it was doing here, and how had it gotten itself stuck under my office, I had no idea.

"That, Sally," Blayde said, putting an arm around my shoulder and waving at the ship, "is a Killian ship."

"What?"

"Yup. The very same Killian ship that you two were supposed to be looking for, and, Zander, please tell me where you found it?"

He shuffled awkwardly, frowning. "Right under my…"

"Right under your feet, that's right." She shook her head. "Remind me to put you through a refresher course when we get back on the road. You're not going to be much of an asset if you suck."

I wasn't listening to her anymore. I was too taken in by the ship, too amazed by the one thing I did not expect to find in the cavern under my office.

After all these weeks, it had been under our feet the whole time. A spaceship. An actual spaceship.

"And I think I've found the Killians." Blayde indicated to a large metal pen with her chin. The light was poor above the large strips of chicken wire covering a small inset in the chasm, but it was enough to see the shadows of oddly-shaped figures enclosed.

Blayde retrieved her laser pointer from Zander, and holding it gently in her hand, she approached the cage. With delicate precision, she worked the lock, springing it within seconds. It fell to the floor, and she ripped the rusty metal chain from the fence, tossing it on the ground with the padlock. She said nothing; she simply walked into the pen without a word to either of us.

She wasn't inside the pen long before walking out, her face tinted a vivid, nauseous green. Blayde had seen more horrors than I could even begin to imagine, yet whatever she saw in there was worse. She looked disgusted, as if she would do anything to burn the world to the ground.

"It's worse than I imagined," she whispered, clutching the fence for support. Her fingers dug into the metal so tightly they turned red. "We can't wait, Zander. We have to act now."

"What is it?" I asked, stepping forward.

Blayde extended a hand, stopping me from going any closer. She shook her head, her lips set in a tight line. "Don't."

"Why not?" I replied. "I've come this far. I want to know the price I've been paying for my job and for the promise of clean energy."

Blayde hesitated and, for the first time since I met her gave me a nervous look. Her brows furrowed and she chewed the inside of her cheek. Even so, she stepped aside saying nothing, though her eyes softened.

"Thank you," I said and ducked my head as I stepped into the enclosure.

The first thing to hit me was the stench. It was as if a barge of rotting fish had been left in the sun. It filled my nostrils and reached for my stomach, the acid inside churning. The cage smelled like decay, like death.

As my eyes adjusted to the lack of light, large brown eyes met mine. They were foggy and covered with mucus, belonging to beings so utterly different from me and in so much pain it was a wonder they were still alive.

I had seen living Killians. I had been on their ship and knew what they were meant to look like. These beings were a poor excuse for what could only be called majesty in comparison. They were cramped so close together it was hard to tell one from another. They were withered. They were drained.

They were barely breathing. Their short, pained breaths seemed dry and cracked. They didn't even try for the door. How could they? They looked ready to die, like they should have died years ago, decades ago, maybe even centuries past, yet something was forcing them to stay alive.

A hand lifted. Three long fingers, a shade of greenish gray, waved then fell, too weak to ask for help.

I hadn't noticed I was running until I stumbled, falling to my knees in the soft sand at the foot of the ship, emptying the contents of my stomach on the ground in front of me. I felt drunk and dizzy, my mind reeling with revulsion. I felt an urge to storm Grisham's office and light everything on fire. My mind was overwhelmed with shock and pain, begging for an escape.

Grisham was a monster.

I pushed myself up, holding back the tears and the second wave of nausea. Grisham was the real alien; he didn't fit into this world—any world. What Grisham had done, was doing, was incomprehensible. Zander and Blayde may have been alien, but they had humanity and empathy. Grisham was just a fraud.

I knew there were men and women on this planet

capable of that kind of horror, people who exploited the lives of others in inhumane ways that I could not imagine. But this was tangible; the horror was in front of me.

Blayde was right—we had to act now.

Her eyes were red, but there were no tears. Zander's face was like stone. He avoided looking at the aliens, eyeing me instead and assessing my reaction just as I was assessing his.

"What ..." I stammered. "What are we going to do?"

"That was recon," Blayde replied. "Now, we go for the head and deliver it to the Alliance, though we can't let them know about our involvement. First, we'll get the victims to safety. We need them out of the way before we can deal with Grisham."

"We're going to jump them away." It was Zander's turn to speak, allowing his sister to study the alien captives. "We're getting them out of here. Off the planet. As far as we can go. We got here right in time."

"In time?" I croaked. "They're dying, Zander."

"Dying, but not dead," said Blayde, snapping her attention back to us. "Sally, this is what we do; we save the day. We—"

A shot exploded through the cavern. Blayde clutched her chest as red seeped through. "Oh, shit, not this again."

There was another shot, tearing through her stomach like putty. She fell to her knees, a bored look on her face as she toppled over, face forward on the dusty floor.

It was as if a mute button had been pressed because

the third shot never even registered. Zander dropped to the ground as the front of his head exploded outwards, leaving him silent and unmoving beside his sister, the red of his blood and the pink of his brains spurting outward into the dirt.

I think I screamed. I could hear no sound, but I felt the breath leave my lungs and burn my throat. The only sensation I was truly aware of was terror. I dashed to Zander's side, tears soaking my face as I ran my hands over his cool skin. My fingers trembled as I searched for a pulse, finding nothing, but getting stickier as they touched more than just skin. Blood stained my skin. Strong arms tore me from him. They dragged me away as I kicked and screamed. My voice echoed off the walls of the cavern. Wide eyes watched the scene from the enclosure, watching me succumb to wracking sobs, staring as their hopes of freedom died on the dirty floor.

I didn't see my attackers. One strong blow against my skull and darkness took me over.

CHAPTER TWENTY-THREE
THE WORLD IS AWFUL AND EVERYTHING SUCKS

A high-pitched whistle filled the air.

It sounded awful. Whoever it was, they couldn't carry a tune.

Back and forth the notes went, rising and falling and rising again, highs and lows and a sputtering cough. The shrill tones hurt my ears, and a persistent ringing filled my head. I let my eyes open slowly, peeling the lids apart one at a time. The world was fuzzy, but I didn't need to see to figure out that I was completely trapped. My hands were bound together behind my back, and my ankles strapped to the chair legs.

As my vision cleared, I saw Grisham parked in front of me, his bulbous face blotched with rage. It was as if I was seeing him clearly for the first time in my life.

It was the face of a monster.

I finally realized where I was—his office. The light from the large bay window poured in, bathing the room in a warmth so bright and comforting, and so completely inappropriate for the situation. The light was too pure to touch anything in here.

"Wakey, wakey, Ms. Webber." He grinned, but I wasn't in the mood to reciprocate.

My friends were dead. On his orders, yet he didn't seem in the slightest bit phased.

Well, fuck him.

I wouldn't give him the pleasure of assigning me to the same fate. I bit my tongue and held back the slew of profanity I wanted to fling at him. And then I saw him—Matt.

He sat at the desk watching wide-eyed. He looked as shocked as I felt. Thousands of possible explanations for why he could be here running through my head, but none of them stuck.

Had he been here when they brought me up? In the wrong place at the wrong time? Grisham had been grooming him as his successor. Was he only now being brought in on the secret?

Or had he been in on it from the beginning?

I shuddered. He couldn't have been. Matt was kind and sweet. His jealous streak didn't make him evil. But he was Grisham's protégé and trusted him to the ends of the earth.

"Awake at last," Grisham said. My eyes snapped back to his. "We've been waiting quite a while, you know? Young Matt and I got bored of playing twenty questions."

I said nothing. I thought of Blayde, not her ripped up corpse, but when she was alive and fuming. I forced my face into one of her trademark sneers.

STARSTRUCK

Everyone in the room is out to kill me, but I have a secret weapon that will destroy Grisham and everything he's ever loved or cared for. I am a star about to go supernova. And I will burn him to the ground.

I knew none of it was true. But Zander had been right, the thought was like fuel. I glared at Grisham with a fury that could have set entire galaxies on fire.

"Aw, come on, now, don't be like that," Grisham continued. "We all want the same thing here."

"The same thing?" I spat. "You murdered my friends, and you killed an innocent woman who had nothing to do with this. You've been exploiting living, breathing people for your own gain. How could you think I would ever want the same thing as a ... as a monster like you!"

Grisham sighed, leaning back into the seat of his scooter. He looked bored. He looked pissed.

"We both want the truth, Ms. Webber. And I want answers—now."

"Then I guess you're going to have to learn to live with the disappointment," I replied, drawing my scowl as wide as I could, "because there is no way in heaven or hell that I'm going to tell you anything."

"Come on, Sally, you want answers too, don't you?" Grisham chuckled. "It's not like I'm unreasonable. We're going to have a nice conversation and then both of us can leave with more answers than we started out with. Sound fair?"

"What makes you think I'd make any kind of deal with you?"

"You want answers," Grisham replied, "and I'm willing to give them to you. And promise that you'll get

306

out of this."

"Out of the door? Not at the end of a gun barrel?"

"That's entirely up to you and how cooperative you are."

"Hold on," Matt interjected, breaking out of whatever trance he was in. "You never said anything about hurting her. I thought you just wanted to talk?"

"That is what I want," said Grisham. A raw smile stretched across his face, yet it didn't reached his eyes. "I want what's best for us. All of us. The trio at the top."

"Huh?" I dropped the Blayde sneer and stared at him.

What the hell was going on here?

"In any case, Sally, you probably have a good idea of what I am," Grisham said, "but it doesn't change who I am. You know me. You've worked with me for months. I am honest to a fault."

I snorted. "I'm pretty sure what I saw downstairs was never brought up."

"Ms. Webber, I have a deal for you," he continued, ignoring me, "and before you answer, you should know that I have a fantastic language chip installed. It translates more than just words. In simple terms, you can't lie to me."

What a load of bull.

I didn't have a single viable reason to believe a word he said. Not a single reason to cooperate with him and his absurd ideas. But it was completely within his power to kill me as soon as he no longer needed me—so, useful I would be.

Well, to a point.

"Let's get started, shall we?" said Grisham. "Are you human?"

"Excuse me?" Matt sputtered, but his boss stuck out his hand to keep him at bay and shut him up in one smooth motion.

Relief washed over me. At least Matt wasn't aware of any of that; although, that was about to change.

"Yes," I replied.

"And your friends?"

"Blayde wasn't." There, testing the waters. Not a lie, but it was a truth his chip could handle, if the so-called chip even existed.

"And—"

"My turn," I snapped, unflinching. "Why are you here? What are you doing, and how does this plant work?"

"You're going to owe me a lot of answers for this one." He shrugged. "The simple answer is money, as it always is. I was in a bit of a pickle back on Hydra, owed a lot of gold to the wrong people. I skipped town and practically stumbled upon this little gem of a ship while on a salvage run. I settled down here, telling myself I'd leave once the fuss blew over, but the ship was more than I anticipated. I thought to myself, why the hell not? I like it here, better make the most of it, help the Earthlings out. The air's a little thick for my liking. Clearing it up would be better for my lungs, you know? Well, I'm getting off track, but—"

"What in the world are you going on about?" Matt sputtered. "What is this shit? You've lost it, you've—"

"Don't interrupt," said Grisham. "Take a seat and shut up. We'll get to you in a minute. Anyway, I got some equipment together and salvaged the ship, only to discover it was Killian. They're quite docile beings, you know; you met a few of them downstairs. In any case, they have this deep empathic BS going on between each other and their spaceship. In an emergency, the ship can feed off the crew's life force to power the life support and keep them and the distress signal going. No one was going to miss them. They've been down there for a few thousand years at least, so I hooked their backup generator to a grid and voila. So long as I keep them fed, they stay alive. They fuel their ship, which fuels the plant, and there you have it—the cleanest energy in the universe."

"What the fuck?" Matt muttered under his breath. "What the absolute fuck?"

"We could report you to the Alliance," I pointed out, knowing full well that I didn't have the first clue how to get in touch with them. "You just told me your entire freaking plan."

"But you wouldn't." My former boss—I really doubted I still had my job at this point—gave me a knowing look. "You don't want to be on the Alliance's radar, not if you're connected to the Siblings." He said the last word with distaste. "And I told you everything because I am absolutely certain that you will be with me by the end of this."

"Are you kidding me?" I spat. "You killed my friends. Why on earth would I want anything to do with you?"

"Because it will be the most incredible thing you will ever do," he proclaimed. "I have always liked you and Matt. You both have much more potential than any other humans I have met. But when you stole my key card. Ah, Sally, that was sly. You're driven, I will give you that. I can see your potential, and you—yes, you—you're destined for great things. Of course, I have no idea what those things will be. I want both of you to join me in building my empire. In making Grisham Corp a household name. What do you say?"

"What if I refuse?" The man was insane if he thought any of this was going to work on me.

On us, I hoped. I thought I knew Matt well enough to know he wasn't going to fall for this shit.

"Well, then there's someplace else you can be useful," Grisham said with a sinister grin. "Killians aren't the only things that can be hooked into the mainframe. How do you feel about helping your planet become just the slightest bit greener, Sally?"

"I think you're insane."

I was shocked. I had thought the words, but I wasn't the one to speak them. Matt stood next to Grisham, his face scrunched with incredulity as he stared at the alien.

"Aw, Matt, come on." Grisham grinned. "You like working here. Why should the fact I am extraterrestrial change our relationship?"

"Maybe because you're exploiting others?" Matt's put his fingers to his own temples. "I mean, what the fuck? You are a fucking psycho. There are aliens? Here? Powering a fucking city, and you murdered Zander? Fucking murdered him? And you think I'm going to help you? Well, tough luck, you mofo."

"Matt," I hissed.

But to my surprise, Matt was the first to act, not Grisham. He grabbed the fire extinguisher from the wall and swung it in a wide arc, slamming it into Grisham's head. Grisham and his scooter crashed to the floor.

His skull had a dent the size and shape of the butt end of the extinguisher. Blood ran from his nose onto the floor, staining the gray carpet.

I gagged. Even after everything I had seen today, the sight of yet another gruesome death turned my stomach. Maybe that was a good thing. I didn't feel the relief I thought I would.

Matt stood, frozen, staring at what he had done. He released the fire extinguisher, it clanging to the floor, and he cupped his face. His body trembled as he gazed upon the awkwardly arched body of his former boss, taking in the crushed skull and blood.

"I ... I quit, Mr. Grisham," he stammered.

He snapped out of his daze and walked over to me, his fingers deftly tugging at the knots as he untied the cords. As he worked the cord around my legs, I leaned on his shoulder, feeling as if someone had ripped my guts to shreds.

"Matt ...?"

"Yes?" His voice was slow and uncertain. He placed a gentle hand on my knee and glanced up, a vacant expression on his face.

"Zander's dead," I whispered, my vision blurring as the words sunk in.

Matt grabbed my hand, squeezing tightly. The shock hung over us like a thick cloud.

"Where ... where did he put them?"

"I don't know," Matt replied, his breaths heavy. "None of this makes sense. I got called up here, and I saw you tied to a chair and Zander is dead. I ... none of this makes sense."

"We were on a recon. We were only supposed to figure out what Grisham was up to. We didn't expect—"

"You were working with them?"

"You ... could say that."

Matt stood up, taking a step back. "What do you mean?"

"We knew something was wrong with Grisham," I replied. I stood, testing my trembling legs, and leaned on the chair for support. "We had to do something."

Matt backed further away. He bumped into the desk, his hand knocking a haggard leather journal and the stunner to the floor. The latter hit the ground, bounced, and with a scream, Matt clutched his foot, which had probably gone to sleep.

"What the hell is going on?" he squawked, picking the gun up with an index finger and thumb. He placed it delicately on the table, still shaking. I would have been, too, if I had just bashed a man's head in. But I was numb, just numb. I felt like the world had been paused. I couldn't believe Zander was dead, and I begged the universe to free me from this hell.

I reached for the journal, my heart sinking when I realized what it was. It looked smaller, more fragile than the first time I had seen it, Blayde showing her brother a memory caught between the yellowing paper. The first of the worn pages was full of text, written in a neat script with a slow progression to lesser, more simplified entries.

It started with some variation of Dear Diary but changed to dear impartial friend, and then to no introduction at all, just some nonsense title. Probably a planet name that I couldn't even imagine knowing or even try to pronounce.

There were illustrations, too: maps and charts, glued into the pages haphazardly or sketched alongside the notes. Creatures I had never seen before, shapes that defied geometry, planets and people and faces in crowds that sent shivers down my spine.

Bodies. Corpses. Death. Life. Everything was caught on the pages. A universe in a book.

I slammed the journal shut, feeling as if I had walked in on someone getting changed. I had seen Blayde nude, but this felt more intrusive than that. I felt the heat in my cheeks, ashamed of having looked, while my mind raced at the wonders captured in my hands. It was Blayde's and she was gone now, but reading the journal felt like a trespass, disturbing a grave that hadn't been made yet.

And then a voice broke the silence that chilled me to the core.

"Get your filthy paws off that, you dirty Earthling."

CHAPTER TWENTY-FOUR
WE FINISH THIS THING ONCE AND FOR ALL

Matt's scream was inhuman as the book was ripped from my hands.

Wide-eyed, I saw the face—the living, breathing face of Blayde, skin covered with a mixture of sweat and blood—snarling as she reclaimed what was rightfully hers.

And then she laughed.

She folded in half as she pointed a finger at my face, roaring with laughter. Zander came up behind her, shoving her out of the way, scowling. "You're being insensitive again," he scoffed, grabbing the stun gun off the table.

"You seriously didn't tell her?" Blayde managed to say between guffaws. "With everything you said? All these months? Not a single hint?"

He said nothing, and she continued laughing. Blayde slapped her leg, and his face flushed bright red. "You stayed out of trouble for two whole months?"

"Yes, I stayed out of mortal danger for two whole months," he snapped. "Why is that so hard to understand? It just … it never came up."

"Because you're you, Zander," she said, wiping tears from her eyes.

"Not every minute of my life is about running around and blowing up things. I can live a day or two without accidentally dying."

With that, a thump resonated through the office. Matt lay unconscious where he had dropped.

And me? I was rooted to the spot. Shocked didn't even begin to cover it.

As if my day couldn't get any weirder, my friends were back from the dead.

Or maybe I was dead?

"Sally?" Zander asked, his voice calm and composed.

He wasn't dead. My eyes took in the figure of my friend, my roommate, my partner in crime, who, despite being shot in the head, was living and breathing and, despite everything, smiling.

Well, it was an awkward smile, but I was used to those.

"Surprise?" he said.

He held up his hands to show he had come in peace. I could have slapped him or kissed him. Or both. Instead, I let out a sound that was something between surprise, confusion, and anger. It sounded a little like someone had stepped on a cat, sending Blayde into further peals of laughter.

"I'm not dead."

Yeah, no shit, Sherlock.

I did the only thing I could possibly do—I hugged

him. I held Zander tight, taking in the fact that he was here, that he was alive while ignoring the blood on his shirt. It stained my blouse, but I didn't care. I cried, and he hugged me back, waiting for me to make sense and come to terms with his return to life.

"My cells regenerate fast," he explained, answering the question I couldn't get past my lips. "Very fast."

"Even after you ... die?" I sputtered. "How is that even possible?"

"I never stay dead for long," Zander replied. "A by-product of having to reassemble my cells every time I want to travel. And no, it doesn't hurt."

I leaned back and slapped his face, silencing Blayde's laughter. The room rang with the force like a storm that had passed. Zander's eyes widened. "What was that for?" he squawked, holding a hand to his cheek, even though he had just told me it would not hurt him.

"It never came up?" I said. "It never came up that you were immortal? Not once, huh?"

"No, it really—"

"I have spent the last two months worrying about keeping you alive, and now you're telling me you can't die?"

"Well, I can, but not for long. I mean—"

"Don't play coy with me, Zander." I spun on my heels, marching to Matt, who was only now stirring. "There were plenty of opportunities for you to let me know you were effing immortal."

"There really weren't, Sally," Zander muttered, his face reddening.

"How about when you got yourself doped up on

316

caffeine?" I snapped. "I thought the coffee was going to kill you."

"Coffee …?" Matt muttered, dazed, as I helped him into a seated position. "So, you two aren't related, are you?"

"Long story," I replied, turning my glare back on Zander. "I just watched you getting shot through the head. You've got blood down your face. I saw your brain! And here you are, hunky-dory and alive. I must be going mad."

"It takes a minute or two for the body to reboot," Blayde interjected. "Gee, this is fun. The look on your face, though. On all your faces. Absolutely hilarious. It's on days like these that I wish I owned a camera or something."

No one said a word, ignoring the chirpy revenant with cold silence. I managed to help Matt to his feet. The color returned to his cheeks, a good sign if I had ever seen one.

"Fine, if no one's going to say it, I am," said Blayde. "We've got more important things to do than sit around waiting for the idiot boss man to wake up. If he ever does wake up, that was an impressive blow."

She turned around, the laser pointer held high as she marched out of the room. Zander gave me an apologetic look, the kind a puppy gives when he knows he's chewed the wrong chair leg, and turned to follow her, stepping over the still unconscious body of Mr. Grisham.

"You don't have to come along," he said, turning to face Matt and me before reaching the door. "We can handle this ourselves, but we won't stop you if you'd like to help."

"What are you going to do?" I asked for the both of us.

"Blow this place to smithereens," he replied, grinning. He pulled the fire alarm with one swift motion and marched out of the room as the sirens blared.

I looked at Matt, who stared at Grisham's body, then at Zander. His eyes rested on me. He shrugged his shoulders. "I'm sure as hell not going to sit this one out."

"You sure you're okay to walk?"

"I could be missing a leg and would still make sure I could walk if it meant being able to stop whatever the fuck is going on. So, are we going or what?"

True to his word, Zander held open the elevator doors for us. Blayde clutched a handful of wires in her right hand, the guts of the elevator exposed to the world. Once the team was complete once more, she jammed them together.

"Better grab onto something." She snickered as the doors slid shut.

The floor dropped from beneath us, and the elevator just kind of gave up and fell. My stomach somersaulted, and I grabbed onto the railing. in terror. And Blayde, well, she laughed, cheered, and floated in the free fall. Shouting like this was reserved for roller coasters, not an elevator plummeting into the abyss.

"She's a psycho!" Matt shouted.

"Oy, watch who you're calling psycho," Blayde replied, her cheers cut short. "Someone took an awfully long time to recognize his own boss was one."

Matt said nothing.

The elevator jolted to a stop, and the four of us hit the floor. The tiny ping filled the air like an afterthought. I caught my breath as the doors slid open, relieved to have stopped, but my heart sank when I saw what was waiting for us.

They were most likely all the security personnel Grisham had hired to protect the plant and its secrets, and they were armed to the teeth. With robotic synchronicity, they turned toward the elevator, ready for us. I shuddered when I realized we were more than outmatched.

Blayde grinned. The smile crawled up her face as she shared a look with Zander.

And just like that, it was over. Blink and you would have missed it. Actually, I had.

The second the doors opened we saw the security guards. Blayde shot out of the elevator like a bullet. Without hesitation, Zander spread his arms to the sides, shoving Matt and me into opposite corners. We were shielded. We were safe.

By the time I had gathered the courage to peek out, nobody was standing in the small atrium other than Zander and Blayde. They had already collected the security guards' weapons, taking out the ammunition before tossing the empty guns into a corner. The men on the ground were unconscious, not dead; although I couldn't tell for sure. I probably shouldn't have made assumptions about their current state, considering how little I knew about my friends.

To my surprise, this didn't scare me.

Matt, however, turned to the potted plant in the atrium and emptied the contents of his stomach. It wasn't the best look for him. His eyes were wide when he turned to face the others, his face gaunt. As he gazed upon the unconscious bodies, he looked as if he were in a dream; a nightmare, maybe.

Blayde grinned at her handiwork. The look on her angular face was that of an artist having finished a piece she was proud of.

"I thought they would have put up more of a fight," Zander grumbled.

"Somebody's gone soft, hasn't he? That would have been over in half the time if you had practiced your forms. Look at you, I'm out of your life for two months and your reaction time doubles."

"It hasn't," he snapped.

"Maybe you were distracted, how's that?"

"Shut up."

Zander rolled his eyes, pocketing the small shiny gun. Finally, he turned back to us with a solemn look.

But I could see right through it. I had seen the look in his eyes when he had died, and I could see the brightness behind those stern eyes now, even if he was attempting to hide it. Zander was more alive at this moment than he had been during his entire stay on the planet.

I shuddered. I guess I was finally meeting the real Zander.

"Are you coming?" he asked, as if he was about to throw out a hand. For a second, I thought he was going to take mine and pull me along, but he turned and headed for the door instead.

"Remind me why the dynamic duo is down here again?" Blayde asked, following her brother into the fake systems room, ignoring both Matt and me as she stormed past.

Zander let out a heavy sigh. "They deserve to be here," he answered coolly, not making eye contact with any party involved. "Matt bashed our boss's head in with a fire extinguisher. I think we owe it to him to see the lives he saved."

"Former boss," Matt squawked.

Zander chuckled. "That goes without saying."

"You don't expect us to take them down to the Killians, do you?" Blayde snorted. "I mean, come on. Sentimentalism? From you—of all people? Zander, we're on a mission. We can't have people like them coming along. They would get in the way. Worse, they could get injured. Killed, even. What were you thinking? We go down, rig the self-destruct, grab the Killians, jump them home, and ... what? Let these two Earthlings find their own way out of an exploding ravine?"

"I was going to take them with us."

Blayde froze mid-stride, her foot dangling awkwardly in the air. Her eyes widened to the as fear rippled through her perfect exterior.

"Take them ... with us?" she sputtered. "Offplanet? During a rescue mission?"

"Yes," said Zander as he flung open the door to the pit. "The return won't be instantaneous. It'll be better if we take them now."

"Take us where?"

Matt was frozen in place too, but for other reasons. He no longer seemed able to move his legs.

"You never even asked him," Blayde scoffed. "Look, you can't take people off their planet willy-nilly.

321

It's called alien abduction, and is frowned upon in respectable circles."

"Sally wants to come," he said, bordering on whining without breaking his calm demeanor. "And she likes Matt, so I thought—"

"Most importantly, Zander, you didn't ask me." Blayde scowled. "And I'm not into the idea of having Earthlings holding us back. We've only just found each other, Zander; we only need each other."

Zander turned his back to her. My eyes met his, and in that second, they said much more than words ever could.

"I owe her, Blayde," he muttered, his lips the only thing to move. His eyes were locked on mine, and the conversation there was still going: I don't want it to end like this. I'm doing everything I can.

"You don't owe it to her to put her in harm's way."

"She's coming with us," he snapped.

My heart thumped in my chest, though not out of fear or nervousness but anticipation. At that moment, in those eyes, I saw it all. I realized there was nothing I wanted more than to leave this planet and see the wonders beyond.

With him.

It was as if my life had been nothing but a movie until that moment, that it had gone by without me actively participating, only watching. In less than a second, I felt pelted into their story, awake and alive.

And living is what I wanted to do.

Holy crap, I really want this.

"Please, Blayde," I said.

Matt slipped his hand into mine. I could feel his

pulse against my skin—fast, hasty. And he was sweaty, still trembling, still reeling from what he had done, but the words that came out of his mouth were those of agreement, of determination.

"I want to come too," he said. "If the offer still stands."

"The offer was never on the table," Blayde snapped, glaring down at the pit. "Sally's clever and all, but she's a deadweight. She could end up being a literal dead-weight."

"But—"

"Let's get those Killians out of harm's way. We'll come back and work out your issues, okay?"

Zander sighed. "So, what about them?"

"When we set off the self-destruct, it's going to blow this plant sky high. I'm glad they got to see your little fight scene, but they need to evacuate with everyone else. They can't come any further."

Zander tilted his head and looked at the pit below. When he turned his head back to us, he was stoic and stern.

"I'll be back, I promise," he said, offering a hint of a smile. "We'll take a well-needed vacation. All four of us. Absolutely anywhere. All right?"

"You've got a deal." My reply was slow, and it was determined. "Be safe down there."

"Hate to be a bummer," Matt piped up, his voice shaken and unsteady, "but how are we meant to get back to the surface? Elevator's bust, last I checked."

"Take this." Blayde grabbed my hand and pressed a cool, metal tube against my skin. The laser pointer. "Sever the blue wire. That'll recall the elevator to the ground floor. Once you get up there, run for it. I'll give you ten minutes, more or less."

"Is it more, or is it less?" Matt sputtered.

"Just get out quickly," Blayde urged. "Zander, take this as proof that I'll keep my word. I'll be back for the laser, and if you lose it, Sally, or damage it, or if it's anything less than in the perfect condition it is in now, I will strip the flesh from your bones. All right?"

I nodded. I had no doubt Blayde would make good on that threat.

"Great. Zander, with me. We'll see you two soon. Now, run."

And with that, she darted to the railing overlooking the pit, grabbed it with both hands, and flung herself into the abyss. Zander followed suit, pausing to toss me a salute, before flinging himself into the chasm.

"What the hell is happening today?" Matt's hands flew to his head, clasping it in a vice-like grip.

"Pretend it's a dream," I offered, clutching the laser pointer to my chest. "We'll wake up tomorrow, and everything will be as it should."

"No aliens and bosses bent on world domination," he muttered. "Oh, god, I killed—"

"Let's get out of here." I grabbed his hand and rushed for the door. "We need to focus. Keep our minds off ... that."

"So, um," he said, as we walked, squeezing my hand tighter, "am I to understand that all those times you were being all, I dunno, shifty, it was because—"

"We were off saving the planet," I replied. "Or something like that. And once because an alien was chilling in my living room."

"Something like saving the planet?" Matt shook his head. "That's pretty impressive."

He didn't know what had hit him.

CHAPTER TWENTY-FIVE
I GET MY FINAL BOSS FIGHT

Matt hit the ground like a sack of potatoes, letting out a pained gasp of air.

My hand still clasped his, and I was flung across the grated floor landing face first on the cold metal. The pointer flew out of my hand, rolling across the grate. I tried to push myself back up, my eyes finally seeing the creature that had knocked Matt down.

My neck strained to pull my head up high enough to see. Just five feet away were large, red things. They were so thin they resembled stilts, except there were six, no eight, no ten crablike appendages.

Holy crap, Grisham was a crab.

I was stunned. The man hadn't been a man at all, at least, not in the sense I was used to. His face looked the same, though the glasses were gone, and if you ignored the bashed in part of his head where the red shell seemed to seep out. The torso was still clothed in a suit, but it was ripped in places. I doubted it was an entirely human chest to begin with.

Everything from his waist down was legs and sharp-edged shell, red and orange like a lobster's, larger than life, clammy and glistening. The legs, if they were indeed legs, must have been hidden inside the scooter, though I could not think how. Their sheer bulk was much larger than the small vehicle.

How had they been folded in there? How had they fit? Wouldn't that have been incredibly painful?

As I took in all this, my mind reeled at the shock of discovering that my former boss—who not only was an alien but much more of an alien than I previously assumed—was somehow still alive. I realized I had frozen, and that Matt was still in danger.

Ignoring the pain, or pushing past it, I couldn't really tell, I pulled myself to my feet. Everything shook, but the rush of adrenaline kicked in and steadied me. I lunged at Grisham, grabbing him around his torso.

What this was meant to accomplish, I wasn't exactly sure, but it still failed dramatically. Grisham did not seem bothered in the slightest, though it distracted him long enough for Matt to roll out the way. I banged on the creature's head, not waiting to think, simply attacking with all I had.

"Die, you scum," I shouted, then, realizing how useless that sounded, I began to screech in Grisham's ear. That would annoy pretty much anyone.

Except it wasn't an ear, so it didn't do anything.

Grisham swung his shoulders, tossing me from his back, and I crashed to the grated floor once again. My mind spun as I felt the shock of the fall, my stomach turning as I saw the chasm bellow. There was light down there, and movement.

Instantly, the memory of New York was back. I began to choke.

But time was not our friend. We had to go. And we had to go now.

One of Grisham's feet came down with a rattle next to my ear, and I rolled over to see Grisham right above me leering with his half-human face. A skin wrap, much like Miko's, flaked, revealing more of that bright red shell and an eye the color of charcoal. He raised a foot again, bringing it down on my other side, close enough to make it look as if he had intended to squash me.

"You cost me everything! You brought them here, to my plant, after everything I did for you!"

I rolled to the side, reaching to drag myself away from the creature, but one of his many legs grabbed my shirt collar, dragging me toward him. There was nowhere for me to crawl.

"It's going to blow!" I shouted, trying to call Grisham to reason, but a grin spread across his face, his joy growing from the terror in mine. I rolled again, trying to avoid his attack, aware he was toying with me like a cat about to kill a mouse.

"I wasn't lying," he hissed. "I see great things in you, Sally: time itself warps around you. You're a turning point in this universe, but you're wasting your talents. And if I can't have you—no one will."

In a sudden spur of madness, I shoved forward, pushing myself under Grisham's many legs, and kicked the soft spot in his undercarriage. He let out a scream, legs folding and cringing, giving me the precious seconds I needed to dash from his reach.

But not long enough.

A claw grabbed my shirt, tearing the fabric. He shoved me under the rail, my hair dangling into the chasm, my neck straining to keep my head from falling back into the void.

The red in his mask was almost purple, as if he steaming in his shell. He held the sharp end of one of his legs above my neck, so close that I could feel it when I breathed. I sucked in a breath.

"Goodbye, Sally Webber," Grisham said with a grimace on his face. "Oh, did I mention you're fired?"

The world darkened. I struggled to breathe, and my breath was raspy as it burned my lungs. My eyes flickered, and I could see stars, beautiful stars.

A scream pierced the stagnant air, filling it with the sound of agonized pain. Grisham's face turned as something flew forward, grabbing him around the neck, and sailed over the railing. The momentum dragged the beast over the edge, and the screaming red mass tumbled after the dark blur.

I pulled myself up, coughing as I tried to breathe again. My neck ached, and my hands were clammy as I watched Grisham fall through the earth. I felt feeling no remorse.

Which was when I realized what the dark blur had been.

"Matt!" I reached for him, but it was too late.

I didn't realize how hard I clutched the railing until I lost the feeling in my fingertips. I didn't care about that. My eyes watered as I tried to make out the forms in the bottom of the pit, but it was too low and too dark to discern anything.

But I knew.

I knew.

With a sound like rolling thunder, the ground erupted into a blossom of red. The explosion shook the room, dislodging stones from the cavern roof. It crashed into the grate, drowning all sounds.

The rumbling burst in my ears as petals of fire stretched and grew, reaching up. Instinct kicked in, forcing me to turn and run for the door. I had to get out, get into that safe, re-enforced room before the flames reached me.

The pointer.

Blayde was going to kill me. I turned back to the carnage, grabbing the tiny metal rod, and ran for the room as flames licked my feet. The world crumbled around me as I propelled myself through the open door.

·····••••●●••••·······

I watched as a body was carried out of the still-crumbling building.

My co-workers had rushed across the street when the plant started to sink and shake. I stood beside them, although no one seemed to notice I was there. Actually, I wasn't all that sure how I had gotten out.

Everyone shook their heads in confusion. Some blinked, staring at their hands like they had woken from a dream, but most watched the building crumble and sink. Some called loved ones to let them know they were safe.

The woman in the fireman's arms didn't look much like a woman anymore. The parts that her tattered clothes didn't cover revealed burns worse than I'd ever seen. She barely looked human. I felt sorry for her. I wondered which of the co-workers she had been.

I felt dead inside.

I climbed into the ambulance with the injured woman, overcome with an urge to keep an eye on her. No one noticed in the controlled panic of trying to save this woman's life. They shouted words I could not recognize, pumping the woman full of things I had never seen before.

She was taken to the hospital's Intensive Care Unit after her surgery, where she was hooked up to more machines. I sat by her bed, watching and waiting, praying for the stranger's survival with a need I had never felt before.

It was almost midnight when her family finally showed up. I heard them before I saw them, and my heart sank when I realized that I knew those voices. I recognized the footsteps, too. I wanted my gut to be wrong, for the people walking into the small room to be strangers.

But they weren't. They were my parents—my mom, my dad. And the look on their faces mirrored those I had seen two years previously.

The same sorrow as when John had died.

I sat on the roof of the hospital that night, trying to cool myself off, rid myself of the terror of that realization. I wasn't sure what it all meant. What was I, if the stranger in the bed was me? Was I a ghost? A memory? Was this what death felt like? If it was, then where was Matt?

Matt, who had no remains to retrieve.

Matt, who had taken Grisham down single-handedly.

I had never understood self-sacrifice, although I hadn't given it much thought until now. I had never pondered what it would be like to be dead, either. Now I wondered how it was possible for me to feel so torn. So amazed by his last action in this world, yet so broken by his death.

The stars were glorious, but they filled me with sorrow. I wondered where Zander was, if he would hold true to his promise and come back for me? How would he react when he knew I was dying—dead? How would he react to Matt's death?

What were we to an immortal, anyway? Maybe he was used to his friends dying around him. Maybe we weren't really friends to begin with. I wasn't sure what I was to him, anyway.

Or what I could do about any of it.

At that moment, I was confused about my own existence.

I mean, duh, lots of questions go through one's mind when in limbo, and I couldn't imagine what else this could be. The body downstairs wasn't dead, not yet, but I was vagabonding around as an invisible ... something. All of this made me quite tired and hungry, so I tried to put the thoughts out of my mind.

Could I eat or sleep like this? Dammit.

I pondered many things in this state. I remembered the feeling I'd had before Zander left, of feeling so alive; that life had only just begun. Why then, had it been ripped away from me so soon? I wanted to be angry but found myself being sad instead.

I left the roof and returned to my body. My parents

had left the bedside and were now in the doctor's office discussing options I didn't want to hear. I had a good idea of what was being said anyway.

The body in the bed didn't even look like me. Maybe it wasn't me now, seeing as I was really, well ... here.

"It's been nice," I said to myself, knowing no one could hear. "It's been nice being you."

I sat down in the chair in the corner. Not that I needed to sit, but I wanted to feel normal. That hadn't been an option for me for a while now.

So, I sat there for a little bit. For a few days, actually. My parents came in, came out, and said words I pretended not to hear. It was only a matter of time, after all. Soon they would have no children at all, and there wasn't anything I could do about it.

Maybe I would be seeing my brother again, soon. The thought thrilled me, if just a little bit. Days and nights where I had been at my worst, unable to move from my bed or my couch, my body and mind at odds with each other, I had wished for nothing else than a permanent end to the pain. To leave this all behind, to join John in whatever existence you had after this one.

After all, anything would have been better than this.

Days when things were better, I felt disgusted at myself for those thoughts. Even if they weren't true, my mind had still been the one to come up with them. My sick, sick brain. Medicine and therapy helped, but it was hard to be honest with a stranger when you couldn't even be honest with yourself.

If I was being honest, though, I hadn't ever felt so good as I had these past months. Maybe we had finally found my perfect dose. And then, right when I was beginning to recover – if there even was a point, for me, where that was possible – I go ahead and get blown up by my roommate.

I thought of who I would rather see right now – my brother, or Zander. But that wasn't a reasonable thought: my mind was, once again, giving me a choice that made no actual sense. John was gone, gone in a different way than Zander ever would be. And though I missed him – I missed him so much – I realized now that I wasn't ready to join my brother just yet.

And then, one night, after all the lights had gone down, after silence became the ruler of their tiny world, he was there.

He didn't use a door. No one had seen him come in, and no one would see him leave. He simply was.

I didn't recognize his clothes, the purest of white from head to toe, his head hooded like a monk. Dried blood stained his right sleeve.

He flipped down the hood, muttering to himself that he didn't remember putting it up. I recognized the hair, and reality crashed down on me. This was real. No matter what this looked like, how surreal it felt, I knew this was no trick or illusion.

"Zander ..." I said, slowly, which of course, he couldn't hear.

Who knew how long it had been at his end. I didn't care. He was here, and the look on his face was evident: he was terrified.

"Oh, Sally." He strode to my side, reaching a hand out for mine, then snapped it back before touching my body, realizing the folly in the gesture. This only seemed to sadden him more.

Of course, the girl in the bed did not, could not, answer. She hadn't answered anyone in a while now.

"It's me," he said as if this would rouse her from sleep. The silence between his words was heavy, broken only by the slow bleeps of the machines in the room and the raspy sound of air being forced into Sally's lungs with a tube.

"Sally, it's good to see you," he continued, awkwardly. He pulled a chair up to the bedside. "How are you doing? Yeah, I see that. I'm really sorry I couldn't come back sooner. You'll know what I mean. Or maybe not. This probably won't mean anything to you, and I'm not sure you'll even remember this meeting. You've been very vague, after all. But I had to come and help. Though I'm not sure if this is the help you need."

He reached over to brush a strand of hair out of her—my—hair out of her face. It was one of the last strands she had, yet it refused to stay off her nose. Just my luck.

"I promised I would come back. And I will. But not yet." He smiled. "Soon, though. Blayde and I are with the Killians right now, if I remember correctly. They treated us like heroes when we took their people back. Seems as though some of the people under the plant were quite important. We're going to be back soon enough, and when we are, Sally, you'd better be alive, d'you hear me? You'd better be alive."

He picked up her hand delicately, holding it for a while, without saying a word. I watched from my chair, distant, unsure of what exactly was happening. What he was saying made no sense. I tried my best to

335

understand, but his words escaped me, no matter how hard I tried to grasp them.

"So, I'm going to put a guarantee on this," he said slowly, rising to his feet, gently placing her arm back on the bed. He pulled a syringe from his pocket—a sleek, tiny thing—and plunged the needle into a vein in his tightened bicep. The chamber filled with thick blood.

"I'm coming back for you, Sally Webber," he promised, taking the tube with her IV and finding the right place for the syringe. Once emptied, he slipped it back into his pocket. "I'm already sorry for the wait."

My arm tingled.

I was feeling it. And it felt weird.

I watched as Zander faded out of existence, gone in a literal blink of the eye. I watched as my body began to twitch and spasm on the bed. And I felt, somehow, as though warm syrup spread through me. The warmth grew to a boil, to a burn, and I felt my entire self consumed by flames.

Oh, how it burned.

Everything darkened, and I trembled. A shiver coursed through me from head to toe, but it wasn't from the cold. Quite the opposite. My body shook as if I had been plugged into an electrical socket: alive, hot, burning, melting.

My eyes flew open, the ceiling blinding white above me.

And I breathed through soft, new lips.

They let me go home within a week.

EPILOGUE
WHERE SOME THINGS FINALLY GO RIGHT

At precisely 2:05 am, there was a sharp buzz at the door. It rang out, loud, filling the entire apartment with electrical noise. But I was already awake, my heart spinning. I had been waiting. I knew this was it.

The sharp buzz trilled again. I felt my bones quivering as I hopped to my feet. I walked to the door, knowing that if I ran, I would lose control. I had to remain calm.

"I'm coming," I shouted to no one in particular, seeing as how no one could hear me with the intercom closed. The person at the buzzer was downstairs, after all. I didn't even have to check the window to know who it was: I could feel them.

"Hello?" I asked, "Who is this?"

Please, please, please.

"I promised, didn't I?" he replied, and my heart fluttered. It was him—Zander was back. He was here.

They were here. They had come back for me like they said they would.

My thumb held the buzzer down for longer than needed. My heart pounded, rushing faster than it had in months. Breathe in, breath out. I had to focus all my energy on just standing, just being. I would explode if I didn't contain my excitement.

I opened the door, and there they were. Blayde wore a skintight flight suit, all blue and striped down the sides, like a fighter pilot in the disco era. Zander wore his suit and tie, the same one, I noted, as he had worn the last time I saw him.

No white monk clothes for him. Just a tattered black suit with dust all over it.

"Sally," he said, picking me up and squeezing me, pure joy and relief in his voice. He swung me around like I was lighter than air. Blayde smiled politely, the way one would smile at a friend's dog. I didn't care. I hugged Zander with the grasp of a thousand men. They were back. He was back.

"We just climbed out of that hole that used to be a power plant," Zander said with a grin. "So, everything went well on your side?" he asked. That was all it took for my heart to sink. He looked around the apartment, his brows furrowing. "What's with the new couch?"

The slap hurt me more than it hurt him. I knew that before I swung my arm, but I did so anyway. Blayde's hands rose to her mouth, a real grin spreading on her porcelain face. She looked like she was going to laugh.

"What was that for?" Zander asked, rubbing his cheek. Not that he had felt the slap. For him, the last slap had been days away, and an immortal douche-canoe like him needed a slap from time to time, seeing as how he didn't feel the pain anyway.

"Two years, Zander!" I shouted, my hands on my hips and my lips on fire. "Two whole years. You said you would be right back, so what is this shit?"

"Two years?" Blayde laughed a hearty laugh where she had to slap her leg to calm herself down. "What a sloppy jump, Zander. I said you were out of practice."

"But ..." The shock on his face was real. He lifted a hand to my face, gently, then pulled it back without touching the skin. He dropped his hand, which had started trembling. "It's been four days since we left the plant."

"Two years."

"You're pranking me, aren't you?"

"I'll make the tea," Blayde interjected, shaking her head, holding back laughter. There were tears in her eyes. "Two years ... da-a-nm."

"We didn't even stay long," Zander muttered. He fell into the armchair, clutching his head in his hands. "I had one drink. One. Then I danced in a line. We left when I got proposed to. The third time."

"It was hilarious, if that makes you feel any better," Blayde called from the kitchen, where she was definitely not making tea. Instead, she had opened the cupboard, found herself a jar of olives, and was eating them with her fingers, wiping the water on my dishtowel.

"Two years, huh ... wow," Zander muttered. "Is everything ... what's changed? How are you and Matt?"

"He's ... all right, Zander. He's all right," I said, giving him a nervous smile. "Our relationship blew up when the plant did. He moved out of state."

The room was basked in silence. No one quite knew what to say, so we stared at our hands, our laps, and in Blayde's case, at each olive as she slowly halved them.

I'm quite sure she swallowed the pits whole.

"So, you're immortal, huh?"

"Yup."

"Like, can't die, ever?"

"Nope."

"That's impressive."

"Somewhat." He smiled, though I didn't feel reassured.

"Anything else I should know about you?"

"Well, I have no pulse, though I'm not sure if that counts as interesting."

"So, are there a lot of people who are like you? Immortal, I mean?"

"I haven't met any, other than Blayde." He stared awkwardly at his thumbs now, as if they were going to tell him something nice. "And that's probably reason numero uno that so many people are after us."

"That, and our keen sense of fashion," Blayde insisted from the kitchen.

It got quiet again, after that.

"Thank you," I said, trying to calm the storm of conflicting emotions within me.

Zander's head snapped up. "For what?"

"For coming back."

"I promised, didn't I?" he replied. "I just wish I hadn't … screwed up."

"You didn't." My mouth was dry as I said the words. "You came back."

"I promised," Zander repeated, "and part of the

promise was that I was going to take you on a trip. Somewhere, anywhere. And Blayde is all right with this, so long as it's just the one—"

"Try to stay longer, and your head will be the only part of you that makes it home," she chided, closing the now-empty olive jar.

"We jump there," Zander continued. "Explore, discover the local cuisine. A completely random jump, anywhere in the universe. When we're done, we jump right back, to the here and hopefully the now. One visit, with one return trip. Are you still up for it?"

"Hell, yes." My smile grew. "What do I need?"

"Coat, toothbrush, maybe some clothes," he said as I raced through the apartment. "You'll need a towel of course. You always have to know where your towel is."

I grabbed the old duffel bag from my closet and tossed everything in sight into it. Clothes, iPod, socks, underwear, and anything else that came to mind. I wanted to grab my laptop and camera, but thought against it. There was a good chance I could lose my things on another planet, and I didn't want to have to deal with that.

"You may want to leave a note with your neighbor," he offered. "I obviously have a few issues with time dilation. You don't want people asking too many questions about where you disappeared to if this trip takes longer than expected."

"On it," I replied, scrawling a few words on some scratch paper. But Jules didn't need to be bothered. My roommate would catch the note when she got back.

Taylor. It's happened. Will be incommunicado for

a little while. Please let people looking for me know I'm all right. — Sally

"That'll do." Zander grinned.

"My pointer," Blayde screeched, flying into the room and grabbing it off my desk. "You left this out for anyone to see?"

"I haven't really had company over, Blayde," I replied sullenly. "It was safe, no worries."

"You'd better hope it still works," she growled, but she was all softness and love to her cherished killer laser.

"Ahem?" Zander cleared his throat in her direction.

"Ah, yes." Blayde shook her head slowly. "Thank you, Sally, for taking good care of the item I entrusted you with. You have no idea how much it means to me that I can trust someone with my shit. Right, ready to go?"

I nodded and slipped my hand into Zander's. He smiled.

My heart raced. And then stopped.

And we jumped.

ACKNOWLEDGEMENTS

They say a book is only 10% the author, and 90% the reader. Well that tiny 10% might be even smaller than that: I have so many people to thank for making this book a reality. My editor and her team; my friends; my family: these amazing people have never stopped believing in *Starstruck* and I can't thank them enough.

To Michelle, my editor. You're incredible. You saw promise in this book and turned it from novelty to novel. I never thought editing a book could be so much fun, and I'm still in awe of how you do it. For helping me work out the details that had been holding me back, for turning my words into quotes.

To my parents, grandparents, and amazing sister. I could not have done it without you. Thank you for encouraging me through the thick and thin, and putting up with all the weird things along the way. I could not ask for a better family. I love you all.

Now to my friends, and this is going to take a while. To Hugo, for always texting me messages of encouragement and giving me silly ideas when I needed them. Your constant support carried me through the hardest times. To Ronnie, for being one of the greatest motivators in the universe. Your insightful wit when I was down, you pushed me to bring this novel together. Your Grave Report and Books of Winter series are too fun to put into words, and you inspire me to be a better writer. To Andrew, for reminding me how much fun it is to be master of your own world. If you hadn't allowed me to read Iris as you were working on it, I probably wouldn't have pulled this dusty manuscript off the shelf and started it up again.

To all my beta readers who told me this book had promise, who enjoyed the novel and immediately asked for more, who helped me every step of the way. I am insanely in your debt.

A huge thank you to my great friends, Alix, Nico, Laura, Kenzie, Victor, Lea, Katika, Liam, for your support!

I left the biggest thank you for last: Joanna. Seven years ago, we were eating turkey when we decided to write a series together. We brainstormed names: Stella, Rand, and that knife lady. We alternated books, writing episodic adventures "that would never be longer than a novella, no." That was seven years ago. You helped bring these characters into the world. You helped craft their world and their adventures. None of this – none of this! – would be here today if it weren't for you. I am eternally in your debt not only for starting this adventure with me, but for handing me the reigns and allowing me to drive it alone. I owe Starstruck to you, which is why I dedicate it to you.

ABOUT THE AUTHOR

S.E. Anderson can't ever tell you where she's from. Not because she doesn't want to, but because it inevitably leads to a confusing conversation where she goes over where she was born (England) where she grew up (France) and where her family is from (USA) and it tends to make things very complicated.

She's lived pretty much her entire life in the South of France, except for a brief stint where she moved to Washington DC, or the eighty years she spent as a queen of Narnia before coming back home five minutes after she had left. Currently, she goes to university in Marseille, where she's studying Physics and aiming for a career in Astrophysics.

When she's not writing, or trying to science, she's either reading, designing, crafting, or attempting to speak with various woodland creatures in an attempt to get them to do household chores for her. She could also be gaming, or pretending she's not watching anything on Netflix.

Did you enjoy *Starstruck*? Tell us about it! Share your thoughts on social media with the hashtag #Starstrucksaga

Please consider leaving a review of this novel.

Website: seandersonauthor.com
Facebook: www.facebook.com/seandersonauthor
Twitter: @sea_author

KEEP READING FOR A SNEAK PREVIEW OF

FIRST RULE OF INTERSTELLAR TRAVEL:
DON'T GET LOST WITHOUT YOUR ALIEN

A STARSTRUCK NOVEL

CHAPTER ONE

THE ART OF SPACE TRAVEL AND HUMAN REPAIR

The universe was a cold, dark, and empty place.

And I loved it.

I drifted in perfect silence, my legs dangling, useless, in the void below, my senses a mere whisper in the back of my head. Everything was pure in the quiet: there was no worry, no stress, nothing to get wrapped up about.

It was amazing.

The darkness extended forever, though it seemed to have some depth. Unlike a cave or a pitch-black room, this kind of darkness had no end.

So it was a little weird I could see my hands. Strange, perhaps, but I wasn't worried. Nothing worried me.

There was no up or down; no left, no right; just eternity. And while I knew it was cold, the temperature didn't bother me. It could have been warm; I didn't care.

For a minute, I thought I must be dead. What did death feel like, anyway?

And then the stars came out.

They blinked into existence, one by one, little holes pocked with pins on a distant black fabric. I reached out as if to touch them, but they were too far away, so very far away. Even so, I felt the heat radiating from them, the warmth that pulsed as they pulsed. They were so beautiful. I wanted to pick them up, pluck them off their celestial shelf and bury them in my chest, keep the warmth forever.

Once again, I wondered where I was. I remembered feeling intense pain, like someone had tried to force me through a slivered crack in a window. Yet all that was left was a dull, vague ache, like a long-forgotten memory bobbing slowly to the surface. I felt my chest with my hands. It was still there, intact. I was fine.

And it didn't matter, anyway.

The stars almost looked like diamonds. They didn't twinkle like the stars watching over Earth. I wondered why they didn't twinkle like they were supposed to. Twinkle, twinkle.

"Is she ... singing?" The voice was angelic, the most beautiful voice I had ever heard. Ethereal, it wrapped me in a sweet, heavenly blanket, lifting me higher in space and filling me with a deep sense of satisfaction. My bliss grew tenfold. The pretty lights around me made me grin.

"Um ... she might be?" another voice answered, just as beautiful, if not more so. It was deeper, resonating in a timbre that took my breath away. I turned, swaying awkwardly in the emptiness, searching for the sound. I listened without hearing, letting the voice wash over me. The pain I thought I remembered was a lie:

there was nothing but beauty here.

"Has this happened to her before?" the higher voice asked. A woman, I realized, wondering why I hadn't noticed before. I could find no sign of where the voice came from, but I was in no rush to find out.

"I can't remember if we've jumped Terrans this far before," the other one replied, worried. "Who knows what we're meant to expect?"

"If her brain's fried, just remember it was your fault; you were steering."

"I thought you were."

"No: your friend, you drive." The voice, though still beautiful, sounded harsh.

"Really?" There was a pause. "We should have a system for jumping friends."

"Yeah, like we have a lot of those."

And as she stopped talking, so the angel left. I reached out for it, letting out a small moan. I begged for the voice to return, to warm me once again.

It was getting cold now.

There was a quiet sigh in the distance—neither melodious nor divine. I realized my arms felt heavy. Were the stars rising? No, I was falling, slowly at first, so slow I didn't notice until it was too late. The stars rushed past me in a dizzying ballet, going faster and faster.

My world shattered, my universe ending. The tightness in my chest grew, and I could do nothing to stop it. I drew wildly at the space around me, wanting to scream, but the pain clutched my windpipe and kept me silent.

"You're saying *I* screwed up, huh?" the male replied,

almost savagely, but beneath it, I heard fear—the same fear in my chest. His voice sent a tremor through my universe. "What should I do? Do I wake her up, or do I—"

"Better not," the other voice said, and I wondered how I ever found it angelic. It was harsh, gruff; crude. "Don't mess with her. She should be fine once it washes over."

"Are you sure? These people can die in their sleep, you know. Combusting, spontaneously, just like that! Poof, they're gone."

"Urban legends, surely."

"It's no joke," the man assured her. "I need to make sure she's okay. I don't want her to—"

"Fine. Your guest, your responsibility. You mess up her brain; it is not my fault. Clear?"

The voices went silent, and the world returned to normal. The stars slowed and I bobbed amidst them, but the sense of peace was gone. I worried about where I'd gone, and what I was doing here. My legs and arms, still dangling beneath me, hurt from their own weight, and it annoyed me that my chest still felt constricted.

And then, suddenly, there was a chill. The cold hit my muscles, making them contract and spasm. The space around me melted: the stars didn't race; they disappeared as if to say they were done with me.

I stifled a scream as the universe crumbled around me. The world was bleak and black, then gone, and then nothing at all.

I threw my hands out to grab the void, to clutch at everything, anything, and found warm flesh. Bouncy, springy, skin. I grabbed onto what I assumed, and hoped was a hand, my anchor to reality. My mind finally pieced itself together, the thoughts flying and reassembling until it all made sense again.

Like rising to the surface after being underwater too long, I floated upwards. My eyes pushed themselves open to reveal a gray ceiling, and a face with a hand clutching it from forehead to chin, from cheek to cheek.

"She's opened her eyes," the voice muttered from under my hand. I pulled it back quickly. My face, which I realized was damp, felt hot—was I blushing? But the man smiled, unperturbed by my facial groping. The next step was to figure out who he was, and what he was doing there.

The woman put her face in front of mine, her halo of bright hair fanning out from her sharp olive-toned features. Red, pink, blue and purple strands fell away from her face, the deep gray eyes scanning me just as intensely as I scanned her.

"Doesn't look too screwed up," the woman muttered. She snapped her fingers next to my ears, then threw up a stiff index finger and brought it back and forth across my line of vision. The man looked annoyed, practically glowering, but if he had anything to say to her, he kept his mouth shut.

"Reactions seem normal enough, but I don't have much of a baseline to go with. This appears to be the norm for lower cognitive life forms. Wait until the word processing boots up and you can have a normal conversation with her. Might take a while but count yourself lucky: she has all her limbs."

I turned my head to the side and let out the contents of my stomach. My throat burned, but I was more focused on how the vomit slashed and hit his shoes. My eyes and nose felt clogged and hot. Instantly there were hands on my neck, but they were there to hold my hair, gently, as I sat up and retched once again.

Ugh, gross. I felt rung out, hungover. Not only that, but I was pretty embarrassed.

It wasn't the woman holding my hair, but the man. He stared at me with a worry so intense I could barely process it.

Was I dying? Sure felt like I was. He looked at me like I had minutes left to live.

I opened my mouth, but before I could utter a sound, it snapped shut. I tried again, taking a deep breath before forcing my jaw open—but the sound leaving my vocal cords didn't resemble words in the slightest. Instead, a prolonged squawk left my throat, my body's awful attempt to take up birdsong. The sound was loud, unstoppable, and most certainly pungent.

The woman let out a snort. The man glared at her, shutting her up. "Not a word," he ordered.

When he turned back, I coaxed my jaw into moving at my command. My lips danced before they managed to let out a sound.

"Hey," I croaked.

"Hey, Sally." A smile spread across his face. "Are you alright? You can hear me okay?"

"Pressure," I said, forcing a yawn to pop the bubbles in my ears. It didn't do much to help. The world was becoming clearer, and their names floated back to the surface: I was not a fan of the real world lagging.

"Zander?" I sputtered, and his eyes lit up.

Zander, the man I hadn't seen in two years, who had returned in the middle of the night to take me to the stars; the man I had hit with my car, the man who had blown up my workplace, the man not of this earth. Or, my earth anyway.

I'm pretty sure we weren't in Kansas anymore. Well, not Kansas, but our solar system probably wasn't anywhere near here.

He had promised to come back and made good on that promise, even if it did come a little late. I wanted to be angry about that, angry at how he had abandoned me to deal with the aftermath of the plant's explosion by myself.

But for him, so he claimed, only a week had passed since leaving Earth: a side effect of his kind of space travel.

As for me, I promised myself I wouldn't mention any of that. I wouldn't let anything ruin this trip, the one I had been waiting for since seeing the stars as a child for the first time. If this was my only shot at leaving my planet, I sure wasn't going to ruin it.

I took his arm, and he helped me up, my legs wobbly and weak. I narrowly avoided the puddle of vomit on the floor. I felt empty and drained, but my muscles were slowly coming back to me.

"Are you well?" the woman asked, perched on the impossibly high windowsill above us, giving me only a second of her gaze. The large window was the only one in the room, and she was staring at the world beyond it, as if she was a sentry, keeping watch, keeping us safe from the shadows. She almost looked comfortable up there; how she had gotten on the sill, I had absolutely no idea, but it was likely she was doing it just to show off.

It sounded like something Blayde would do.

Blayde, the living weapon, an amazingly dangerous military panoply in the form of a petite, muscular woman. Not human, though she sure looked it. I had no idea what she was, seeing as how she and her brother hadn't told me about their planet of origin or anything.

Not that it would have meant anything to me if they had.

"I'm fine, I think, thank you." I pretended I didn't know that Blayde didn't care about my well-being. I regretted speaking almost instantly: the words rang like cymbals in my ears, crushingly loud, every syllable a blow to the eardrums.

She was colder, now, despite only having been gone for a week. Was that normal? I had thought Blayde was warming up to me when we brought down Grisham. She had allowed me to come along on this trip, and I was under the impression that was massive coming from her. But it seemed whatever I had done to deserve merit in her eyes has washed away in her week with the Killians. I guess liking me a tiny bit wasn't the same as wanting me to tag along.

I tried to take a step on my own, shaking off Zander's helpful hand. My feet shuffled zombie-like on the cold stone floor, legs shaking as I put weight on them. Finally, though, I stood on my own, and I was proud of that, but now my mind was free to worry about other things, and it mainly focused on what I was doing here.

"What happened?" I asked, teetering on my still

weak limbs.

Blayde shrugged. "You blacked out." It was obvious from her tone she didn't care.

"Nothing bad or anything," Zander was quick to say, his face all smiles and nods. "Your body reacted a little differently to the jump than expected. There's nothing to worry about. The first time can be a little traumatic for some. It's not a very pleasant process, having your body reduced to atoms and sent to the other side of the universe in less than an instant."

"Oh, okay." I smiled sheepishly at my crutch. "I can see why that's problematic ... for some."

I gave him my best attempt at a reassuring grin. The look on Zander's face said he didn't buy it.

"You sure you're alright?" he asked.

"Positive."

To prove it, I distanced myself from his grasp and managed a few tentative steps. I really was fine, it seemed. What a relief.

I wondered why the floor felt so cold, even through my Chucks. And then I wondered where in the universe we could be, and the cold faded away. I had more interesting things to think about.

"You see?" I cracked a real smile this time, the excitement pulsing through me. "Totally fine. Nothing to worry about. So, where are we?"

At first glance, the answer was simple: we were in someone's garage. The room looked somewhere between a barn loft and a cathedral, with vaulted ceilings and the one large window high on the wall. The floors looked like they were made of stone, and the rafters of wood; nothing seemed otherworldly in the slightest. We could have been anywhere in the US.

A large tarp covered a vehicle in the middle of the room, something bigger than a car but smaller than a truck. Larger in sheer bulk, maybe, but it sat on the floor rather low, only reaching my hip. I had an incredible urge to rip the tarp off, go '*aha*,' and discover a spaceship. But we were technically trespassing, and I should probably limit what I touched.

No matter how exciting those things were.

I was relieved my duffel bag had arrived in one piece. I rifled through it while waiting for someone to answer me, feeling odd and out of place and not sure when it was polite to repeat myself, like when I was a kid and invited to a friend's house for the first time. I pretended to focus on my bag to stifle the awkwardness.

Still, it was awkward.

"Not quite sure, yet," Blayde said excitedly, slipping down from her perch. "The reason we have so little light is because there's a huge billboard blocking most of the window. That isn't sunlight in here: it's artificial UV, pumped in to make this place seem more natural in exchange for stealing their view. Great for the owner, sucks for us. We're going to have to go out."

"Hold on, what?" I jumped to my feet, wide-eyed.

"Which part has got your head in a twist?" Blayde made the sweetest, most patronizing smile a face could make. "Was it the UV light thing? Or the problem of being a real estate owner in a universe where anyone can pop into your home?"

"Go back to the part where you don't know where the hell we are."

"Oh, yeah, that." She shrugged. "Zander didn't tell

you? Universal lottery. We jump; see where the solar winds blow us. Destination: anywhere."

"So we could be anywhere in the … entire universe?"

"Yup."

"So the air out there might be poisonous and destroy our lungs and burn our faces off."

"It could." She shrugged again. "But it won't. Back me up here, Zander."

"Jumping may be random, but we never arrive anywhere where the atmosphere hates us. That would be awful."

"Okay, great," I said, "Coming from people who can't die … totally reassuring."

"Blayde and I can survive pretty much anything, but it doesn't mean we like breathing sulfuric acid."

This was, after all, the deal I had struck to see a different corner of the universe. We can jump somewhere at random, then back to the starting point: but further than that, and we can never go back. Dangerous, but it wasn't every day I got to leave the planet, and it wasn't as if Zander hadn't explained the situation.

Well, two whole years ago.

"Not to mention, I'm a fantastic driver," Zander said proudly, running a hand through his hair. Blayde let out a loud snort.

"Oh please," she said, "until ten minutes ago you thought I was the one doing the steering. We arrived safely through wishing and praying. A whole lot of praying. Thankfully that hasn't done any of us in yet."

"It's a good thing I remember how to get back to Earth, then."

She turned her attention to the wall, drawing her

hands over it like she was caressing a body. Her hands were gentle and delicate, running over cracks and crevasses, searching for something. Her eyes were focused, determined.

Zander watched her, somewhat excitedly, as if wanting to join her, and with a start, I realized I was holding him back.

"So, um," I said, trying to break the silence. I was determined not to be the third wheel on this interstellar trip. "How do we get out of here? I don't see a door."

"It's probably hiding," Zander replied, "it's what happens when you max-up your privacy settings."

"So how do we ... where can we find it? Can we find it?"

"You have to coax it out," Blayde grunted, but it was invitation enough: Zander and me joined her by the wall, running my hands over the stone-like interior, trying to find anything out of place, though not sure exactly what I was looking for.

I wondered again what the walls were made of; it felt like stone but was wrong, somehow, like it was artificial. My mind shouted Alien Tech, over and over again. I took a long sniff, taking in the scent of damp stone. It smelled like the musty cellar of an old English home.

There were no drafts to follow for a clue to the door's whereabouts, but the noise coming from outside—or rather, the loud buzz—seemed louder at one end of the room. Blayde paused and inspected that side a little more intently.

Her strange methods of searching for an exit had to be the culmination of years of experience in finding herself in tight spots; her fingers tapped the walls as if she were playing the piano; her right foot coming down more forcefully on the floor than her left, leaving a slight pause for her to listen.

My eye caught the tarp again. I left the duo to their search and snuck over to it, determined to have a peek. I lifted a small corner to see the fender of a bright red sports car. At least, it looked like a sports car. I was disappointed: I had expected something a little more futuristic.

I jumped as someone touched my elbow: Zander crouched beside me, taking the tarp from my hand and letting it fall back in place. "We're trespassing, remember?"

I nodded, feeling like I had been lectured by a teacher. A bit embarrassing, but Zander was still smiling, no hard feelings.

"I barfed in the corner."

"We should probably clean that up."

"Ah, here," Blayde said from across the room. She ran her hand along the wall, and an arch lit up in the dust, a bright blue light glowed from inside the stone itself. Within seconds, a door materialized as if it had been there all along.

"What the ...?" I stammered, and Blayde gave me a proud smirk.

"They don't have this on your backwater planet, do they?" She sniggered. Zander rolled his eyes.

"Security. The door only exists when you need it," he explained, "and Blayde, calm down, will you? Be polite. We're all—"

"Yeah, yeah, rainbows and sunshine," she muttered.

"Anyway, ready?"

I wondered if giant bees inhabited the world outside: Maybe we'd get stung to death by killer bees in a strange twist of fate. Part of me wanted the door to stay safely shut forever.

But the rest of me wanted to see the world beyond. That's why I had come along, after all; I wanted to see the universe, if only for one short day. To quench my astrolust. A brief trip with my best friend, who happened to be a space-hopping alien.

Life had stopped making sense the second I hit him with my car.

Blayde and Zander were ecstatic, their faces radiant with joy and excitement, though they did not voice this aloud. After a long look shared with her brother, Blayde ceremoniously took out her laser pointer, adjusting a small dial on its short handle, pointing the tip at the crack between the door and its frame. She severed the lock with surgical precision, a motion she had obviously performed many times before.

She threw the door open, and my heart skipped as I prepared to lay eyes on my very first alien planet.

Sally's ADVENTURE CONTINUES
IN ALIENATION

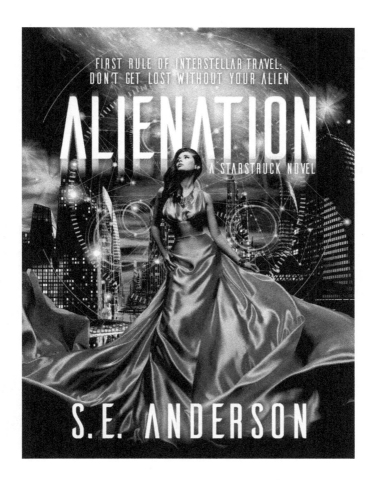

CPSIA information can be obtained
at www.ICGtesting.com
Printed in the USA
BVHW041131050420
576897BV00018B/939

9 780995 778917